Gathering Storm

The Order of the Black Swan, Book 5

Victoria Danann

Special THANK YOU'S...

Thank you to my assistants, Judy Fox and Sarah Nicole Blausey.

Thank you to Kelly Danann who gave me the confidence to publish the first book.

Thank you to Julie Roberts, world's best editor.

Thank you to my friend and bridge partner, native French speaker, Michele Murphy, for translation.

Thank you to my husband, my biggest cheerleader, who values every book sale and gets excited about every milestone.

Victoria is a big fan of A Team.

Anna-Marie Coomber
Anna Salamatin
Brandy Ralston
Cheryl Lewis Fennimore
Cristi Riquelme
Crystal Lehmann

Dawn Dow
Dee Bowerman
Elizabeth Quincy Nix
Ellen Sandberg
Gina Whitney
Jennifer Tracy
Joanette Fountain
JoBeth Sexton-Harris
Kim Staley Schommer
Laura E. Wolf
Laurie Johnson
Laurie Peterson
Leah Barbush
Leslie Miner
Lisa Jon Jung
Maggie Nolan
Michelle Stein
Mountain Crew
Nelta Baldwin Mathias
Pam James
Patricia Smith
Rebecca Stigers
Robyn Byrd
Rochelle Taves
Shan Harris McKinney
Shanna Rankin
Susan Blanford Westerman
Sylvia Ashford

Tabitha Schneider
Talisa Martin
Teri Zuwala
Ticia Morton Hall
Tifinie Henry
Tori Whitaker
Vicki Turner Simpson

Victoria Danann

PROLOGUE

This series is also a serial saga in the sense that each book begins where the previous book ended. **READING IN ORDER IS <u>STRONGLY</u> RECOMMENDED** in order to fully enjoy the rich complexities of this tapestry in book form.

There is a very old and secret society of paranormal investigators and protectors known as The Order of the Black Swan. In modern times, in a dimension similar to our own, they continue to operate, as they always have, to keep the human population safe. For centuries they have relied on a formula that outlines recruitment of certain second sons, in their early, post-pubescent youth, who match a narrow and highly specialized psychological profile. Those who agree to forego the ordinary pleasures and freedoms of adolescence receive the best education available anywhere along with the training and discipline necessary for a possible future as active operatives in the Hunters Division. In recognition of the personal sacrifice and inherent danger, The Order bestows knighthoods on those who accept.

BOOK ONE. *My Familiar Stranger: Romancing the Vampire Hunters.*

The elite B Team of Jefferson Unit in New York, also known as Bad Company, was devastated by the loss of one of its four members in a battle with vampire. A few days later Elora Laiken, an accidental pilgrim from another dimension, literally landed at their feet so physically damaged by the journey they weren't even sure of her species. After a lengthy recovery, they discovered that she had gained amazing speed and strength through the cross-dimension translation. She earned the trust and respect of the knights of B Team and eventually replaced the fourth member, who had been killed in the line of duty.

She was also forced to choose between three suitors: Istvan Baka, a devastatingly seductive six-hundred-year-old vampire, who worked as a consultant to neutralize an epidemic of vampire abductions, Engel Storm, the noble and stalwart leader of B Team who saved her life twice; and Rammel Hawking, the elf who persuaded her that she was destined to be his alone.

BOOK TWO. *The Witch's Dream: A Love Letter to Paranormal Romance*

Ten months later everyone was gathered at Rammel's home in Derry, Ireland. B Team had been temporarily assigned to The Order's Headquarters office in Edinburgh, but they had been given leave for a week to celebrate an elftale handfasting for Ram and Elora, who were expecting.

Ram's younger sister, Aelsong, went to Edinburgh with B Team after being recruited for her exceptional psychic skills. Shortly after arriving, Kay's fiancé was abducted by a demon with a vendetta, who slipped her to a dimension out of reach. Their only hope to locate Katrina and retrieve her was Litha Brandywine, the witch tracker, who had fallen in love with Storm at first sight.

Storm was assigned to escort the witch, who slowly penetrated the ice that had formed around his heart when he lost Elora to Ram. Litha tracked the demon and took Katrina's place as hostage after learning that he, Deliverance, was her biological father. The story ended with all members of B Team happily married and retired from active duty.

BOOK THREE. *A Summoner's Tale: The Vampire's Confessor*

Istvan Baka was captured by vampire in the Edinburgh underground and reinfected with the vampire virus. His assistant, Heaven McBride, was found to be a "summoner", a person who can compel others to come to them when they play the flute. She also turned out to be the reincarnation of the young wife who was Baka's first victim as a new vampire six hundred years before.

Elora Laiken was studying a pack of wolves hoping to get puppies for her new breed of dog. While Rammel was overseeing the renovation of their new home, she and Blackie were caught in a snowstorm in the New Forest. At the same time assassins from her world, agents of the clan who massacred her family, found her isolated in a remote location without the ability to communicate. She gave birth to her baby alone except for the company of her dog, Blackie, and the wolf pack.

Heaven was instrumental in calling vampire to her so that they could be intercepted and given the curative vaccine. Baka was found, restored, and given the opportunity for a "do over" with the wife who had waited for many lifetimes to spend just one with him.

BOOK FOUR. *Moonlight: The Big Bad Wolf*

Ram and Elora moved into temporary quarters at Jefferson Unit to protect mother and baby. Sol asked Storm to prepare to replace him as Jefferson Unit Sovereign so that he could retire in two years. Storm declined, but suggested twenty-year-old trainee, Glendennon Catch for the job.

Litha uncovered a shocking discovery about the vampire virus by accidentally leading five immortal host vampire back to Jefferson Unit. Deliverance struck a deal with Litha to assist Black Swan with two issues: the old vampire and an interdimensional migration of Stalkson Grey's werewolf tribe.

In the process of averting possible extinction of his tribe, the king of the Elk Mountain werewolves, Stalkson Grey, fell in love with a cult slave and abducted her with the demon's assistance. He eventually won his captive's heart and took his new mate to the New Elk Mountain werewolf colony in Lunark Dimension where the wolf people's ancestors had settled centuries before.

Throughout this portion of the story, Litha's pregnancy developed at an alarming rate. Since there had been no previous instance of progeny with the baby's genetic heritage, no one knew what to expect. The baby arrived months ahead of schedule. The birth was dramatic and unique because Storm's and Litha's new daughter, Elora Rose, "Rosie", skipped the usual delivery with a twelve inch ride through the passes and appeared on the outside of Litha's body.

•

Victoria Danann

PREFACE I

Stagsnare Dimension

Archer jerked awake when the science fiction book he was reading fell from his hand. He'd been having trouble sleeping ever since a team of twenty of the Ralengclan's finest had left on a mission to assassinate the last surviving member of the Laiwynn clan, Elora Laiken. That was three weeks ago. None had returned. All were presumed dead.

He thought about Rystrome and knew it seemed silly to use the term "innocent" when describing someone who was also an assassin, but the young soldier left that impression. He had taken the job so that he could educate his children and buy his wife a flute to replace the one that had been taken from her. Like all of them, he had stories to tell about Laiwynn ruthlessness, which meant that he also had good reasons to hate the Laiwynn.

That zealot, Rothesay, was so obsessed with making sure all Laiwynn were exterminated that the deaths incurred in pursuit of that goal were shoved into the "acceptable loss" column and forgotten. At least by him.

Since none of the twenty had returned, they didn't know any more about how to prepare for a mission than they had the first time. Nothing had been gained. Nothing had been learned. And a lot of lives had been lost.

They had speculation about what *may* have happened, but no facts.

Archer was the sort who dealt in facts and didn't have much patience with other modalities. Belief in gods? Until there was evidentiary proof, there was nothing to discuss. Sun coming up every day? The only thing that could be said with certainty was that "sunrise" had been happening lately in cosmic terms. Life after death? Don't be ridiculous.

PREFACE II

Dunkilly, Ireland

Glendennon Catch caught the eye of the bartender who simply pointed toward a back corner. He couldn't see what the man pointed to, but he nodded his thanks and began making his way toward the rear of the pub.

He wound through a crowd of people standing, holding glass mugs and talking loudly to be heard over the music. When he was closer to the back, a rear corner snug came into view. It was close to a window so there was enough light to see, even with the thick haze of smoke hanging in the air, that the bartender had been right in surmising that he was looking for Z Team.

There they were, the farthest thing from inconspicuous. Glen couldn't begin to guess how they had managed to be successful vampire slayers when everything about them drew attention and broadcasted vibes of this-is-your-last-chance-to-run. It was a message that floated around them like a diaphanous cloud of warning.

The four of them fit comfortably in a snug designed for eight. That was partly because of their size and partly because they had a casual way of draping arms and legs so that they took up more space than was normally allotted for a civilized person, even a large one. The posturing also communicated disdain for established notions of propriety. Glen knew instinctively that even the word "propriety" would make Black Swan's infamous misfits laugh out loud.

One of them was wearing a sleeveless shirt that had once been a denim jacket. His left arm had been transformed into a tattooed sleeve by an intricately inked mural of muted colors. Bare biceps seemed out of place in a part of the world where it was brittle-dick cold outside, but Glen supposed that if he'd made *that* much of an investment in ink he might want to show it off, too.

Glen's initial impression of the guy sitting next to Sleeve was that he should have the nickname, Dark, or Black. He wore black jeans, a black metal band shirt that was probably vintage, maybe collectable, and his spiky hair was so blue black it had to have been dyed that color. He was eye-catching, all that black paired with eyes so pale he could almost get away with going undercover as a vamp. He wasn't wearing eyeliner, but the contrast between his ice-color irises and those thick ebony lashes made his eyes pop in a dramatic way that probably drew interest from a lot of babes. *The Black Knight.* Glen smiled a little to himself, enjoying the company of his own voice in his head and his own offbeat sense of humor.

The third wore a plain gray long sleeve tee that covered his upper body, but Glen could see black ink climbing out of the neck of the guy's shirt, stopping just below his pronounced jaw line. Either tribal pattern or angel glyph. Hard to tell with just snake tails in view. He had a serious case of bed head going, maybe by design, maybe not, and one eyebrow that was raised and had been since he'd noticed Glen standing there watching them.

He said something to the others. Then the fourth, the one facing away with one long arm draped over the back of the snug, turned to look at Glen over his shoulder. That shift revealed elfin ears outlined by light brown hair with titian streaks. Same curl as Sir Hawking. Had to be Torrent Finngarick.

Somehow they looked exactly the way Glen had expected them to look. Hard. Tough. And like they belonged together. He was thinking, *so they're Black Swan knights with a little bit of a nasty reputation. They put their pants on one leg at a time just like me. Right?*

As internal pep talks go, it was adequate, but he just wasn't feeling it. Even so, he decided to stick with Plan A, which was taking life straight ahead, one step at a time. Glen had a reputation of his own for being easy-going, but he made an exception for passive aggressive nonsense. He didn't like it, didn't like people who habitually avoided the front door, and didn't mind letting his irritation with bullshit bubble over if it got to be too much.

Plan A it was. It meant walking straight up to them, stating his business, hoping for the best, but being prepared for the worst. That was the thought bouncing around in his mind as he observed their reactions to seeing him approach.

Once he was standing over them, he looked around the table and said, "I'm Glendennon Catch." Then he zeroed in on Torn. "Sorry for your loss, Sir Finngarick." He said "Sir" quietly enough so that only they heard him, but they got the message. Sir was a small little honorific that could also serve as code, as good as a secret handshake. "The office sent me with a message from the HR department."

They left him standing there for a minute without saying anything or changing expression. They just stared.

It was a thinly disguised intimidation strategy to get him to reveal nervousness, timidity, or some other weakness that would register as a flaw in their eyes. As tactics went, it was almost sure to get results, but not with somebody who had inherited a dominant werewolf gene. Glen could stand there all day breathing normally without flinching or looking away, patiently waiting for them to get tired of practicing Mind Fuck 101.

Finally, the big guy with the glyphs crawling up his neck grinned, showing dimples that seemed entirely out of place against the persona he'd so carefully crafted. "So go ahead and deliver your memo, Sweet Cheeks. We're listening."

The other three chuckled softly without taking their eyes off of him. Glen laughed openly and good-naturedly, but let the sound trail off and end in a low-level growl, incongruent with the smile on his face. The growl wasn't loud enough to draw attention from the wake-goers, but it was definitely heard by Z Team. They all sat up a little straighter and took another look at the kid. He had their interest, but that was worlds away from respect.

Looking at Glyphs, he said, "My briefing didn't mention that any of you are hard of hearing. If you want to call me by a name, it's Glen."

Finngarick's blue eyes twinkled in a way that brought Sir Hawking to mind, while the other two laughed at the fact that Glyphs had been challenged by a kid who was years away from growing into his lanky, big-boned frame.

"Long way to deliver a message. Would you no' have a pint with us then? Glen." He reached out with a long leg, put the toe of his scuffed boot through the leg brace of an unoccupied chair, pulled it closer to the snug, and waved toward it in a gesture of invitation. "We're no' much on formalities. Call me Torn."

Glen nodded then looked at the others. Torn pointed at the guy with the sleeves and said, "This is Gunnar. That's Raif." He raised his chin in the direction of 'black knight'. "The fella with the questionable personality is Bob."

"Gunnar. Raif, Torn, And Bob. No way."

Finngarick's eyes twinkled with that special sparkle that had elf written all over it. "Aye. Make no mistake. The bugger's name is Bob."

Glen shook his head. "Let's rename him."

Finngarick looked at Bob and then back at Glen. "What we have here, gentlemen, is a cool, gloomy Irish day with no place to go and no' a thin' to do other than have another pint. So I say we should try playin' Glen's game. What would you be callin' the man if 'twas up to you, young emissary?" Glen shrugged. "Come now. No ideas?"

"Well, yeah, I sort of named him in my head on the walk across the bar."

"Pub," Torn corrected.

"Yes. Pub. Sorry."

Bob raised both brows. "I, for one, cannot wait to hear what *you* named me in your head on your walk across the... pub."

Glen looked at him with speculation trying to decide whether or not to tell the truth. "Glyphs."

While Bob studied Glen, his three teammates studied Bob in turn, like they were trying it on for size. Bob lowered his eyebrows and rolled his big shoulders in approval.

Finally Torn nodded as if to say he'd reached a conclusion. "Right you are. Now that you point it out, 'tis plain as day he's no' a Bob. Glyphs suits him fine. Congratulations. You just nicknamed a knight. No' an easy thin' to do. Had he no' liked it, well, shall we say 'tis good he did."

Torn Finngarick called for a Guinness Extra Stout to be served to Glen, who wasn't used to alcohol at all and certainly wasn't ready for Irish black beer. He took a manly mouthful, thinking he had arrived, and promptly spewed it all over Torn in a spectacular demonstration of human fountain power. The other three members of Z Team laughed so hard they had to wipe tears.

"... almost as funny as the night that Chokarzi stripper puked half a gallon of half-digested Cuervo in your face. In the middle of a lap dance."

Glen borrowed a wet bar towel and offered it to Finngarick with a blush. "I'd offer to clean you up, but your file says you're heterosexual."

Torn took the towel without a word, but with a glint of amusement in his eyes. When he was as clean as was possible without a shower and fresh clothes, he handed the towel to Glen. "Go get yourself somethin' else. Drinks are on me. Milk maybe?" he teased.

When Glen returned with a mug of root beer, no one asked him what was in the glass. Torn simply motioned to the chair. "So. They record sexual preference in our files, do they?"

Glen sat, but didn't answer that question. "You're needed at Jefferson Unit. You're to accompany me to Fort Dixon after the funeral. Your things are being gathered and moved as we speak."

As Glen looked from one to another, he saw no discernible reaction. They were a cool bunch. He'd give them that.

Glyphs shrugged, saying, "New York's no worse than any other place. Maybe better than some."

Finngarick looked at Glen like he was a lab specimen on a microscopic slide. "Would you be happenin' to know why we're *needed* so urgently?"

Glen thought about it for a minute and decided there was no reason to withhold the truth. "Yes."

A ghost of a smile seemed to cross Finngarick's handsome elven face. "And will you be sharin' with us then?"

"Sorry. No."

Torn glanced at his teammates as if the four could communicate telepathically. "See. The thin' is, we're accustomed to hearin' The Order needs to sweep us further under the rug. No' brin' us into the light. We would no' be the least surprised if you came to say we're bein' transferred to Antarctica. But this? Naturally we're curious, you understand."

"Of course I understand. But I'm not at liberty to say."

Torn nodded thoughtfully. "Well, then. Might you be at liberty to say why you, in particular, were sent to escort us?"

It took Glen less than a second to process whether there could be ramifications to divulging that information. "The Jefferson Unit sovereign is retiring. I'm being given a try-out for his job. He sent me to get you." Z Team stared at Glen as if they were waiting for the punch line. Finally, he said, "No. Really."

Gunnar cleared his throat. "So. You're saying that, at some point, we could be calling you boss?"

Glen responded with a shit-eating grin so big, it begged for retaliation. Gunnar swept his gaze around the snug before it settled on Glen with a disturbing mix of challenge, mischief and amusement.

Torn leaned forward. "Seems we have limited time for the application of a right proper hazin' then, Glen."

Four sets of eyes darted to the movement in Glen's throat when he swallowed.

"'Tis a good thin' that Stormy and I put the bad in Bad Company, else the two of us might be intimidated by unhappy mates standin' o'er us with mean faces and hands on delectably curvy hips."

"I concur," added Storm.

"You can *concur* until the cows come home, *Sir* Storm, but you are still NOT playing in the Jefferson Unit Annual Rugby Match." Litha's voice was loud enough to make the babies get quiet and listen.

"Yeah. What she said." Elora couldn't really see what more could be added.

"We're playin'."

"We are," Storm confirmed.

"You. Are. Retired!" Elora countered.

"Retired is no' dead."

"*And,*" said Storm, "I'd like to add that we retired *early*. Lots of active duty hunters are older than we are and they'll be playing. There's *never* been a match that didn't have B Team represented and there's not going to be one this year either."

Elora huffed. "Since they retired B Team as an honor to you..."

"*And* you," Storm added.

"Thank you for the thought, but not really. And I don't think any of you would enjoy having me

23

play. Stop trying to distract me. I'm in the middle of asking if you plan to still be repping for B Team when you're ninety."

The husbands looked at each other. They both sat on the sofa in Ram's and Elora's Jefferson Unit apartment with their arms crossed, looking like they had dug in to be stubborn.

"She might have a point," Storm said to Ram.

"We're no' givin' any points nor any ground. With them 'tis always a slippery slope slidin' toward capitulation."

Storm looked at Elora. "We're not ninety *now*. We'll torch that bridge when we come to it. We're not even nearing thirty. And we're playing."

"Aye. We are."

Ram and Storm uncrossed their arms long enough to give each other a fist bump.

"Look," Elora began, "you're both young, strong, still in your prime and tough as they come."

"We'll no' be fallin' for the flattery approach."

"I'm just saying that you're all that, but you're also husbands and fathers with bones that can be broken and organs that can be ruptured." Elora deliberately omitted the part about how she hated overhearing female spectators objectifying her husband. She already knew that he was the stuff of nocturnal fantasy and didn't need to have that driven home by listening to women talk about imagining him when they were with somebody else. Ugh!

The men were silent and resolute. Resolutely silent.

When it was clear they were not being moved from their position, at all, Litha whispered something in Elora's ear and they withdrew to the bedroom, closing the door behind them.

"What do you think they're doin' in there?"

"I think they are saying that they will have better luck with a divide-and-conquer strategy."

"Aye. 'Tis my thought as well."

"Pact?"

"My man."

"Lust to dust."

"Sperm to worm."

"Womb to tomb."

Elora whispered to Litha. "Quiet. Ram's ears are amazing."

"Then let's duck out for a coffee. Or cocoa," she corrected.

When Elora nodded, Litha closed her fingers around her fellow conspirator's wrist and they popped into the lounge downstairs. The trip wasn't far enough to disturb equilibrium. It was no worse than a fast elevator drop.

"It won't hurt them to watch the babies for a little while."

Elora chuckled. "Neat trick."

They picked out two of the comfiest chairs, the ones that made sitting feel like getting a hug, and sat down facing each other.

"Hmmm. Well, I'm thinking that we're not going to get anywhere as long as they're together. They're feeding off of each other and ratcheting up the resolve. We need to interrupt that feed."

"Brilliant. Let us have yummy drinks and then go to our separate bedrooms to see if we can't get their arms uncrossed."

Litha smiled knowingly and initiated a soft five.

"Is it occurrin' to you that they're bein' *too* quiet?"

"It's your bedroom. You go check."

Ram opened the door and said. "Great Paddy loves a fuck. They're gone."

"What?" Storm got up.

"Gone. G.O.N.E. As in your wife always brin's an unknown factor to the mix. Great Paddy, I'm glad we were never assigned to hunt somethin' like her." Ram ran a hand through his hair and looked at Storm. "So. Guess who's babysittin'?"

Since moving back to Jefferson Unit, Elora had settled into a comfortable routine that included the luxury of a balanced life - equal parts family, social and work. In her case, work meant passing on the rigors of her clan's semi-secret martial arts, acquired from her training as one of the king's potential bodyguards when she was growing up in Stagsnare dimension. She had always found it gratifying to work with the active duty knights, knowing that some little change in posture or delivery might save a life.

In fact, teaching had originally been her suggestion. But since returning to Jefferson Unit, she found that she liked working with the trainees even more.

When she looked at those kids, she couldn't help thinking about the fact that each of them was some woman's baby. Understanding what that meant ratcheted her desire to teach them everything she could to keep them safe. She came to think of it as a sacred duty. And every day she was glad that Helm was a first born and not a second son. Of course she knew that exceptions had been made to that rule, but they were relatively rare. Her son would not be one of those exceptions.

She worked the boys hard in hand-to-hand and also taught an elective on weaponry, modern and ancient, for those who were interested. Some of them used it as an excuse to spend more time in the company of the famous knight who was centerfold gorgeous. And fun. But regardless of motivation, the result was a better trained class of future knights.

Elora made no secret of the fact that she thought "her" boys were going to be so much better than the active duty knights because she had gotten them young. When Storm was available, she used her influence to persuade him to stop by her extra-curriculum class and give firearms instruction.

The Lady Laiken made people feel golden in a way that was natural to her personality. She bragged to Storm about what fine hunters the kids were going to be and boasted to the trainees that nobody anywhere was better with firearms than Sir Storm.

At the end of class one cold winter day, the boys followed Sir Storm and Lady Laiken to the Hub level. Storm was in the middle of saying goodbye by postulating his thoughts on the importance of discipline when the normally noisy Hub suddenly became all but silent. Storm, Elora, and their students looked up to see Glen coming toward them, trailed by four ruffians who could not possibly pass for Black Swan knights.

Without taking his eyes away from Z Team, Storm finished his thought. "If you don't believe what I'm saying about self-discipline, just take a look at the alternative."

Elora's eyes roamed over Z Team and they responded with conspicuous ogling. Glen headed straight to Storm with a big grin on his face.

"Signed, sealed, and delivered, sir."

Glen glanced behind him like he was making sure his charges were still following. Storm greeted his protégé with a warm smile and a handshake just before turning an icy stare on the misfits. "I thought I'd take them straight to the Sovereign and report."

Storm nodded. "That would be standard procedure. By all means, proceed." He hit the down button to call an elevator car and stepped out of the way. Noticing that the boys were still standing in the same place practically gaping at Zed Company, Storm turned to Elora. "Class is dismissed, isn't it?"

Pulling her attention away from the human spectacle Glen had dragged in, she addressed the little cluster of boys. "The big guy's right. See you next time. If you put in extra practice, don't forget to log it. I want to know."

The kids started away slowly, making it pretty clear that the arrival of the exiled knights was definitely more interesting than anything else they might have planned for free time.

Storm leaned into Elora so that only she could hear and said quietly, "Think I'm going to accompany the circus to Sol's office and make sure he gives my boy the props he has coming." When he drew back, Elora nodded and Storm's face broke into a boyish smile that was definitely mischievous. "Plus, I need to pick up the proceeds from a little wager."

Glen left Z Team waiting in the hallway outside Sol's office with their duffels. Storm glared at them on his way past. Glyphs shot a what-the-fuck look at Torn who just shrugged and shook his head with a minimum of movement.

Storm knocked once on the closed door and entered without waiting for an invitation, a move that would have earned him a severed head when he'd been active duty under Sol. He shut the door behind him with a quiet snick as Sol looked up and waved him in.

"Just telling Catch here that he performed adequately and can take the rest of the day off."

"Adequately?" Storm turned to Glen. "I think that's the Sovereign's way of saying that there aren't half a dozen men in the world who could have gotten those losers here on time and without incident. You should get a medal."

Sol gave Storm a dirty look. "Just because you're no longer on my payroll doesn't mean you can speak for me. I said what I had to say."

"Okay." Storm raised his brows in judgment.

"Catch. You're dismissed."

"Yes sir. What should I tell the, uh, Z Team waiting in the hallway, sir?"

Sol picked up his phone and pushed a button. "Farnsworth! Send me runners to escort the new arrivals to their quarters." He slammed the phone into its cradle.

Storm whistled softly. "The woman you're engaged to lets you talk to her like that?" As he watched the blood drain from Sol's face on realizing what he'd done, Storm almost laughed out loud. Yeah. The man was in for it alright.

Sol recovered his grumpy pants quick enough and stepped out into the hallway. His greeting was brusque and efficient. If you took away the scowl, it could have been delivered by a robot.

"Welcome to Jefferson Unit. People are on the way to show you to your digs. Get settled in. Briefing tomorrow afternoon." He started back into his office then turned back. "And stay out of trouble till then." He slammed the door.

Glen smiled at the Zs and hunched his shoulders in apology for Sol. "Like he said, welcome to Jefferson Unit. See you around?"

Torn stuck out his hand. "Sure, kid. We'll be seein' you 'round."

The next couple of days were relatively quiet except for a catfight between two nurses of all things. Rumor was that it had something to do with Torn Finngarick, but he wasn't overly talkative on the subject and neither were the two women with nail scratches on their faces that were so deep they were practically gouges.

Halcyon Dimension, Fifteen years earlier.

Angel Wolfram Storm seemed to have been born knowing things, like math for instance. His mind would grab on to a concept on first presentation and then, while his classmates struggled, he would look around for something to occupy his busy mind. That *something* usually ended up being disruption.

His parents loved him, but the school faculty misunderstood his gift for disruption. He was smart, bored, and went about doing whatever he pleased while ignoring objections to the contrary. In short, no one in his life up to that point had given him an adequate reason to think that anarchy was not the best policy.

The majority of his time in school was either spent in the hallway outside class or in the waiting room outside the vice principal's office. His parents agonized over what to do, but never found the answer.

One day he was sent to the V.P.'s office under protest claiming that, for once, he hadn't done anything wrong. Maybe he didn't have a right to feel self-righteous about being wrongly accused, but if they'd been paying attention, they would have realized that he'd never shrunk from taking responsibility for his antics. Yeah. He got in trouble a lot, but he hadn't tried to weasel out and claim innocence.

He sat down in his usual chair to wait for the usual carpet ride thinking about the obvious chasm that exists between stoically silent and, "I didn't do it." When his dad showed up looking even more grim than usual, he knew it was that final hammer. He wasn't being suspended. He was being expelled.

The V.P. opened his door and leaned out. "Storm. Your father is here to take you home. Clean out your locker. Don't dawdle. Don't talk to the other children. And, do a thorough job because you won't be coming back."

Angel didn't miss the fact that Mr. Rodgers sounded happy. Well, the feeling was mutual.

His dad waited in the car while he cleaned out his locker. His mind was a blur of possible scenarios about what no school might mean and none of them were good. He stopped long enough to think about missing his friends and realized that he didn't have any friends who were important enough to miss. On the way out he passed the classroom with the ugly ass teacher who had ejected him for the last time. Class was in session, but the door to the hallway stood open.

Prune Face Blackmon followed the eyes of her students to the open door. "Mr. Storm. Do you not have someplace you need to be?"

He stared at her for a couple of beats while he processed that question. Actually no. Thanks to her and Mr. Rodgers he didn't have any place where he needed to be.

He looked to his right toward the front exit. If he went that way he would find his dad was waiting for him in the car. Then he looked to his left down the long polished hallway that led to a rear door. It takes a fraction of a second to make a choice that alters the course of a life so profoundly and irreparably that everything from that moment forward is a result, reward, or consequence of that one little choice. One of hundreds of choices routinely made in a day's cycle.

Angel Storm gave Blackmon the finger, and trotted away toward the rear exit, away from the weary father who waited, away from everything he'd known. He was grinning at the uproar of laughter from the poor douches who were going to be stuck in that hellhole the rest of the hour.

"Not a bad exit," he thought to himself. "Points shaved for lack of planning, but..."

He didn't know where he was going or what he was going to do. But, if he could have looked into his future, even for a moment, he wouldn't have been grinning.

He was fourteen.

The day after Elora Rose was born, the proud parents brought her home to the villa they had each dreamed about since adolescence.

Litha was stretched out on one of the two long leather sofas that faced each other. "I'm falling asleep. Again."

"Go ahead, Mama." Storm looked at the baby sleeping in his arm and brought her up to rest on his shoulder as easily as if he'd been performing that maneuver for years. "We've got this covered."

"You need to put that baby down sometimes, Beautiful. You're gonna make her sore."

He looked over at Litha with a half smirk. "I think that's an old wives tale."

"You're *not* calling me an old wife."

"If you say so."

"Do you smell something burning?"

Storm tightened his abs to help suppress a laugh so that the movement wouldn't wake Rosie. "You know that threat's starting to lose some of its punch. I think there's more blowing smoke than burning fire."

That taunt woke Litha up just enough to give him a smile so wicked he was instantly sorry he'd thrown that gauntlet in her direction. After all, she was only going to be in a weakened state for a short time. She had a long memory and, like most hereditary witches, believed that few things are sweeter than payback. The witchy DNA combined with demon blood meant that his spouse had an internal magick bag of tricks, any one of which packed a punch potent enough to put the fear of the gods into the gods themselves. Yeah. He was going to be sorry he'd started something.

Thinking about that made him heave a big sigh. Just the distraction needed because it earned him a whiff of pure heavenly new baby scent.

He glanced at Litha who was sleeping peacefully, turned on her side facing him. He was watching her when she jerked from the sound of a whistle coming from the kitchen. *Crap. Guess who's here?*

Deliverance came striding into the living room, loud, chipper, irritating as hell, which come to think of it, could be behind the reason why demons ended up associated with the fiery underworld of mythology.

"Ding dong. The witch gives head."

Litha was startled awake, which couldn't feel good to a bunch of internal organs desperately trying to resize, reshape, and put themselves back in the right place. The baby was startled as well and was wiggling around, close to erupting into a full-blown fuss.

"Oops. Everybody sleeping?"

Storm shot the self-centered, inconsiderate, asshole of a demon a look that should have killed him where he stood. "Not anymore."

"Hi, Dad," Litha said softly, sounding tired and drowsy.

The incubus smiled at her and waved then dropped to his knees next to where Storm held the baby. "Can I hold her?"

"Oh. Now you want to use inside voices?" Storm wasn't the least fond of his father-in-law, but it was impossible to hate a creature who looked at his child with an adoration so complete that it was borderline worship. "Okay. Here's the deal. I let you hold the baby for fifteen minutes and then you go get Litha's favorite pasta primavera from Corelli's."

"Done," the demon grinned. He was ever so much happier to be offered an equitable trade than he would have been to get off Scot free. Demons are like that. It's all about the deal.

Rosie had just begun to settle back down when Storm stood carefully, trying not to disturb her further. He gestured for the demon to sit where he'd been and then transferred the baby onto the shoulder of her grandfather, the incubus.

Storm shook his head. *Waking Woden. What a family.*

The child seemed more than content on the new shoulder and sighed audibly. Storm held his watch up and made sure Deliverance saw him point to the time. The demon gave him a wide smile that said, "Holding me to my bargain. Lovely. Maybe you're not so bad, dickwad."

Turning back to check on Litha, Storm saw that she'd drifted off again. Using the stealth he'd acquired as a Black Swan hunter, he headed toward the kitchen without waking his girls. He checked his intelliphone for texts while keeping an eye on the time. One thing he'd learned about Deliverance was that, if the demon managed to exceed the contractually agreed time – in that case, fifteen minutes, he would lose respect for his son-in-law.

Storm could care less about having the respect of an incubus except for the fact that things seem to go smoother with it than without it. So for Litha's sake, he made adjustments for kookiness that sometimes stretched way beyond the pale.

He stepped into the kitchen archway to check on Litha when he thought he heard quiet voices coming from the living room. She still looked sleepy and hadn't moved, but her eyes were open and she was talking to her father.

Storm arrived in time to hear Deliverance say in a near whisper, "She's so perfect in every way. Even her name. I *love* that you named her Rosie."

"I'm glad you like it. And she is. Perfect in every way."

"She looks like you."

Litha smiled and shook her head without raising up from the pillow. "No dad. You're not looking through clear eyes. See those long fingers? And look at that tiny scowl on her brow. She's intense even when she's asleep. She has my hair and maybe my eyes, but she's Storm all over. And I'm thrilled about that. He's the beauty in the family." Storm had to smile at that. What guy didn't want to know his wife thought he was beautiful?

"But look at the bloom in her cheeks and the way her nose turns up a little at the end, like a pixie."

"All babies' noses turn up a little," she chuckled. "That's so they can nurse without being suffocated."

Deliverance didn't look convinced.

Storm cleared his throat then tapped his watch face as he came around the sofa. He reached for the baby. The incubus pouted, but handed her over after planting a soft kiss on her little cheek.

"Stop that," Storm said, trying to wipe the kiss off Rosie's cheek with the corner of a pink baby blanket. "There's no telling where those lips have been."

Deliverance snickered and held out his hand for money. Storm mined his pocket and slapped a hundred dollar bill in the demon's hand. "Tell them to put the Alfredo sauce on the side. She's very particular about how much and likes to put it on herself. And don't think you're fooling anybody about the money. I know you're not going to pay for that."

Litha's dad glanced at her, snickered again, and vanished.

"You want to hold her while I set the table?"

Litha's eyes lit up and that was all the answer needed. He placed the sleeping baby on the sofa next to her mother.

Rosie's eyes might have opened a slit, but it was impossible to tell. She rubbed a tiny fist against her nose and went back to sleep.

Storm finished getting the kitchen ready for dinner delivered by demon and had just started back into the living room to check on his girls, when Deliverance appeared. Storm wondered for the hundredth time why Litha was the only one who didn't jump when the demon popped in.

"Hi ho." Deliverance announced raising two bulging brown paper sacks, one clutched in each hand, and looking as pleased with himself as if he'd retrieved the Golden Fleece.

Litha's mouth suggested a wisp of a smile. "I keep telling you not to call me a ho."

The demon giggled and handed the bags to Storm one at a time. "Done and done." He knelt down next to the sofa where Litha was stretched out and ran the back of his index finger over Rosie's cheek. "Have I mentioned that you're the two most beautiful females in the universe?"

Litha's eyes sparkled. "You haven't, but you're pretty good at communicating your emotions. I guessed you felt that way."

Deliverance stood and gave his daughter an adoring look, nodded to Storm and disappeared.

Litha gathered up the baby before trying to swing her legs to the floor. Storm made two long-legged strides.

"Here. Let me do that." He scooped Rosie into the crook of his arm and used the other hand to help Litha stand. "I can bring the food in here if you'd rather."

"Don't be silly. I'm not an invalid. In fact, since our daughter is the most considerate baby in the history of babies, I can only imagine that I'm doing a hundred times better than most moms with one-day-olds." She cut Storm a suggestive leer. "There could be some benefits to you as well."

"Like..."

"Sex sooner. Less wear and tear on the equipment." She wiggled her eyebrows.

"Okay, stop. I get it."

"Am I making you uncomfortable? Please tell me you're not going to be one of those men who loses interest once the hot mama becomes a mama."

Storm grinned. "That had better not be wishful thinking on your part because, no." He used his free arm to gingerly pull her in close to his side then looked down at her with a sexy little crooked grin full of the promise of lots of living yet to come. "I'm never gonna give up any part of you."

"Well said, knight. Is that pasta primavera I smell?"

"Indeed. A feast worthy of my lady."

For almost six weeks after Rosie's birth, everything proceeded normally. Storm's mother stopped over every few days to bring flowers or food or flowers and food. And hold the baby, of course. She was over the moon and kept calling grandparenthood a transcendent experience.

Six weeks to the day after they brought her home from the hospital, Rosie slept through the night without waking. Storm and Litha had gone to sleep facing each other, talking quietly about the future, reveling in the simple pleasure of their little family's cocoon. Storm said he was looking forward to teaching Rosie how to swim and ride a bike.

When they woke they were still facing each other. Hearing the baby's cry, they opened their eyes and watched each other's features transform into surprise when they realized it was light already.

"She slept all night." Storm said it like he had not really believed that would ever happen. Then his mouth curved up to show how much he appreciated that it had.

Litha returned his smile as she pulled on her robe and padded down the hall. Storm stretched in their bed enjoying the feeling of sleeping naked between clean sheets. The thought crossed his mind that he was going to have to give up that luxury, sooner or later, with a daughter in the house.

He was completely relaxed and completely content, when he heard Litha call his name in a way that couldn't be good.

"Storm!"

He scrambled up, not bothering with clothes, and hurried to the nursery next door. Litha was standing just inside the door with wide eyes and her hand over her mouth.

Rosie was sitting up staring at them like she was waiting to see what they would do next. In her hand she held the diaper that had come off during the night. She waved it a few times to show them she had learned a new trick of coordination. There was no question that the child in the crib was Rosie, but it was a lot to process all at once.

Her black hair was three inches longer and falling around her pixie face in waves. Her blue eyes had changed color and were going toward green. The yellow nightgown that she'd been wearing when she went to sleep, which cinched like a sack several inches below her feet, now gaped around her chubby little knees and the upper body was stretched so tight it looked like it might have to be ripped away.

The doorbell rang. Litha looked at Storm in a panic.

"It's probably your mother. You're going to have to make up a story. She can't see Rosie."

Storm practically leaped into a pair of jeans and pulled a tee shirt over his head as he was jogging toward the front door.

When he opened the door and didn't step aside to welcome her in, his mother looked him up and down. "What's wrong?"

"Um. Baby's sick. We were up with her all night." *Thank Paddy.* Ram's ability to lie on cue must have finally rubbed off on him.

"Oh. I'm sorry. Let me make breakfast."

"No, mom, that's wonderful of you, but we want to find out what the doctor says before we expose her to any more people. You understand."

"Yes. Well. You'll let me know if I can do something?"

"Of course. Thank you. Sorry to shuffle you off. I'll call you soon as we're cleared for company."

"I'm not company!" She sounded offended.

"No... I... ah...."

"Never mind. I know what you meant. Take care of Litha and Rose."

"Rosie," he corrected. "And I will. Talk to you later." He felt like a scumbag for closing the door in his mother's face, but he had bigger problems than a mom with hurt feelings.

Way bigger.

He walked back to the nursery halfway hoping that, when he arrived, he would find a six-week-old baby. No such luck.

The next hour was a blur. Litha estimated Rosie's age at six months. She fashioned a makeshift diaper out of a dish towel and sat down in the rocking chair to feed the baby. Rosie was happy enough to lie in her mother's arms while she ate, but she promptly took the bottle away from Litha and held it in her own two hands. Litha looked down into green eyes that mirrored her own and said, "I wasn't ready to give that up yet, little girl."

Rosie stopped sucking for a minute like she was contemplating what was being said. She smiled, but she didn't offer to relinquish the bottle. That smile stole Litha's breath. She was sure she'd never seen anything as beautiful since the day the gorgeous

knight had walked into the Headquarters building in
Edinburgh.

Storm returned home with clothes and diapers
to fit a six-month-old and jars of organic baby food to
supplement the formula.

"How did you know what kind of baby food to
get?"

"I Giggled it."

"Oh." Litha started looking through the
selection. "What is Tutti Fruiti?"

"Ah. Mixed fruit?" Litha read the label,
looked at Storm like he was a moron, and
unceremoniously dropped the jar in the trash. He
pinched the bridge of his nose. "I'm guessing there's a
learning curve."

Elora was eager to see the reported changes in
Rosie, so she was invited to come to what had been
known for a while as Thursday Night Dinner With
Glen.

Glen arrived first. He and the demon popped
in as Litha was on the verge of giving Storm a lecture
on nutrition. She stopped when she saw that Glen had
arrived. Turning toward him with the baby straddling
her hip, Litha smiled and opened her mouth to
welcome her husband's protégé, but the greeting was
upstaged by Rosie's delighted giggle. The baby
clapped her little hands, making up for what she
lacked in coordination with enthusiasm and squealed,
"Glen!"

Deliverance, who had dropped Glen and gone
back for Elora, arrived with the auntie in tow seconds

later. They found three adults frozen and staring at Rosie.

Elora looked around the room. "What'd I miss?"

Sol summoned Storm to Jefferson Unit. It was easy enough for him to get a ride with Deliverance because the demon showed up to gush over Rosie every damn day.

"You wanted to see me?"

"Sir Storm. Come in. Should thank you for not just barging in whenever the hell you feel like it."

"You do know I'm retired and have absolutely no obligation whatsoever to come when you call. So. You're welcome."

Sol harrumphed. "I need something from you."

"Imagine that."

The Sovereign narrowed his eyes. "Is this attitude new or have you been hiding a belligerent side all along?"

Storm smiled brightly. "You'll never know."

"The reason why I asked you here is this. Things are kind of quiet for a change so I'm thinking I might slip away for a few days of vacation."

Storm barked out a laugh.

"Vacation? That's how you're gonna play it? Come on. You churned up a shit storm with your future bride and had to promise a romantic getaway to smooth things over."

Sol's brows drew together. "How did you know that?"

Storm plopped into a chair laughing.

"How indeed? I told you you've got a lot to learn about women." He leaned forward with mischief written all over his normally serious face. "And I hope this make-up interlude costs you dearly."

"What did I ever do to you?"

Storm gaped, then looked at his watch. "You have the rest of the day for me to get started on that list?"

Sol stared at Storm for a few beats, clearly uncomfortable with the idea of asking for favors. "The point is that I need somebody to cover for me. I thought maybe I could leave you in charge with Catch acting as assistant."

"For how long?"

"Four weeks."

Storm started chuckling all over again. "Four weeks? You really did bite it, didn't you?" Sol looked a little beaten and confused so Storm gave him a little pity slack.

"Neither one of us has ever done vacation. We've got years of paid leave in accrual. I figure it might take a couple of weeks just for workaholics like the two of us to figure out how to 'do' vacation. There's never going to be a better time. Jefferson making the transition to research and training, well, you and I both know the place doesn't really need someone like me."

Storm studied Sol for a minute, trying to read between the lines. With a guy like Sol there was always more going on that would be spoken out loud.

"Tell you what. I'll come in for half a day and make sure the building is still standing for triple time and a half. Glen can handle the rest for trainee allowance."

Sol pursed his lips. "Triple time and a half. That the best I can get?"

"Final offer. I've learned a lot about negotiating from my wife. And I have a kid to send to college." Sol nodded his agreement like he couldn't bring himself to vocalize the word yes. "When are you leaving?"

"Tomorrow."

"Tomorrow." Storm repeated with his eyebrows raised. "Got your speedo packed?"

"Out!"

Storm left laughing to himself, enjoying Sol's discomfort with stepping outside his comfort zone immensely. He planned to get in a quick workout before heading home and was still chuckling when he got to the elevator.

Elora was getting off. "What's so funny?"

"The image of Sol on a romantic vacation."

"Okay. Not sure I want to share your vision. But I wanted to ask you about something else. What's the deal with Z Team? You have some bad history with them?"

"Not exactly. I just think that bestowing knighthoods on them is ludicrous. It makes a laughing stock of us all."

"Why?"

"Because, Elora, they're loose cannons. Rebellious anarchists who are proud of their non-conformity, and their first loyalty is to their teammates and not to The Order."

Elora laughed in his face. "Storm! You just described B Team. It sounds like the only difference

between them and us is that we dress better,
sometimes, and don't wear ink."

"You know what the other knights call them?
Team Fuck Up! Say what you want, but B Team
didn't end up in Marrakesh, the last outpost before
you fall off the Earth."

"Okay. Okay. Calm down. You just act like
they're a personal affront."

"They are. That's what I'm trying to tell you."

"You resent them."

"Yes." Elora tried to make her features as
blank as possible. "You think I'm being a self-
righteous prick."

"I did not say that."

"Well, you didn't have to. I know you."

"Not that well."

"Really? Then tell me I'm wrong about what
you were thinking." Elora opened her mouth to argue,
but ended up laughing because he'd nailed it. "Like I
said. I. Know. You."

"Kay. Have a good day."

He smiled and saluted.

As a favor to his daughter, Deliverance agreed
to help simplify things by showing up at the vineyard
every day to give Storm a "ride" to work at Jefferson
Unit and stopping in to pick him up and return him
six hours later.

The next morning Storm and Litha awoke to
the sounds of a happy little girl coming from the next
room. As they lay in bed and looked into each other's
eyes, each wondered if the other was reading their
thoughts, which were a conflicting mixture of delight

and dread. They couldn't wait to see what changes in Rosie the morning might bring. At the same time, they were in no hurry to see what might have happened overnight.

When they heard the sweetest voice in the universe say, "Momma. Daddy," they watched each other as they mirrored a reaction that went from slack-jaw surprise to smiling eyes. Okay. So it wasn't going to be an average family living an average life. Had either of them been naïve enough to expect that? Well, maybe. But people who were extra-human, married to other people who were extra-human, should be smart enough to know better. These were the thoughts that ran through the minds of Rosie's parents as they watched each other silently come to terms with their unusual circumstances.

Storm pulled Litha close for a quick snuggle and a smooch on the lips.

"We better go get our little girl before she starts calling Child Protective Services."

Litha smiled. "Go ahead and joke, but she probably knows how to use a phone."

The two of them rolled out on opposite sides of the bed and then raced each other to the nursery giggling, eager to see what the day had in store for the three of them. As they suspected, it was an adventure in parenting. A unique adventure.

Rosie was standing up holding onto the end of her crib, laughing at them as they came through the door. Her dark curly hair was a tousled mess, three inches longer than the day before and her eyes had settled into the deep emerald gemstone color of Litha's.

"Hey, little girl." Litha reached to pick her up.

Storm said, "Are you sure you should be lifting her? I don't think your body is healing at the same rate she's maturing."

"I'm fine," Litha said smiling at Rosie.

Rosie hummed and leaned toward Storm. She reached a fat little dimpled hand toward his cheek and patted. He was already a fool for the child, but that affectionate little gesture tightened the bindings around his heart making fatherhood feel almost painful.

"Oh. So you like the big guy, do you? Well, who could blame you? He's one of a kind. And you could certainly do worse."

He swallowed a lump that caught in his throat while he listened to Litha massage Rosie's little spirit with soothing mother talk. She got the baby out of a tight wet nightgown to ready her for a bath. While they were so occupied, Storm called Glen and explained the situation.

"I don't have to tell you that this is FYI. She appears to be maturing about six months every day. If this continues, she'll be grown in a month."

"Wow."

"Yeah. Exactly. Here's the thing. It's priority organization time and she's my priority. I'm not going to miss being here while she grows up. So here's what I'm going to do. I'll get Deliverance to bring me to lunch every day at one and pick me up at two. If you need to bounce something off me, or run it by me, you'll get an hour a day. Can you handle that?"

Glen was such a natural for the job of

substitute sovereign that he wouldn't require much supervision, or even guidance. He might not know that yet, but Storm was sure of it.

"I think so. If a decision had to be made that I didn't feel good about making on my own, I could get you on the phone. Right?"

"Absolutely, but highly unlikely. You've got instincts that work overtime. I should probably call you with my parenting questions."

Glen laughed. "No, sir. Jefferson Unit's not that hard to manage, but I'm not taking responsibility for that baby."

Litha padded into the kitchen barefoot carrying a clean, happy toddler on her hip. Storm relayed his decision and his conversation with Glen.

"Can we arrange her schedule so that she's napping then? At least for the first couple of days? If the pattern holds true, I'm guessing she'll be too old for naps by the end of the week."

The wave of sadness that came over Litha's face made his stomach clench.

"I'm sorry," she whispered.

He moved toward her with a purposeful determination that never failed to make her glad that Storm was her man. *Fearlessness. Beautiful.*

Putting his arms around both his girls, he kissed Litha's temple. "Baby, which thing do you think was the biggest clue that we weren't candidates for an ordinary life:

"A. The fact that you're a witch?

"B. The fact that you're a demon's daughter?

"C. The fact that you're a firestarter?

"Or D. the fact that I'm a vampire hunter who's also part demon?'

That earned him a tentative smile. "We knew we signed on for an adventure. This is just part of it."

He turned her to face him and ducked down so he could look directly into her eyes.

"I wouldn't trade *us* for *anything* else. You know that. Right?" She nodded, trying to hide a misty sniffle. "We're going to make every minute count. I'm still going to get to teach her to ride a bike. Even if I have to do it quick."

Litha cocked her head to the side. "That's the second time you've mentioned that."

"Is it?"

"Yes. Is there a reason why?"

"Was a good memory for me. My dad out in the street in front of our house, full of encouragement. I guess I want to recreate it. Who taught you?"

"Brother Morrighausey." She laughed. "He was probably the last person in the world who ought to be teaching a coordination skill. He knew seven ancient languages but could barely walk without tripping."

Rosie laughed out loud, mimicking her mother, then said, "Maury!"

Litha gave Rosie a strange look. "Yeah. That's what we called him. And he *was* funny."

Rosie hiccupped another little giggle.

Elora saw Monq's profile pic come to the face of her phone, the ridiculous one with the mouse ears.

She was en route to S2, where Monq's research facilities were located, among other things.

"I'm on my way. Hold on to your mouse costume or whatever else you might be wearing. Can't wait to find out what's got you in such a fit of impatience."

"Just hurry up."

Just then she pushed through the main lab door and said, "Okay!" as she closed the phone and dropped it in the outer pouch of her messenger bag.

"Don't take that tone with me, young lady. I'm the one who's been working night and day to save your beautiful...," Monq caught himself just before he finished that sentence with an unrefined word. "...self."

"Really? Well, if you're going to persist in calling me *young lady*, I'm not sure I want to be saved. Just kill me now." Monq ignored that as completely as if she hadn't spoken at all. "And if you keep taking all my blood, I'm not going to be able to make enough milk for my elfling."

He waved his hand. "We're done with that." Then looking away as if something had caught his interest, he said, "At least I think so.

"Here. Sit. Let me tell you the news."

"Should I call the press?"

"This is not a joking matter, Elora."

"Lady Laiken."

"Is Rammel standing behind you with his hand up your shirt?"

She looked stunned. "Monq! You made a joke!"

"Pffft. Will you just stop and listen? Please?"

"Yes, I will. I'm all yours."

"I *never* use your blood frivolously. In fact I used some that was collected before you left for Edinburgh to mutate a strain of rats for testing purposes."

"You did what?!?"

"So I've been using the rats to test an airborne chemical that would weaken potential assailants from your home world."

"Deliverance says it's called Stagsnare Dimension in his circles."

"Um-hum. Stagsnare Dimension. The biggest obstacle was coming up with a chemical solution that has no harmful side effects to other species that might frequent Jefferson Unit. So I've been testing on both normal rats and Elora rats."

"Elora rats? Please. I'm begging you. Tell me you did *not* name a species of rats *Elora Rats*."

Refusing to be distracted, he dismissed that with a characteristic wave of his hand. "And I think we've got it."

She stared and blinked a few times. "Are you saying that, in the event of an attack by natives of Stagsnare Dimension, you could gas the intruders without adverse effects to Jefferson personnel?"

"Yes. I believe we understand each other."

"And they'll be weakened to mimic indigenous physical ability?"

"Yes."

"Why not just terminate while you're at it?"

"Good question. Because then there would be side effects. Bad ones."

"Okay. So the assassins will lose the edge

they would normally get from slipping to this dimension." He nodded. "And that's without any negative consequence to the rest of us. Including the *tiniest* of us," she said pointedly.

"Um. More or less. Do you want the good news or the bad news?"

Elora's shoulders sagged as she sat back in the chair and sighed deeply. "It has been my experience that, when you ask that question, there's usually a teeny weeny tiny tidbit of microscopic good news and a shitload of bad."

"Young lady...!"

"Especially when you add 'more or less' to that."

"Just give me the news."

"Very well. There's no way to make *you* immune from the effects. It's what they call a trade-off. You wouldn't retain superior strength and speed, but neither would others from your dimension of origin. They wouldn't have any advantage over those who come to your aid. And there will always be people at Jefferson Unit ready to come to your aid. Capable people. So you'd have a better than good chance against them. It wouldn't be just you. Alone."

It was easy to read both concern and sincerity on Monq's face. There was no question in her mind that he cared about her in his own way. Maybe not as much as the Monq who had been her tutor growing up and had taught her everything from Latin to horseshoes, but still.

"And you're ready to test it on me. Monq. You *do* realize that I'm nursing."

He pursed his lips. "I can't tell you what to do

about that, but I think staying alive is more important.
I can give you something to dry up your milk quickly
and painlessly and without having any detrimental
effect on your, uh, natural shape." Monq turned pink
when trying to communicate that last bit of info.

"You mean feed Helm formula milk instead."

"You could wait until he weans naturally,
but..."

"I get it. I'll talk it over with Ram tonight.
Maybe I'll look into baby formula."

"Already done. I put Allicent on it. We had
some flown in with the last passing. Just in case. It's
expensive. Made in Switzerland."

"Just in case," she said dryly. "You've
thought of everything."

"I should hope so since that *is* my job."

When Ram finished music practice, he hurried
"home" to the Jefferson Unit apartment he hoped
would be temporary quarters. When he opened the
door, he saw Elora sitting at the table next to Helm's
crib, hands on the portaputer keyboard.

"Hey. What's up?" With a Ram-style smile
that lit up the room, he headed straight for his mate,
gave her a kiss in passing on his way to pick up
Helm, but made sure to linger long enough so that she
knew it was heartfelt and not routine.

As he lifted the baby, she said, "Something we
should discuss."

"Sounds serious."

"Hmmm. Depends on how you look at it. Can
you sit?"

Ram sat and listened intently without interrupting. "'Tis no question about what you're goin' to do. Is there?"

She looked thoughtful. "I didn't want to make a final decision without talking to you. I've done a little research and I think Helm will be okay so long as I still spend the same time with him and hold him the same way I would if I was nursing."

"Helm is strappin'. Just look at him." She had to smile at the pride so evident in Ram's voice. "What our boy needs is for his mum to be survivin'."

"So we're decided."

"Great Paddy, Elora! O' course."

An hour after Elora informed Monq of their decision, six of the trainees showed up at the apartment door wearing boyish expressions – a cross between sheepishly shy and eagerness to get a look at the private life of their instructor. Each was carrying two cases of expensive Swiss formula. Ram directed the stacking of the boxes while Elora smiled and thanked them for their help.

Elsbeth stopped in after her shift in the clinic to give a crash course on the proper preparation of bottles. It wasn't part of her nurses training, but she had a sister-in-law who had done bottle feeding.

Elora walked Elsbeth down the hall to the elevator.

"So don't think I didn't notice that special glow, which can only mean one thing where you're concerned. *Hot* date."

"Not per se. More like a get together." Elsbeth managed to look coy, which was a remarkable feat considering the level of her worldliness and experience.

Elora laughed in her face. "Keep it to yourself if you want. I'm just sayin'."

"Well, you know I've been seeing Dirk."

"No. Who's Dirk?"

"Fennimore?"

"Oh. Dirk is his first name? I didn't know that. The knights all call him Fenn."

"I think he goes by Fenn with them because of the razzing about his first name."

Elora nodded. "Yeah. I can see that."

"Anyway."

"Yes? Anyway? Go on."

Elsbeth grinned. "I like him."

"And that's supposed to be a revelation?" Elora pulled her friend to a stop. "Really?"

"Okay, yeah, I like him a lot," she chuckled.

"You really need to work on your impulsivity."

"Really?" Elsbeth looked concerned.

"No! Not really! You need to borrow a nickel for the jar and go see Monq."

"What do you mean?"

"Never mind. I guess that's a service for knights. Forget I said anything. Back to Fenn... uh, Dirk. I've got to tell you it feels weird to call him that. Like my tongue is resisting."

They had just reached the elevator doors when Elsbeth leaned in and whispered, "I get it. I'm terrified that one of these nights I'm going to accidentally shout Dick instead of Dirk."

When the doors opened, none other than Sir

Fennimore was standing there being treated to the sight of two grown women locked in a fit of giggles that would make any tween proud. Fenn, who lived about halfway down the section hallway on Elora's floor, gave them a sexy little smile that said he was both charmed and amused.

"Ladies." He addressed both women, but had eyes only for Elsbeth. As he and Elsbeth changed places, her taking his place on the elevator, he looked down lowered lids with an expression of male smugness and said, "Later." The unmistakable undertone filled the air with suggestion. Elora looked at Elsbeth and crossed her eyes.

Walking back toward her apartment, Fennimore fell into step with Elora, but said nothing more. When they neared his door, she said, "Have fun tonight, Dirk."

Elora suppressed a smile when she caught a little hitch in his stride.

The next afternoon Elora returned to the apartment looking a little dazed. The experiment hadn't been painful. She'd breathed into a gas mask twice, then Monq said, "That's it."

"You sure? I don't think anything happened."

He smirked. "Okay. See you later."

Elora shrugged as she started to get up. She made it as far as a crouch and sat back down. Hard. "What the hell, Monq?"

He chuckled and did a little jig. "It works!!" She gaped at him with a mix of confusion and betrayal. "You've grown used to wearing a superwoman suit, my dear. The gas just took it away from you, as it would any visitor from your dimension of origin. If you ever have to function under the effects of the Equalizer, you're going to need to make some adjustments."

"Adjustments? I feel like I'm seventy years old."

Monq cocked his head. "How do you know what seventy feels like?"

"I have a good imagination. This isn't going to work. If I was being attacked I wouldn't be able to defend myself. Or my family. Or my friends. Or anybody else for that matter."

"Sure you could. You'd just be reduced to the same physical resources as any other woman. You still have your angry martial skills."

"Angry martial skills?" She stared. He nodded. "Do you mean *mad* skills?"

"Whatever."

She shook her head and mumbled to herself, "Who would have ever thought I'd be correcting somebody on pop phraseology?"

"*And!* You're still you."

"And that means what?"

"That means it's just another challenge. You'll find a work-around. It's what knights do."

"Right. How long will this last?"

"That's part of the experiment. I need you to call in as soon as you no longer feel the effect so we can log it." She moved toward the door, a lot slower than usual. "Don't forget."

"Oh! Like that's possible!"

"Good to see the sarcasm is unaffected." He

didn't look up from his monitor to see the withering look he got in response.

She trudged home feeling heavy and dejected. That last part was resented in the worst way because she knew she was feeling pissy and spoiled and didn't like the way either one fit. Monq was right. She'd gotten comfortable in her role as semi-invincible. *So this is life as a mere mortal.* She chastised herself for feeling entitled to the privilege of extra strength and speed.

Ram was holding Helm above his lap and laughing while the baby did a tiptoe jig on his da's thighs. He looked up when Elora came in. "Somethin' wrong?"

"It takes a little getting used to."

Walking over, slowly, she reached to pick up the baby and give him a smooch. And almost dropped him.

"Great Paddy! This child weighs a ton!"

Ram snickered. "'Tis the word on the street. Never thought to be hearin' it from you though."

She sat down on the sofa next to Ram with Helm on her lap, looking thoughtful as she jiggled him. "You know…" her eyes cut toward her mate, "all the way from the lab I've been trying to find an upside to this predicament."

"Um-hmm?" Ram leaned into her side and nuzzled her neck below her ear, as if he knew what she was thinking.

"Monq calls the chemical the Equalizer."

"Uh-huh," he said absently as he continued nuzzling.

"And I was thinking that we've never made love as two ordinary elves."

He drew back and looked into Elora's eyes with an expression suddenly grown serious. "Ordinary elves is it? Ordinariness is no' possible for you, Elora. Do you no' know that? No' even if you put a paper bag over your head."

"Please tell me that's not a fantasy."

He laughed, shaking his head. "No. No' at all."

"Thank you for the lovely compliment. Back to what I was saying; aren't you curious about what it would be like? I think I might enjoy no restraint, not having to worry about squeezing too tight or raking my nails down your back."

Rammel's pupils dilated as he went instantly hard, making his eyes look navy blue. He searched her face for less than two seconds. "Call Elsbeth."

"She's got plans."

"Cook's always askin'."

"It's early enough in the day that she might have a couple of hours." Rammel grinned. "You call her. I'll get a diaper bag ready to go."

After a lengthy experience of sex with native Loti strength, Rammel bore the marks of no-holds-barred fucking and reveled in every one of them.

"Great Paddy, would you look at me, woman?" Ram turned his naked body first one way and then the other while he admired himself in the full-length mirror. "I'm shredded. If I ever get you without your extras again, we will be trimmin' your nails first."

"I hear your words, but they're bouncing off that smile."

He laughed and sailed through the air then bounced on the bed next to Elora. "Aye. Will suffer pain for your pleasure any day."

She leaned up on an elbow and looked down at him, then lowered her head to place a kiss in one of the valleys of his abs. Since he was relaxed and not aroused, he was ticklish. He tried to roll away, but she held him down without effort, which immediately drained away the fun.

Elora looked at her watch and sent Monq a text. Three hours, seventeen minutes.

Ram pulled up to his elbows. "What's wrong?"

She turned back to look at him.

"I clocked three hours, seventeen minutes that the gas was effective on me. I was just sitting here wondering what would happen if that wasn't enough time to… take care of things. And I was thinking about sending Monq another text asking if there is enough Equalizing gas in the system to deliver a second round."

Ram reached out and ran his fingertips down her spine, which gave her a pleasant shiver from head to toe.

"You're worryin' the thin' more than you should. I'm gettin' there is wisdom in precaution to a point. But the chance of Jefferson Unit comin' under attack? Dwellin' on it is just silly. 'Tis why we live here, you know."

She turned and grinned at him. "Oh. Is *that*

why we're here? I thought it was for the free and plentiful babysitting."

"'Aye. 'Tis a nice perk and one we shall miss when we leave."

Stagsnare Dimension

Archer had looked at the equation from every angle. A thousand times. He couldn't solve for the unknown because he was missing a critical factor. His superiors wanted results immediately. Nothing new about that. When had they ever said, "We want results. Take your time."? The face that the puzzle was missing essential pieces was irrelevant so far as they were concerned.

He sighed, turned over, and looked at the bright LED display on the alarm clock, the only light in the darkness. Sleeplessness had been more rule than exception for a long time. He spent his nights tossing, turning and cursing at himself. At the moment he was engaged in his usual nocturnal pastime, staring at the clock that mocked him. Time. It was his biggest problem. Because he'd run out of it.

The Council had decided that a second expedition would be launched to find the escaped Laiwynn royal. It had been less than three months since the last had claimed the lives of twelve young healthy Ralengclan males, each of whom would have been an asset to the gene pool. They were officially classified as MIA rather than KIA, but if anyone thought there was a chance that they'd survived, they weren't optimists. They were fools.

Of course there were a few detractors who were cynical enough to realize that MIA meant not having to pay the families death benefits. Bastards.

Politics followed its normal course of bureaucratic ineptitude and rewarded the idiot in charge of the senseless debacle, Lt. Rothesay, with a promotion to Council membership.

Although Archer had no proof, he had theorized that a "placeholder" was required for each life signature in a particular dimension. He wished he could claim authorship of the idea, but the truth was that there was an obscure reference to something of the sort in a fragment recovered from Monq's journals.

If the princess had survived the trip to another dimension – and there was no proof of that - she would theoretically have gone to a dimension where two conditions were met: a life signature matching Monq's and a "placeholder" for her. In other words, someone who matched her unique life pattern, but was deceased.

The Council had been in far too big a hurry to explore that possibility. When the first team failed to return on the appointed date, or any thereafter, Council members had decided to grant Archer three months to better prepare for the next trip.

Archer had tried to impress upon them that, if his theory was correct and he sent someone to a dimension where the matching life signature was occupied, they would simply cease to exist - as in vanish or disappear. The idea of that had chilled him before. After having been instrumental in wiping out the lives of the entire expedition, his conscience was bruised and constantly throbbing. No doubt the root cause of his insomnia.

Truthfully, the additional time had done little to change anything. He continued to cling to the original premise of his working theory, but the reprieve of three months had rendered nothing in the way of new evidence. Just guessing, guessing and more guessing.

Archer wasn't into guessing. Scientists pride themselves on dealing in facts. Nothing was more uncomfortable than playing parlor games with cosmic operations and yet that was exactly what he found himself doing.

Without the benefit of reliable data and replicable results, there was nowhere to turn except to gut feeling. His mother's intuition had been fodder for inside family joking that bordered on ridicule, but that intuition was also typically unerring in a way that had been disturbing to a budding young scientist. There was an effect without an explainable cause.

The chasm between physics and metaphysics was not easily bridged because adherents of each were passionate about their dissimilar beliefs, not to mention that both sides were convinced that they were "right".

Still, he found himself hoping, to gods he didn't believe in, that he had inherited a little bit of his mother's intuitive gift. Another crop of young lives depended on it.

Of course, someone was in line to feed the universal constant of sacrifice, but at least that sacrifice would be on the part of nameless, faceless young men who had no connection to him and their nameless, faceless mothers, wives, siblings, friends and maybe children. He wouldn't again make the mistake of engaging any of the probable victims in conversation as he'd done with Rystrome. He would send them on their way without so much as making eye contact. Better for everybody that way.

While he lay in the dark alone, wide awake and staring at the red LED light on the clock, thinking about the course of events that he would put in motion the next day, he tried – hard - to *not* focus on the likely outcome of the mission.

He blamed himself for the entire thing. Himself and his big mouth. If he hadn't revealed that he'd deciphered the code Monq had used to map the Laiwynn's destination, he could have claimed – honestly – that the search was infinitely hopeless, a grain of sand in the Sahara. But he had reason to believe it was narrowed down to less than twenty possible destinations.

When he began to make out gray stripes on the ceiling, it meant first light was streaming past shutter slats. It was a relief of sorts. He could set all hope of sleep aside and move on. So he threw off the covers, grateful for an excuse to get up and fill the silence with noise and other distractions.

He showered, shaved, pulled on clothes and made his way to work. That meant opening his apartment door and walking fifteen feet to his main computer. He'd taken over the basement complex that had formerly belonged to Thelonius M. Monq. It included a well-stocked study-library, a large lab and a bachelor apartment that was comfortable and stylish in a medieval minimalist way. He'd been given a generous allowance to make changes, but found that the setup suited him as it was. So the allowance had been funneled into a scholarship program for Lt. Rystrome's children. That was why Rystrome had volunteered – to get the money to educate his children. Archer shook his head and then shook off thinking about that.

He glanced at his watch. One hour until commencement of the death parade. That wasn't the official name of the project, of course, but it's what he called it in his own head. Before his assignment was complete there were going to be a lot of corpses. It was inevitable. And it was a waste. All the lives that would be cut short, all the squandered potential, just for a dubious seek-and-destroy with one inconsequential Laiwynn girl as the target. One who most likely died in her escape attempt. What a gigantic waste of resources! He didn't agree with it, but was powerless to stop it.

One hour to get breakfast before the countdown. After checking in with his system, he opted for coffee only. He could always eat when and if his appetite ever returned.

Archer had lined up twenty sacrificial lambs except that, unlike ancient tradition, they weren't lambs and they weren't healthy. They were men who were walking around in bodies that had medically-established expiration dates. Yeah. Terminal illnesses.

The new Ralengclan government made deals with the guys. If they survived transport and returned, they'd be given the opportunity to serve their clansmen in a legendary way. The new offer was that, either way, the families' circumstances would be elevated to a state of luxurious security. Archer's superiors hadn't been happy about coughing up funds for the program, but he'd played the old we're-better-than Laiwynn card, which usually turned the key in the lock. And, truthfully, he'd been surprised by the number of volunteers.

Right on schedule the first walking dead was escorted in. The guy was tall, fortyish and lean in a way that suggested either illness or a very hard life. Maybe both. His cheeks were gaunt and the skin around his eyes was gray, but he was upright with an alert gleam in his eye that looked out of place with the rest of him.

Archer offered his hand out of courtesy and motioned for the man to sit for final instructions.

"I know you've been through this many times, but just to be sure, let's go over it once more. When all motion has ceased, step outside the device and run the locator program exactly the way you practiced. Don't linger. Don't walk around. Don't spend time looking around. The transport is programmed to open and readmit you in three minutes. Turn around and get back on the machine.

"If the light is red, you will automatically proceed to the next stop and repeat. If the light is green, board the transport and push the big green button. You'll return immediately.

"If all goes well, I'll see you back here shortly and we'll have a drink. Questions?"

The man – his name was Tarriman – just shook his head no. Archer started the tumbler rotating and motioned the man to enter. Unlike the pre-experimental version that had taken Elora Laiken to another life, the new transport was equipped with a smooth titanium lining that remained both stationary and stable while the tumbler moved around it.

When the tumbler was whirring so fast that it was no longer visible without mechanical apparatus, Archer closed the door and nodded to his assistant to enter the countdown sequence. As the panel slid to lock position, his eyes locked with Tarriman's. He'd sworn he wasn't going to look any of them in the eye, but when it came down to it, he couldn't treat the poor devil like scrap metal. The least he could do for the guy was give him the respect of looking at him as he sent him to his fucking useless death. If Archer had been a gambling personality he might have held onto some hope of seeing Tarriman again, but he was too well acquainted with the odds to let himself go there.

The prospect of sharing that drink depended on Tarriman making it to the dimension where there was both a placeholder for his life signature *and* a version of Elora Laiken Laiwynn whose anatomical makeup matched Stagsnare biology and whose presence had not been detected earlier than two years before, to be confirmed by the biolocator. Of course it was possible. They just might have to go through a couple hundred termies on the way to bingo.

Ninety-six minutes later, the transport "docked" with a roar and a power surge before the whirring of the tumbler slowed. Five people waited with eyes glued to the panel door: Archer, three assistants, and Rothesay. It slid open with a hydraulic-sounding hiss. Empty. The compartment was empty.

Rothesay turned away throwing Archer a menacing look like it was his fault and strode toward the exit while barking out two words. "Tomorrow! Again!"

Archer stood looking at the empty cylinder, feeling as tired as a man who had never slept once in his whole life. He hadn't expected to see Tarriman again so he couldn't explain the sudden onset of bone-crushing weariness. He heaved a sigh and gave a simple order over his shoulder, "Notify the family."

Number 17

By the seventeenth day, Archer was in the throes of his predawn ritual, staring at the LED light on his alarm clock and thinking about how he would go about committing suicide, if he should ever decide to check out. He wasn't serious. It was a game, albeit a morbid one. Just something to occupy his mind, a way to fill the hours of silence and loneliness while trying to elbow guilt and remorse aside.

Archer hadn't had a day off since the death parade began. By the time they reached the eleventh guy he'd stopped asking their names. It was easier to think of them as numbers. He worked harder at not making any kind of connection with them. He didn't shake their hands. He didn't look in their faces. He ran through instructions like an automaton and pointed to the tumbler.

So far as Archer was concerned he was no longer a scientist or inventor or investigator. He was an executioner, the modern equivalent of a shirtless guy wearing a hooded mask, carrying a nice sharp ax.

When number seventeen was escorted in, he didn't look up. He spoke the text of the instructions by rote, in a monotone, and waved toward the machine. Forty-seven minutes later the interdimensional transport returned. Archer looked at the clock so that he could log the time, but didn't bother to turn around when the door hissed open, at least not until he heard cheering and clapping. His head came around to see number seventeen shuffling toward him offering the biolocator.

Rothesay was beaming, no doubt imagining his next promotion.

So Archer looked at number seventeen, really looked. He accepted the biolocator with thanks and verified that the light was indeed green. There was a match between number seventeen and the first stop on his tour. The *first* stop.

Archer had thought it so unlikely that Phase Two would ever be implemented, that he hadn't given much thought to how he would feel about the inherent operations of a third mission. It was looking like he'd better get with the program fast. Because that's how things were going to start moving. Fast.

BLACK SWAN TRAINING MANUAL, STANDARD PROCEDURES.
Section II: Knights. Chapter 1, #2

A knight of The Order of the Black Swan

*comports himself with honor, dignity, and in
accordance with the wisdom of the guiding principle,
that service is a privilege.*

 Glen had found that there were a lot of
surprising things about performing the day-to-day
duties of Sovereign. It didn't take long to figure out
that it wasn't a glam job. First, it involved lots of
lonely butt-in-chair hours staring at spreadsheets on a
monitor. Second, when he did get to interact with
other people, it was usually under circumstances that
were unpleasant for the person on the other side of his
desk.

 That was never more true than in the case of
disciplining trainees. He'd never really given much
thought to the fact that the Sovereign of a training
facility acted in a capacity corresponding to that of
Principal or Vice Principal in more typical schools.
Dressing down a seventeen-year-old when he could
only claim to be older by the technicality of two plus
years? It went beyond feeling ridiculous, past
preposterous, and kept going right on into the
sublimely silly.

 The day that he had to discipline Kristoph
Falcon and Rolfe Wakenmann, a.k.a. Kris and
Wakey, gave him reason to rethink his suitability for
the Sovereign gig. Kris was seventeen. Wakey was
sixteen, but just three months younger. The two of
them had sneaked out of trainee quarters and stowed
away on a Manhattan-bound Whister, behind the back
seats of the last row. They'd gotten a quiet, smooth
state-of-the-art ride to the city and weren't nabbed

until they tried to disembark or decopter or get off or whatever you call it when you leave a Whister behind. They were promptly returned to Jefferson with the promise of punishment, to be determined by the acting Sovereign.

The next morning they were escorted to the hallway outside Sol's door where Glen was inside feeling like a kid playing "dress up". The trainee who had been assigned as Sovereign's gofer from eight to eleven knocked on the door.

"Come in, Mr. Barrock."

Glen's morning boy came in with a quiet dignity that seemed mature for nineteen. "Thank you, sir."

Glen sighed. "Look. I know that calling me sir has got to sound as eff'd to you as it does to me. So let's make a deal. If I should be cursed by ending up riding this desk in Excel hell permanently, gods forbid, then you'll have to call me sir. Till then, Glen is good by me. Deal?"

The other boy grinned. "Sure."

"So what's going on?"

"Two for A.A., si..." He cut off the last consonant and smiled.

"What's A.A., Barrock?"

"Sovereign Nemamiah's code for discipline. It stands for attitude adjustment. He says consequences are the bedrock of civilization."

The big burgundy tufted leather chair creaked when Glen leaned back, the corners of his mouth curving with amusement. "Does he? And what does discipline usually entail?"

"Well, he's old school about some things, but

he doesn't believe in corporal punishment, something about knights not hitting other knights, even knights-to-be. Actually, there's kind of an ingenious creativity to his approach that scares the guys more than knowing what's coming."

"Scared of the unknown. I can see that. So give me some examples. I need a feel for comparison's sake, action and reaction."

"Um. Okay. Let's see.

"Eidelman pretended to stumble into one of the nurses so he could grab a feel. Sol made him cross-dress for a day, complete with wig, makeup, and falsies." Barrock leveled a look and gestured with his hands in front of his chest. "Big ones." Glen snorted while he tapped a pencil. He didn't actually use pencils, but he liked having something to do with his hands. "The guys had a field day with telling him how cute and sexy he was. And, really, between you and me, he kind of was. That's why some of the guys call him Queenie Eidelman."

Glen nodded, clearly enjoying this. "So it's the punishment that never stops giving." Barrock nodded. "What else?"

"Another time, somebody made fun of Crisp when he was close enough to overhear. Called him a fag. I heard what Crisp said when he came down here and talked to Sol. He said he didn't like tattling, but that part of his job was to assist in making sure the young twigs were bent in the right direction."

Glen barked out a laugh. "He did *not* say that!"

Barrock's ears turned red when he grinned. "Yeah. He did, but he didn't give any indication that he realized…."

"Got it. Sorry to interrupt. Go on with your story."

"Um, oh yeah, he was saying that it wasn't the principle, but the pejorative, that a knight could be a person of character and call him gay, but the prejudice implied by the term 'fag' was beneath Black Swan ideals.

"The Sovereign agreed. He sent me to the library to find a book and bring it back. Then he had me go get Wakey, um, Mr. Wakenmann – and he's one of the two who are outside waiting right now –he had me go get him out of class and bring him to the office. He told Wakey that his behavior was unbecoming of a knight in training and that it would require restitution.

"Wakey said, 'You want me to pay Crisp off?' The Sovereign said, 'No. You can't buy your way out of dishonor. Restitution has to be made in deeds, not currency. Then he gave Wakey the book, which was *Love Sonnets,* and a little spiral notebook.

"He said Wakey had twenty four hours to complete the task and return with both items. The spiral notebook needed to have the names of twelve different poems from the book and each one had to have the signature of one of his peers. They had to confirm with their signatures that he'd read them the poem, *slowly and with feeling*. The Sovereign emphasized that last part.

"After coming back here for approval, he had to take the book and the notebook to Crisp and apologize, saying that, 'Love must be respected in all its forms. That is a creed worthy of a knight.

Difference must be respected when it harms none. That is a principle worthy of a gentleman.'

"The Sovereign made him memorize that last part."

Glen sat back in his chair tapping the pencil on his thigh. "Sounds like it made an impression on you as well." Barrock said nothing. He just nodded. "So what have Wakey and..." Glen looked around Barrock like he could see through the door. "Who else is out there?"

"Kristoph Falcon."

"Hmm. Of what are they accused?"

Barrock smiled at the formality of the question. "Away from quarters after hours. Away from quarters without permission. Misuse of Order equipment and personnel..."

"English."

"They snuck out last night. Stowed away on a Whister. Got nabbed on a Manhattan roof pad and were brought back here."

Glen wheeled the chair around and looked out the window for a couple of minutes, leaving his gofer waiting.

Barrock was right. He had to hand it to Sol. Points for thinking outside traditional methods. Points for maintaining a climate of uncertainty for the wards. The old guy had made an art form out of designer punishments, making them fit the crime in deliciously inventive ways. Glen spun back around.

"Send 'em in."

The two boys shuffled in and stood in front of Glen's desk in silence. He took his time looking them over.

"So what was your destination?"

Wakey looked down at his feet, but Kris looked Glen straight in the eye. "Strip bars."

Glen's eyebrows shot up. "You turn drinking age without us knowing about it?"

Wakey glanced at Kris, who seemed to be the agreed upon spokesperson.

"Little cash acts like lube. Know what I mean?"

Of course Glen understood, but decided fraternization could unravel the illusion of authority.

"No. I don't know what you mean. Why don't you explain it like the well-educated gentleman you're supposed to be?"

Wakey spoke up. "He means that there are some dives in the thirties that look the other way if you have a couple of big bills ready at the door."

Glen nodded. "And how many rules did you think you were breaking in association with this illicit outing?"

Kris looked defiant.

Wakenmann said, "We didn't count."

"Um-hum. Okay. Tell you what we're going to do.

"For the next three months you will report to the pilots' station at five o'clock a.m., Monday through Friday. You will spend two hours every day learning to fly Whisters. When the pilots have signed off that you're cleared to co-pilot, you will spend your weekends shuttling people back and forth to Manhattan. People who are *authorized* to go. You will not leave your Whister unless you are on the Jefferson Unit roof pad." Wakey glanced over at Kris for his reaction. "Last, except for pilot duty, you will not leave Jefferson Unit for three months."

Glen could see that it was taking every bit of self-discipline and training they had undergone to keep from groaning out a protest. He pulled up his calendar and identified the date when they would regain the normal life of a Black Swan trainee, which was anything but normal by most standards. He pointed to a calendar date.

"This is when you will have completed your obligation to me. Dismissed."

"Yes sir," they both mumbled.

"Whatever. Out."

As they closed the door behind them, Glen was thinking that he was going to have a story to tell at dinner that night at the vineyard. He had dinner with Storm and Litha every Thursday night. She either picked him up right at nine or sent Deliverance. It made an early dinner for them on Pacific time, but it seemed to work.

There was a soft knock on his door. "Come in."

Barrock stuck his head in. "Good one, si… Glen."

Glen cocked his head. "You heard that?" Barrock nodded. "I guess I didn't think anything about your reporting of those other incidents. How are you managing to know everything that goes on in here?"

"I put my ear against the door, si… Glen." Sol's gofer didn't hesitate to answer or bother with trying to look sheepish. As far as he was concerned, knowing what was doing was one of the perks of the job.

"Oh. Okay. Thanks. And either call me sir or call me Glen. Sir Glen sounds stupid."

"Yes, si…" He closed the door.

Almost immediately there was another knock.

"What is it now, Barrock?"

Elora opened the door and stuck her head in. "Name's Laiken, Rookie."

Glen's face lit up in a way that left no mistake he was glad to see her. He jumped up and came around the desk. "Sorry. I just had to lower the boom on two trainees who are two years younger than I am. Everything about it was…"

"Weird."

He nodded. "To say the least."

"You're doing great, kiddo. It takes some enormous… um, confidence to sit in the chair."

He grinned. "Some enormous confidence?"

"Um-hmm. So there's a reason why I'm honoring you with a visit."

"Hey. That was my line. You stole my line."

"Okay. I take it back."

"To what do I owe the honor of your visit?"

"You remember that thing you were doing for me. What I asked before we left Ireland?"

"You thought I forgot."

"Well…"

"Of course you would think that. I should have let you know I'm on it. It's a worthy mystery, tough enough to be fun, cool enough to be interesting. I was at the latest in a series of dead ends, but I've got a new lead. So the trail is heating up again. As soon as Sol gets back I'll request some time off and a pass ride."

"Good news."

"I don't know yet."

"Well, I'm hoping. I wish I could tell you why I need the intel so badly, but just to reiterate, it's important to some people I know. Really, really, really important."

Glen cocked his head. "Abandon-my-post important? Or work-on-it-when-I-can important?"

"Scale of one to ten. One means if we never find out it's no big deal. Ten is the end of days. I'm putting this between seven and eight."

"Okay. You know I don't have any free time while Sol's gone and not much when he's here. And the lead I need to follow requires travel with flex time and a long leash."

"When Sol gets back, let me know what you need and I'll make it happen."

"Done, my Lady." He gave her a little chivalrous bow.

"You know I never thought I'd live to see the acting Jefferson Unit Sovereign bow to me – and in his own office at that. Sol would have a coronary. Got to go."

"Where you off to?"

"Trainee Mid, hand-to-hand." She specified "Mid" because the twenty four trainees were divided into two classes of twelve each. The younger boys were beginning. The older boys were midlevel. The active duty knights were advanced.

Glen looked at his watch absently. "Would you drop this in Monq's box on your way by?" He handed her a file.

"Sure. Later."

Elora exited Elevator 3 a couple of steps behind Kristoph Falcon and Rolfe Wakenmann, who had been on Elevator 2. Some of the boys were gathered in the hall outside the sparring room. When Kris and Wakey walked up, one of the loiterers said, "Yo, Wakey. Let me see your eyes." Wakey gave him a funny look. "Yep. Bottomless pools, clear and deep as a cloudless night."

Amid a round of youthful laughter, Wakey responded with, "Fuck you!" Then he noticed that everyone stood straight as all eyes shifted to something behind him. He turned to come face to face with his instructor, the famous and formidable Lady Laiken. Taking a step back, he dropped his eyes.

She looked over the group. "Go on in and warm up. I want a private word with Mr. Wakenmann." Once the boys had filed inside and closed the door, leaving the two of them alone in the hallway, she turned to Wakey. "You know, Sovereign Nemamiah has strong feelings about minors – that would be you, and expletives – that would be the last two words that came out of your mouth."

"Yes, ma'am."

"Personally, I wouldn't care. My husband is quite partial to colorful language and I've grown used to it. But as long as you and I are on these premises, working with this organization, we're going to respect the Sovereign's wishes on the matter. Not because it's the rules, but because he's earned the right to set the rules. If I've learned anything since being here, it's that he always has good reasons for what he does.

"Was that clear, Mr. Wakenmann?"

"Yes, ma'am."

"Then get to the friggin' mats now."

He grinned. "Yes, ma'am."

"Oh, and Wakey?"

"Yes, ma'am?"

"You do have eyes as clear as a cloudless night."

He spit out a laugh and jogged toward the door to the sparring room.

Halcyon Dimension, Present Day.

Angel was done for the night. When it first opened, Divas Dive had shown some promise as a club. It was a little different in look and atmosphere and often drew yupsters who wanted to check out clubbing in his tawdry neck of the borough. It had even been named in the hopes of drawing uptown curiosity seekers. *Come walk on the wild side.* He sneered at that. Like a couple of hours of pounding bass and undulating bodies could make you worldly.

It's not so easy. *Real* corruption takes practice. For some it even takes dedication.

The ladies had been given a chance to interest him. He'd held court at the bar for an hour while a parade of cartoon tits and well-used tail came and went. They offered the usual, immediate availability and tipsy gushing about his beautiful eyes and broad shoulders. He was almost as tired of that old song as he was of being groped without his permission. Almost.

It was a waste of time, like standing in front of the butcher's premium case, staring at the strips and filets, when you're in the mood for fish and not meat.

He decided to hit the men's room before he left. As he came back out into the dim hallway a girl stepped in front of him. She pressed the front of her body up against him and purred his name. Between the pale blond hair and the white dress, she was glowing like radiation in the semi-black lighting. He'd been with her last week, in a stall on the other side of the men's room door. Maybe she'd given her name and maybe she hadn't. It was irrelevant because he couldn't remember either way.

"Okay look, doll, it's not happening, right?"

He tried to ease her away, but she pressed closer, thinking she was being seductive.

"What's the hurry? Stick around. See what I've got for you."

He grabbed her biceps, his big hands completely circling her arms, and swung her around so that her back was against the wall. When he shoved three fingers inside her, none too gently, she went bug-eyed and gasped. The skirt was so short and the thong so tiny that he didn't even have to work for it.

"Oh, yeah, been there." The words were vicious, but his actions were even more brutal. He wiggled his fingers around while her mouth hung wide open in shock. "And once was enough. See ya."

When he withdrew his fingers, she gasped all

over again, maybe even louder. "You dick!"

He laughed right in her face. She jerked and squeezed her eyes shut when she felt spittle.

"That's right, no name. You loiter outside the men's room and make your twat that accessible, somebody's gonna take advantage."

He wiped his hand on the leg of his jeans and walked off thinking that he'd done the piece a service. He hadn't left anything open for misunderstanding. Even though he didn't remember the details of that particular encounter, he was confident that he'd been honest about his part of the bargain. He never led women on. Never said, "Sure. I'll call," or any such shit. It was what you might call a policy of his.

Actually, thinking more about it, he realized he'd just schooled her up on one of the downsides to indiscriminate fucking. Yeah. He chuckled to himself. He should actually be recognized for philanthropy in the area of saving women from guys like him. Like the song says, sometimes you have to be cruel to be kind.

Angel had never had to work for pussy. Even when his features were completely at rest, his natural intensity mimicked the look of sexually fueled passion. The promise of something forbidden radiating from those black eyes drew women like a Nordstrom going-out-of-business sale. Of course his perfectly proportioned anatomy didn't hurt either.

When he landed himself on the streets as a young teen, he'd survived at first by stealing. It didn't take long before other kids on the street gravitated to him. They seemed to congregate around him and then stand nearby looking at him like he was supposed to know what to do next. So he put them to work stealing for him. He liked to think of himself as a community organizer. Angel loved tongue-in-cheek.

It wasn't a bad gig. He found places where they could be safe to crash, some even had working plumbing. He spent enough of the proceeds on clothes and grooming so that none of the kids would ever be taken for homeless. He taught them how to look and act like suburban kids in the city for a shopping trip, thereby appearing completely non-threatening so that no mark would ever be on their guard.

The big moneymaker was lunchtime in the shopping districts. Nicer restaurants. Women hung their purses off the backs of chairs and then got busy talking to their friends. Lots of people coming and going past tables. If somebody walked by, smoothly eased a bag off a chair back, and kept walking, no one would be the wiser until it was time to pay the check. Then the budding criminal would meet friends around the corner and pass out the plastic. By the time the credit card companies were involved, the nice-looking kids with the fresh faces and conservative clothes could have run up thousands in purchases. The cards, along with the bag and the rest of its contents - except cash – would be in a dumpster within a couple of hours.

He ran the Fagin racket for two or three years before learning - almost by accident - that he had skills to make *real* money.

One of the other boys had pocketed a deck of playing cards on the way out of a convenience store, even though that kind of minimum return risk was strictly against Angel's rules. The other kid taught him the rules of poker.

There was no way to judge how good he was, playing other street kids. He could beat them, all of them, without trying, but that didn't tell him what he needed to know. So he asked around about low stakes street games. Nothing fancy. Something affordable with a cap on bets. He took the gang's take for the week, which was a big gamble in itself, and tripled the money. Since the other kids had provided the funding – even though they hadn't known about the plan, he divided the total take in half, kept half for himself and split the other half equally among the others, which meant they profited as well.

Within six months he had enough money to play with big boys. Maybe not the biggest boys, but hefty nonetheless.

When it came to poker, Angel was special. Even more so than he ever could have imagined because that talent was the result of demon blood that enhanced his intuitive ability.

If he'd been satisfied with playing poker, he could have led a cushy, carefree life and had anything he wanted with minimal effort. He'd already made more money than his parents would earn in their lifetime.

There was just one little problem. Angel liked betting on the horses. He liked it even more than playing poker but unlike poker, he didn't always win. After a while he fell into a cycle of addiction. The only reason he played poker was to get money to bet on horses, which he was sure to lose.

While he could always pull a win with poker,

because the energy of cards is static, the energy of living things - like horses - was unstable. Horses have fluctuations in their biological and psychic patterns and they come with personality factors just like all mammals. Some days they feel like running. Some days they don't. Some days they *have* to win. Some days they don't mind being second. Then there are the unforeseeable factors like accidents that complicate things even more.

Even though a life ruled by compulsion wasn't a recipe for happiness, it could have been okay. All he had to do was bet the track with poker winnings and go home. But the fever escalated beyond that and he ended up borrowing. No matter how much he won at poker, he could always manage to lose *more* at the track. From the outside looking in, it was an exquisite form of psychological masochism.

He'd had some close calls with the shark, the guy he called Baph, but he'd always managed it out before it got too dicey and won enough to pay off his debts in money, not blood. At least that was what had always happened before.

Just like every day, Deliverance came at half past nine so that he'd have half an hour to play with Rosie before taking Storm to Jefferson Unit. At ten, Storm picked up his beautiful three-year-old and gave her smooches on her ticklish little neck until she laughed hysterically.

"Say bye Daddy," he prompted.

"Bye Daddy."

"See you later."

"See you later."

Litha's emerald eyes seemed to sparkle with iridescence whenever she watched that exchange. When Storm turned toward her, she was clearly eager for her turn. She got a sweet and thorough kiss and giggled like Rosie when he turned around and came back for another.

Storm left with a grin on his face, loving every second of his two emerald-eyed girls waving goodbye. It was a vision so perfect that it burned into his memory like a brand. It would be a memory that he would recall thousands of times.

The trip from the Black Swan Vineyard on the Pacific Coast to Jefferson Unit at Fort Dixon, New Jersey normally took about three minutes. According to the habit they had already formed, Deliverance created a portal in his mind just outside the Sovereign's office at J.U. before taking Storm in tow by gripping his son-in-law's forearm.

Perhaps the demon became relaxed in the habit. Perhaps there was interference from another entity traveling the same network of passes. The reason is less important than the result, which was that Deliverance arrived outside Sol's office alone.

The demon was over eight hundred years old and, in all that time, he'd never once had reason to panic. The rise of that emotion, common to humans, was as shocking and dramatic to him as a heart attack might be to a man.

Glen was just glancing at his watch when his door was opened without a knock. Deliverance

looked stricken and the expression was made more
alarming by the fact that his olive complexion looked
wan.

"Have you seen Storm?"

Glen's brows pulled down into a scowl.

"No." Though he was getting a very bad
feeling about the exchange, he posed his next
question evenly and deliberately. "Have you?"

Deliverance was looking a little wild-eyed.
"Um. Yes. He was with me?"

Glen stood up slowly. *Calm. Remain calm.*
"What do you mean *was* with you?"

It was a good thing that Glen was calm
because the incubus was headed toward full-fledged
hysteria. Not because he was tight with his son-in-
law, but because he knew his little girl would be
every possible version of angry about Storm getting
himself lost en route.

"I mean I picked him up at home, but he's not
here!! What else might I mean, human?!?"

Glen's hands had involuntarily curled into
fists and his molars were clenched shut so tight he felt
like he had lockjaw. "Deliverance. What are our
options?"

"I don't know! Nothing like this has ever
happened before. Maybe there's a reason why we
don't carry inferior…"

"DON'T EVEN THINK ABOUT
FINISHING THAT SENTENCE! THIS IS NO TIME
FOR BETTER-THAN-YOU BULLSHIT!"

"Okay."

"Options. THINK!" Deliverance stared
straight ahead, frozen. Nothing was forthcoming.

"Can you retrace your route and find him?"

"No. The passes aren't stationary. They're like… I don't know, tides? They move around. He could be any one of a thousand places."

"So how do you propose we find him?"

The demon was fidgeting from side to side like a child who'd been caught doing something very naughty. "Search party?"

Glen was infuriated and looked it, but did his best to keep a handle on the emotion. "Search party. Okay. Good. Good. Who are you going to get to search?"

"Friends?"

"I'm very glad to hear you have friends, demon. You need to get started on that pronto, but first you've got to let Litha know what's going on."

Deliverance was shaking his head from side to side violently. "No."

"That is NOT an option. She has to know and she has to know now. For one thing, she's going to want to help look for him. Have her bring Rosie here. We'll look after her." The demon didn't respond. "You're wasting valuable time. Man up and go tell your daughter you lost her husband." Still no reaction. "If you're waiting for me to offer to go with you…?" Glen finished that thought by chuffing out a disgusted breath and reached for the phone. "I can call her, but she's never going to respect you again if she hears this from me over the phone."

Glen looked down to speed dial. When he looked back up, the demon was gone.

Rosie was playing on the kitchen floor. Litha

was emptying the dishwasher, when she felt the atmosphere shift. Storm always wondered why she was never startled by the demon's popping in and out. It was because she had enough demon blood to sense the change when another entity opened a portal into her immediate environment.

Litha turned toward him. "Dad. Why are you back so…?" The question hung in the air when she got a look at his face. "What's happened?"

She'd never seen Deliverance look so unsettled and it scared her. "Is it Storm?" *Oh gods.* His lips parted and he looked like a person who had something to say and couldn't decide how to say it. Losing patience, she took a step toward him. "Say it. What's wrong? Where's Storm?"

He was shaking his head just a little. "I don't know."

"You don't know? What do you mean you don't know?"

"We left here…"

"I know that."

"And I was the only one who…"

Litha felt her knees go weak and had to grab onto the countertop behind her. "You didn't lose him in the passes." She felt tears well up. Litha hated tears. She hated looking weak. She hated feeling weak. She hated crying. And she hated her father for making her feel everything she was feeling at that moment. She whispered, "Please tell me you didn't lose him in the passes."

"I'm going to form a… a search party." Litha's eyes glazed over. "Glen said I should come tell you first, that you would want to help look, and to bring Rosie to him. He said they would take care of her."

There was no response. Litha's eyes continued to be out of focus. She looked dazed. As a frequent traveler of the passes, she had every good reason to react that way.

Deliverance glanced at Rosie who was looking at him with accusation all over her little face. It was an odd look on a toddler. He was starting to get a little worried about Litha's reaction. Or lack of.

"Litha. I know this is bad, but I'll fix it. I'll get him back. I promise."

She blinked. Once. Twice. Then slowly her eyes slid toward his.

"You're damned right you will. You'll find him if it's the last thing you ever do."

Litha didn't know it was possible to be so angry or so scared. The combination of two such powerful emotions smacking up against each other was debilitating. She felt like her body was going to go on overload and explode.

"Who's in this search party? And how are they going to look for him?"

"I need something personal so his life imprint can be read, something he's worn maybe. I'll call in some favors, go to the Sylphic Warriors first. They'll be the fastest."

"I know some angels who will help."

"ANGELS!?!"

"YES!!! And you will work with them and you will *like* it." He crossed his arms over his chest in a huff and pouted like a petulant teen. "Save it. I'm warning you." She stood up straight even though she was feeling a little lightheaded. "Watch Rosie while I go get something of Storm's."

In a couple of minutes she returned with a black tee shirt that hadn't been laundered yet.

"Will this do?" He took the shirt, closed his eyes for a second, and nodded. "I'm taking Rosie to Elora. Then I'm going looking for my husband. We need a system so that we don't have people looking in the same place and a way to cross off dimensions that have been checked."

She was thinking while she was gathering up Rosie's things. She called Glen. When he answered she said, "You're going to be our point person. You're the best one for the job."

"Whatever you need."

"We'll be there in a couple of minutes. Will you please contact Elora for me and let her know I'm bringing Rosie to her?"

"Yes. See you in a few."

Litha handed two bags full of stuff to Deliverance. "Carry these." Rosie reached up as her mother bent to lift her. Coolly, but to the point she ground out, "*I'll* bring her."

In his office, Litha briefed Glen on the only plan they had. Glen then sent Barrock to set up two smart boards in the conference room and declare the floor off limits to everyone except himself, Sir Hawking and Lady Laiken.

"Until further notice, no one gets off the elevator on this level. Is that understood?" Barrock nodded and turned to leave. "And Barrock?"

"Yes, Si…Glen?"

"Whatever you may have overheard, this secret is a real secret. Do you understand me?"

"I do."

Elora arrived within a few minutes. She looked like her level of shock rivaled Litha's.

"Come to Auntie." She reached for her namesake and Rosie leaned toward her. To Litha she said, "I can call Baka and get the vampire to join the search if that will help."

Litha had held it together, but when she opened her mouth to tell Elora yes, a choked sort of garbled noise came out instead. Rosie reacted to her mother's distress by starting to cry. Elora shushed Rosie and reached out to wrap Litha in the arm that wasn't holding the toddler.

"We'll find him. He's married to the best tracker in the world. Everybody knows that."

Litha nodded. It was more a signal of resolve than agreement. She shushed Rosie again lovingly and gave her a round of kisses on her pretty plump cheek. "S'okay, baby."

Glen began interrogating Deliverance in an attempt to apply logic to the proposition of looking for a needle in a meadow full of haystacks. While he was doing that, Litha went to find Kellareal and enlist his help. Elora stepped out in the hall to call Baka. She kissed the little fingers that tried to grab the phone while she waited for him to answer.

"Lady Laiken."

"We're going to need your boys."

"Should I ask?"

"That demon lost Storm."

"What do you mean lost?" Silence. "Oh."

Like everybody else, Baka's first thought was, *Gods. Not him.*

"Where do you want us?"

"Sol's conference room. Soon as you can."

"Litha?"

Elora looked back toward the conference room. "Um, holding up. She's gone to get help looking. I've got the baby."

"Okay. We'll be there."

"Hey. Wait. Not that I don't always want to see you, but we need pass riders. I'm afraid the rest of us are benched for this one."

"If I *really* can't be of help, I may not stay, but I'll at least come and say something to Litha." He paused. "Rammel's going to…"

"Be hard to handle. I know."

"The main thing is to bring Jean-Etienne so he can ride herd."

"Agreed." He hesitated to hang up. "This is… I feel…"

"Yeah. Same here."

She hung up. Ram would probably be finishing his workout and heading back to the apartment. She ducked back into the conference room. "Going home to tell Ram." Glen stopped when the weight of that sunk in and nodded. "Don't be surprised if he shows up down here and tries to take over."

"Honestly. I'd like his help."

Elora noticed that all of a sudden Glen looked a good bit older than twenty.

By the time Ram reached the conference

Victoria Danann

room, it was as noisy as a political convention. Elementals, angels, demons of every sort, and a few unidentifiable species, all talking and arguing at the same time and not necessarily in the same language.

Litha sat in a chair looking shell shocked. Glen stood at one of the smart boards with a pointer in hand, hoping for an excuse to feel useful.

Ram, his hair still wet from a shower, leaped up on top of the conference table, put three fingers in his mouth and let loose an ear-splitting whistle. The room went instantly quiet.

"Who is takin' responsibility for findin' my friend?" No one answered. "Everyone who is no' takin' responsibility, be quiet and do no' say another fuckin' thin' unless you're bein' asked." He turned to Glen. "Where are we?"

Clearly frustrated, Glen ran his free hand over the bed head he was rocking. "I can't tell."

While Ram was looking at Glen, someone at the back of the room yelled, "Angels rule!"

Ram's head jerked in that direction. "Exceedin'ly immature for creatures claimin' to be superior. There's no room for politics and games here. This woman…" He pointed at Litha. "…is missin' her husband. 'Tis scary for her. Do you no' get that?

"We're grateful if you're here to help. If you're no' here to help, get out so the rest of us can get down to business."

Elora was standing toward the back of the room, feeling a little numb. Her mind was on alert and trying to mount a defense against thoughts she didn't want to think. *What if we don't get him back?*

Seeing movement out of the corner of her eye, she brought her head around to see Baka quietly slipping in with five vampire close behind. He nodded as he spotted Elora and started drifting her way.

When he reached her side, she leaned over and whispered, "Good to see you. Thanks for coming."

He rolled his eyes. "Like there was a question. What's going on here?"

"Ram is trying to sort things out and get the search started."

Baka's head jerked toward her. "No one's looking?"

Elora shook her head and Baka could read the worry on her face. "Not yet."

"Christ." He rubbed a hand over his mouth.

When no one met Ram's challenge by leaving, he turned on Deliverance and didn't try to hide the fact that he would have loved to turn the demon into a pillar of salt. On the spot. With no fanfare beforehand and no marker afterward. The only thing that kept him from plotting the murder was the fact that they probably couldn't find Storm without the one who lost him.

"I do no' know anythin' about the geography of passes. Can you take the route you used to get here, divide it into sections and assign these different…" He looked around the room as the thought flitted through his mind that dozens of academic types employed by The Order would have a field day if turned loose on that gathering of creatures heretofore thought mythological. "…factions an area to cover?"

"It won't be exact, but we can do something kind of like that."

Ram marshaled every bit of the example of control Storm had set for him so that he could pin Deliverance with a level look and calmly say, "Then will you do that please? Wherever he is, I'm certain he's wishin' he was here instead. So, I'm thinkin' sooner is better than later." He glanced at Litha and back to the demon. "Do you understand me?"

Ram noticed Javier behind Elora. He'd been inching closer and was now leaning in to smell her hair with a dreamy look on his face when Ram stopped him with a pointed finger.

"Step away from my wife now, motherfucker!"

Following Ram's finger, Elora turned around and bared her teeth. She was utterly without patience for adolescent shenanigans. "I suggest you do as my husband says quickly unless you want to end up with another ruined blouse."

Javier looked down at his chest as if he was remembering a flagpole protruding from his front and took a step back. Baka gave him a dirty look. Javier shrugged in response as if to say, "You cannot blame an immortal vampire at the height of his sexual urges for trying."

Ram turned back to Deliverance muttering something that began with, "Great Paddy..."

The incubus nodded his agreement with the plan and started around the room letting the searchers get a fix on Storm by his shirt. He then began giving assignments and calling them out to Glen so he could write it on the board.

Ram's voice carried over the room. "Be sure to check in with Mr. Catch or myself every so often. When you find Sir Storm," Ram was careful to say 'when' rather than 'if' for Litha's benefit. "...report here right away. One of us will be here."

In a short time there were four left. Rammel, Glen, Litha, and her father. Baka had left when the vampire were given their search parameters after extracting a promise that someone would call him immediately when there was word. Elora had gone upstairs to take over looking after Helm and Rosie.

Litha turned to the demon, feeling exhausted, but determined to ignore it.

"Give me an assignment and tell me what to do."

Ram sat down next to her and spoke quietly. "Litha, we have..." He looked at Glen. "How many are out searchin' right now?"

"Thirty-nine."

"Would it no' be better to take care of Rosie?" He lowered his voice so that it was soft and comforting. "I hear she's growin' up pretty fast."

She looked into Ram's face. She wondered if her husband really knew how lucky he was to have so many people who loved him. Tears welled in her eyes and overflowed without warning. Rammel immediately moved closer to offer a shoulder, which she took, gratefully.

"He didn't want to miss anything," she said. "I could hardly get him to go to sleep. He wanted to just sit by her bed at night and watch her."

Ram felt his own breath catch in his throat and

curled his fists tight when the overwhelming emotion threatened to overtake him as well. He blinked rapidly. He wouldn't allow himself to entertain the possibility that Storm wouldn't be back. That outcome was just too impossible to imagine. Through all the years of close, close calls, he'd accepted that each of them would probably end up like Lan. *Not like this. Not this!*

When Litha began to quiet and pulled back, he said, "Come upstairs. Have some dinner with us. My wife is beside herself with worry about you."

Litha narrowed her eyes. "Nice try. She's worried about Storm."

He cocked his head to the side a little. "She loves you, too, Litha. Do you no' know that?"

She nodded. "I do. I'm just cranky. I'm too anxious to have dinner and wait. I need to do something. I'll go out for a while. If I don't find him, I'll come get Rosie and take her home to sleep in her own bed."

"Whatever you want."

When Litha and Deliverance left to pursue their separate hunts, Ram heaved a weary sigh. After a short pause he looked at Glen.

"Let's take twelve hour shifts. I'll be back at nine. I can sleep on that couch over there."

"You sure about that, old man? You might get a crick in your neck."

"I'll take my chances."

At eight thirty, Elora had just put Rosie's little white nightgown on her. She was too beautiful for words, with Litha's stunning emerald-green eyes set into a feminine version of Storm's face. It was the latter that loosened Elora's tear ducts, not that it ever took much to harvest tears from Elora. Rosie, who seemed to have a wide streak of empathy, immediately started to cry along.

Elora swiped at her face. "No. No. Precious baby. Auntie just loves that you look so much like your daddy."

"Daddy."

"Yes. He'll be home soon. And then we're going to have a big party with balloons."

"Balloons," Rosie repeated and confirmed.

Elora hoped to all the gods that she was telling the truth.

Storm had been whizzing along toward his daily lunch briefing with Glen, thinking about how cute Rosie was with Litha's monks and how much they fussed over her like she was the second coming. Without warning he was stopped dead still. The haze that surrounded him continued to swirl in shades of gray and rose constantly mixing, separating, and reforming like a living abstract of colored smoke. He yelled for Deliverance, but knew the volume of his raised voice had been swallowed by the white noise the currents made. His voice even sounded far away to his own ears.

He told himself not to panic. If there was anything that had been drilled into Black Swan knights since they were little more than babies, it was that panic is never useful. He willed himself to calm and, within seconds, was decided on the only course of action that was both logical and reasonable. That was to do nothing.

If he stayed exactly where he was, Deliverance would come back for him. So he set about trying to stay where he was, but the strength of the current in the pass made it impossible, like standing in ocean water up to your chest. The sand changing form underneath your feet and the motion of the waves would move you around whether you agreed to it or not.

After a while, the exertion from just trying to stay upright was taking its toll on Storm's muscles. It seemed to him that he'd been at it for hours, struggling to stay where he could be found. He knew his body was succumbing. His mind was trying to organize a Plan B, but he was exhausted.

That's when he was clipped by a passerby. It wasn't done with malice. It wasn't even intentional. Entities who travel the passes don't expect to encounter a stationary object – like a humanoid at full stop - any more than an autobahn driver expects a single car to be at a standstill in the fast lane.

The impact wasn't enough to do damage, not even a bruise, but it was enough to cause Storm to take a step to regain his balance so that he didn't go down. Unfortunately that single, fateful step took him out of the pass and into another dimension. Storm didn't need a life signature placeholder to keep from having his own life extinguished on contact with a dimension where a counterpart might live. His demon blood negated his susceptibility. He could have a conversation with another version of himself if the opportunity presented. But if he had needed a placeholder, it would have been there for him.

The Storm who was native to that dimension had mistreated a former one night stand outside the men's room of a club a couple of nights before. She had been so incensed by his humiliating rejection and malicious cruelty that she had taken out a tiny pistol with mother of pearl on the handle and shot him in the face at point blank range. She'd had the presence of mind to take his wallet before she slipped out the alley exit. That was how that dimension's version of Storm ended up a John Doe in the morgue, with no one who was close enough to him to realize he'd gone missing. Somewhere he had a mother who cared whether he lived or died, but he hadn't seen her or talked to her in years.

The newly arrived pilgrim, Storm, knew exactly where he was. When he'd been recruited by Sol Nemamiah, the first training facility he landed in was right on the edge of Golden Gate Park. He'd spent time in San Francisco and knew China Town when he saw it. He wasn't actually in China Town at the moment, but if he crossed the street, he would be.

Storm didn't know he was in a different dimension, but he knew something had gone wrong and he knew his nerve endings were pricking painfully. He stood in the street for a few minutes grimacing, waiting for the pain to subside, which it did after a few minutes, when his body adjusted to a different vibration. The human in him didn't appreciate dimension slipping.

When he'd left home it was ten in the morning. The street he was standing on wasn't completely deserted, but it was clear it was after hours.

He took out his phone and dialed Litha. No service.

Shop fronts were closed. Most eateries were closed. Scanning up and down the block it seemed he had two options. A walk-up donut shop that looked like they could use a mop, or a bar with part of the neon winking on a sign that read, HALCYON. The donut shop had customers, hard as that was to believe, and he didn't want to wait in line to ask to borrow a phone. So the bar it was. An establishment called Halcyon couldn't be all bad. Right? And the warmth would feel good. He'd left home in jeans and a black long sleeved tee thinking he was going straight from his kitchen at the vineyard to Glen's office. The temperature was forty-something where he stood, but with wind chill, it felt colder.

He let the red door swing closed behind him and looked around. It was nothing special, just the kind of place you might go to hide out in the dark and lose yourself in one kind of amber liquid or another. Place had an old Wurlitzer playing mellow, bluesy music. No revving. Just the right mood music for a melancholy drink alone.

Nobody was sitting at the bar, but the guy behind it was just finishing a wipe down. He threw the damp towel over his shoulder as his eyes darted around the room. He was a big fella, about the same size as Storm. Maybe thirty years before he'd had the same flat stomach.

He tracked Storm's approach, giving him the once over and watching until he reached the bar and stopped.

"Help you?"

"Ah, yeah. My phone's not getting a signal and I've got to make a call. Do you have one I can use?" The bartender studied him for a few beats, then reached into his pocket and withdrew a phone. "Don't walk off with it."

Storm nodded, continuing to look the man in the eye so that he'd be reassured he wasn't making a mistake by giving trust to a stranger. Storm was self-aware enough to know that he was tall and dark with an intense look that could easily be interpreted as menacing. "Very kind of you. I'll be just at the other end of the bar."

His hands were itching to dial Litha's number. He told himself he wasn't scared, just anxious. He had made a habit of manually dialing every so often instead of relying on speed dial for this very reason – in case he ever needed to call her number from memory. He held his breath when the number rang once, but the little bit of hope didn't last long. The ring was cut short by an annoying set of discordant electronic tones and a recorded voice saying that was not a working number.

His heart was hammering in his chest, but he tried to tell himself not to jump to conclusions. No sense borrowing trouble. Maybe he'd misdialed. He touched the numbers on the screen again. Slower. Double checking each digit. One ring followed by a recorded voice that was the last thing in the universe he wanted to hear.

He figured he didn't have to be a genius to come to the conclusion that Deliverance had abandoned him to another gods forsaken dimension. And he was alone. He could hear his heart beating in his ears then realized that was because he'd forgotten to breathe. He looked around and met the curious eyes of the bartender who'd been glancing in his direction now and then.

Storm made his way back to the other end of the bar and handed the phone over. The bartender took it out of his hand and looked Storm over. Again.

"Not good news, huh?"

Storm shook his head and looked around to see if anyone was watching. "I need to ask you something. You're going to think it's real strange, but maybe you can think of it as a dare or a practical joke or something like that?"

The bartender put both hands flat on the bar and leaned in looking thoughtful. "Sure. It's been slow tonight. I could use a good joke."

Storm took his wallet out of his pocket, pulled out a hundred dollar bill, and put it down on the bar face up. "Does that look like real money or play money to you?"

Looking from the bill up to Storm's face, the man eyes narrowed. "If that's a joke, I've got to admit I've heard better."

Storm blinked. "Play money?"

"It would be a pretty good copy except that, so far as I know, hundred dollar bills come with Thomas Jefferson's face on the front. That's why they're called Tom J's? You know?"

"Tom J's."

"Listen, friend, you seem a little lost."

Storm barked out a laugh that was so sudden

and out of place, the bartender recoiled a little reflexively.

"Lost. Yeah. Understatement of the… millennium."

"You want a drink?"

Storm shook his head and smiled. thinking he might have landed in hell. Is that the way Elora felt? So completely alone? Everything familiar, but not? He chuckled again at his own misfortune. "No money."

The bartender looked Storm over. Again. "Excuse me for saying so, but I wouldn't take you for down and out."

"No?"

"No. Take your clothes, for instance. Threads are top shelf. Close shave. Nice cologne. Healthy. Clean. Clear eyes. What am I missing?"

Storm shook his head again, knocked two knuckles on the wood bar and said, "Thank you for letting me use your phone."

He started to turn away when the bartender stopped him.

"Hold on." The man set a shot glass down and started pouring Jack. "On the house."

Storm was the sort of person who was way too generous to turn down generosity when it was pointed at him. He knew that a gracious acceptance is a kind of return gift. So he didn't hesitate to pick up the glass, throw his head back, and let the contents drain down his throat. He savored the after burn.

If ever I needed a drink…

When he set the glass down, the bartender grabbed up the bottle and made a question of motioning toward the empty glass with it. In answer, Storm looked in the guy's eyes and silently slid the glass closer to the bottle.

"So. I'm guessing you don't have any *real* money in that wallet." Storm said nothing. "I'm also guessing there's a story that goes along with that."

Storm scrubbed a hand down his face and offered a "fuck me" smile. "You have no idea."

"Just so happens I collect stories." He poured again. "You don't have any money. And you don't have any place to go, do you?"

Storm gave his host an appraising look.

"Who wants to know?"

Bartender took the towel off his shoulder, wiped his hands, and stuck a palm out.

"Name's Hal. Hal Cyon."

Storm's mind flew through a catalog of things to say, rejecting each one as fast as it came to mind. He finally decided on keeping his features as even as if Hal's name was unremarkable. He clasped the hand offered to him.

"Engel Storm. So this is your place."

Hal smiled in response and glanced around as if to reaffirm to himself that, yes, indeed he was the owner and also to try and see the bar, as if it was for the first time, through someone else's eyes.

"Angel Storm? Well, there's one thing we have in common, Mr. Storm. Names that are conversation starters. Now, about my question…"

"No. I don't have any money. And I don't have any place to go. When you close this fine establishment, I'm going to be looking for a park bench and hoping it doesn't rain." Storm reached up and scratched his chin. "You don't happen to have a big cardboard box back there, do you? And one of those plastic rain poncho things?"

"Look. Since you're not in any hurry, why don't you sit down there?" He pointed to the stool in front of him. "Let me check on my customers. When I get back, we'll talk about that box."

Storm watched Hal stop at each of the four occupied tables. Twice he returned to the bar with a tray full of empties, filled orders from memory, and delivered fresh rounds. There was a little digital clock behind the bar that caught his eye. It read thirteen minutes after eleven. He looked at his analog watch, which also read thirteen minutes after eleven – an exact twelve hour difference between where he sat and where he should be sitting having lunch with Glen.

Watching Hal take trays back and forth, he wondered if the bar had been busier earlier and, if it had, how Hal had managed to handle things without help. When he realized where his thoughts had taken him, he almost laughed out loud at himself. He was in an alien dimension with no money, where he knew no one, which probably went without saying, and he was pretty sure that his ID would come off just as fake as the money he had on him. The sane response to that predicament would be hysteria.

When Hal returned to his station behind the bar, he gave his hands a quick pass under the bar sink faucet, dried them on the towel he wore over his shoulder, and, just for good measure, wiped them on the white waist apron he wore. Luckily, Hal didn't serve food. Just drinks.

"You probably noticed I'm here by myself. Had a girl working for me up until this afternoon."

"That's too bad."

"At least she called, which was a refreshing change." Storm nodded. "Thing is, I'm semi-retired. Or trying to be. I work during times when we need two people. When I find somebody who can handle it alone, I enjoy my golden years doing other things." Somebody from one of the tables shouted something and Hal looked away. "'Scuse me a minute."

He walked over, talked, nodded, came back long enough to grab a Texas long neck, delivered it and dumped empties into an already full sink. Turning back to Storm he said, "And that's what it's all about. So. You ever done any bartending?"

Storm sat up a little straighter as the conversation suddenly came into crystal clear focus. He was being interviewed for a job that, well, it meant he might not have to live in a box and steal for the bare necessities. Hal was treated to the full weight of Storm's intensity.

"I've never done bartending, but I have worked as a bouncer and I helped my friend study the mixed drinks manual when he was learning to bartend."

Hal lifted his chin. "I'd bet the farm that you're a quick study."

"You have a farm?"

Hal chuckled. "No, but I've got a studio apartment in the back. I put it in a few years ago when the wife and I were in a bad patch. It's got a fridge and a nuke. Not much, but guys don't need much. Right? It's a sight better than a box."

He leaned on the bar. "A year later she left town with a thirty-year-old. I reclaimed the house and moved back in. Now I got a girlfriend who rooms with me." He winked.

"Anyway, it's just sitting back there not bein' used. You know?"

Of all the times to feel like a damn lucky son-of-a-bitch, being stranded wouldn't be the most likely candidate. But there he stood agreeing with Hal that, indeed, a modest room and a job in a place where he had no resources and no way to prove he should exist, was feeling like a mighty big blessing.

"You could finish studying up on drinks. We don't get a lot of call for Pink Poodle Saharas and shit. Most of my customers want just what you'd expect. Straight and easy. We get an occasional request for a somethin'-tini or a cosmo. That's about it.

"I'm thinking that, if you help me work the late shift and watch the place after hours, you can have the job with the room thrown in. Package deal."

Storm looked into Hal's face for a couple more seconds. He started to say thank you, but his voice caught just a little and he had to try again. "Thank you."

Hal grinned. "Nah. You're the one doing me a favor, kid." Hal opened the cash register and produced two keys on a generic chain, which he laid on the bar.

Storm looked down at the old-fashioned polished wood then reached out to finger the keys.

"This might sound ungrateful. I don't mean it that way and I hope you don't take it that way." He raised his eyes to meet Hal's. "Why?"

"Guy wanders in off the street looking lost, asks me if funny money is real, and then says he's homeless. Who wouldn't give that guy a key to his business?" Storm just stared, unsure what to think or say about that. Finally, Hal laughed. "Just pumping you. Truth is, night in, night out, bartenders serve drinks to people so wounded they've forgot how to keep their shields up. Enough years go by, a sixth sense of a thing starts to come on. Know what I mean?"

"You a mind reader?"

"Like the Dear Dora Psychic Line?" He shook his head, clearly amused. "It's not mindreading. More like sensing the core of a person. Their real stuff. You know?"

Storm's brows had come together. In an off-the-beaten-path sort of way, he did think he understood what Hal was saying. Maybe. The guy probably was part clairvoyant, part philosopher. "And your sense told you to trust me?"

"'Bout sums it up."

"Okay." Storm picked the keys up and put them in his pocket. "I'm much obliged. Just one thing."

"Yeah?"

"I, ah, might have to leave in a hurry and I might not be able to get the keys back to you. I wouldn't want to leave you in a bad, um…"

Hal grew serious. "Don't worry about it, kid. If you have to leave in a hurry, I won't be any worse off than the way you found me. Right?"

Storm wanted to give Hal a smile in return,

but was suddenly afraid that, if he tried to smile, he might mist up instead. So he nodded and looked away.

"Then it's settled. Here's the plan. We open at four and close at two. You'll be on from six to two. I'll come in and get things started at four and stay until one person can handle it. Like now. You'll close up."

Storm looked around. It wasn't yet midnight and the place had cleared out except for one guy sitting by himself in a corner booth nursing a long neck like he was in an ice house. Of course, it was a week night. Weekends might be different. Probably were.

"Alright."

Hal turned toward the cash register, opened it again, pulled out a small stack of cash and laid it on the bar where the keys had been.

"Consider this an advance. You're going to need some stuff that play money of yours won't buy. Hope you're not hungry 'cause there's nothing open."

"I saw a donut shop down the block."

Hal's eyes flicked over Storm's upper body.

"Guy your size needs real food. Not puffy fried cardboard dusted with sugar. There's some frozen stuff in the apartment, but it's probably not much better for you." He waved his hand at the bar. "Obviously something to drink is not a problem.

"There's a little pocket grocery two blocks east opens at seven. I think. Run by Chinese, but they carry regular stuff. Nice people.

"So I'll close up tonight. You go on and get settled. Tomorrow I'll show you the ropes." He motioned toward a door behind the bar. "That way. Have a good night."

Storm looked toward the door and back at Hal. "Thank you. I…"

"Okay, look. If you really want to thank me proper, then one of these days when you think the time is right, I'd like to hear your story. Got a feeling it's a collectable." He nodded toward the back. "Go on now."

Storm wandered through the swinging door behind the bar. There was only one locked door, so he figured he was at the right place. Hal was right. It wasn't much.

He closed the door. The space had a half bath, a little dinette with two chairs, although Storm seriously doubted Hal had ever entertained a guest. One window facing the alley had iron bars. A low two-shelf book case that was filled with books. Alarm clock. No TV. He was going to have the company of the constant hum of the refrigerator. It was white with a curved top, about as tall as his chest, and it looked like it could qualify for display in the Smithsonian Americana section.

There was an old porcelain sink with a few black scars where chunks of the porcelain were missing. The room seemed to be clean though. No dust. Bed was made. He hoped the sheets hadn't been slept on. *But beggars can't be choosers.*

Sitting on the side of the single bed that wasn't really long enough for him, he indulged in a deep sigh while he studied the mock marble veins on the linoleum floor tiles and remembered the picture of his beautiful girls saying goodbye, thinking he'd be home in a little over an hour. He looked at his watch and thought, "Right about now."

His mind wandered to a mental candid of his idea of a perfect day. He and Litha had bought their vineyard and given the previous owners the two weeks they requested to vacate. Since the newlyweds had nowhere in particular to be, they reasoned that there might never be another time so opportune for sightseeing Northern California.

The picture that came to his mind was of a day driving the red convertible Aston Martin south on the Pacific Coast Highway from Eureka. The top was down. A cloudless sky met a cerulean blue sea on the western horizon and the water shimmered with the magic of reflected sunlight.

As he looked over at his new wife, her loosely bound hair whipping behind her in the wind, he was thinking that paradise could not hope to be as perfect as that moment. As if reading his mind, she turned toward him and laughed.

He could almost hear the sound of that laugh bounce around the walls of the little studio apartment. He saw a drop of something fall on his jeans. *Oh, shit no. Black Swan knights don't leak. Not unless they're Elora.* At least not over something as trivial as being temporarily misplaced.

Storm considered that he didn't have a lot of experience with sadness. He had parents who loved him. He'd gotten what he wanted for Yule when he was a kid.

From the moment Sol recruited him, he'd been busy learning and drilling. Then patrolling and fighting. He had a mission to occupy his drive and his needs were taken care of so that he could focus on the work.

The closest he'd ever come to sadness was when Elora chose Rammel, but if what he was feeling at the moment was sadness, then getting on that plane without Elora would have to be categorized as a minor annoyance.

He told himself to pull it tight and get ready to wait it out. He would be found. He knew that Litha would *never* stop looking until he was back at home.

His fuck up of a father-in-law would have to do something right for a change. Storm's mood lightened a little when he imagined what Litha would be saying to the incubus when she found out. She'd put him through seven levels of Hades.

Litha.

A week had passed without finding Storm. Both hope and enthusiasm were starting to wane. Every day fewer searchers showed up to help.

Litha's friend, the angel Kellareal, was committed and pressed his crew to keep looking.

As for Deliverance, over the past eight hundred years, he'd made more fans than friends, most of whom were human women and, therefore, not equipped to help with the search.

There were hoards of Elementals who owed him favors though. Nothing kept a significant female from suspicion or curiosity like being preoccupied by her own tryst with an incubus, which meant that Deliverance was always in demand among philandering male Elementals.

The problem wasn't that he had lots of favors available to collect. The problem was in trying to collect those favors. Many of the entities he could tap for a U. O. Me couldn't be found unless they wanted to be found.

Nonetheless, between friends, fans, and favors, he'd produced a respectable search party. The fact that there was nothing to show for their effort really wasn't because of lack of trying. Glen's smart board had turned into a chaotic mess with the numbers of searched quadrants struck through.

Under his own authority and initiative, Glen hung photos of Storm, enlarged to poster size, around the conference room. He knew the Elementals who were searching weren't using sight to find him, but being human, it seemed to him that a search and rescue war room ought to have photos of the missing person. Maybe he also needed a visual reminder to keep him from leaning toward despair, because he and Ram were both starting to show some frazzle around the edges. They had no way of calculating the odds of getting Storm back, but every day that ended without finding him made it feel like the chances were growing fainter.

Litha was a mess emotionally and constantly berated herself for that. Her little girl was being raised by other people while she searched. When her mother was at home, Rosie was exposed to pure stress and that made Litha feel even guiltier.

Rosie was three when Storm had disappeared. She now appeared to be around six and a half.

Just the right age to be learning to ride a bike.

She'd had that thought in the middle of having dinner with her little girl and had burst into tears.

"Don't cry, Mama."

"No. I won't." Litha shook her head, smiled, and tried to compose herself quickly. "I'm not going to cry. It's just that your Daddy wanted to teach you to ride a bike and I think you're at the perfect age right now."

Rosie looked back at her with an expression of intelligence that was arresting. "Then I won't learn to ride a bike until he comes home."

Litha was grateful for that sentiment and feeling pensive. "Rosie. Do you remember your daddy?"

She beamed in response and nodded enthusiastically. "I know everything about him."

Litha cocked her head. "What do you mean?"

"I know everything from when he was a little boy."

"I don't understand. You mean you've heard stories about little boys?"

She giggled and shook her head like her mother was being silly. "No. I remember."

Litha frowned. "You remember what exactly, darling?"

"I *remember* from when Daddy was a little boy."

Litha felt her heart speed up, but tried to keep her voice calm.

"Rosie. Tell me a story from when Daddy was a little boy."

"Okay. When Daddy was a little boy, his favorite thing to do was to go to work with his daddy."

"What did they do at work?"

"They looked at the rows where the grapes were planted. They looked at the big barrels. Stuff like that."

Litha knew that to be true because Storm had told her how much he loved going to the vineyard where his father worked.

"What else do you know about?"

"I know *everything* about you, too, Mama."

Litha's breath gushed out in a laugh or a sob. She wasn't sure which. As if it wasn't already unusual enough to have a little girl who was aging six months a day and transporting anywhere she pleased with a thought.

"Oh my." More tears slid down Litha's face as she made a mental list of things she wouldn't want her child to know about her. Nothing said 'lack of privacy' like someone who had your memories.

"It's alright, Mama. Until Daddy gets back we have Auntie Elora and Grandy and the seven monkeys."

"Rosie! Don't call them that! It's disrespectful. They're *monks*."

"I know. But they don't mind. They laugh when I say it."

"And don't talk to me about Grandy."

"He's sorry, Mama. He really is. He didn't mean to lose Daddy and he's sad all the time that you're mad at him."

"Good."

Rosie pressed her lips together and looked at her mother with condemnation. In a moment of turning the tables that was almost weirder than the rest of it.

"You can just stop looking at me like that because I'm not taking it back."

Rosie raised her little eyebrows and perfectly mimicked that head jiggle mannerism that Deliverance had passed on to Litha. And now Rosie, too. Apparently.

"And we have Glen." Rosie had the oddest little smile on her face, like she had a secret.

Glen finished another twelve hour shift almost too exhausted to think. He'd been running Jefferson Unit from the conference room. He was afraid that, if he stepped away, one of the searchers would return with news and he wouldn't be there. During his shift, he ate his meals there, slept there, and had Barrock stand watch when he needed a toilet break. The stress of the constant barrage of emotion was scraping him raw.

He was furious with Deliverance and worried like hell about Storm. Every time someone or some thing popped into the conference room, his hope spiked like a jack-in-the-box and then crashed when it turned out to be nothing but a no-go report.

Of all the times for Sol to take a vacation. Of all the times for Storm to get lost. When *he* was in charge feeling like the furthest thing from a boy wonder.

In one of the few quiet moments, Glen summoned Monq to talk about the mishap and was shocked that he came.

"I've been thinking that you need to come up

with a way to be certain this doesn't happen again. Ever."

"By 'this', you mean the displacement of Sir Storm?"

Glen glared at him, with too little energy left in emotional reserve to be polite.

"Yes. That's what I mean. And for now, until Sol gets back and makes a final decision, we need to classify this accident as Top Secret. If it gets around that you can get lost when piggybacking the passes, how many employees or associates are going to volunteer for that ride in the future?"

"I see what you mean. Reluctance could ensue."

"You have a gift for understatement, Dr. Monq. I want you to come up with something that will prevent a repeat."

"I'll look into it."

"And keep me up on the progress."

Monq nodded and left. He could see that Glen was on the verge of collapse and didn't think it would be a good time to protest more work. But the truth was that he was busy overseeing the outfitting of the entire A/C system for emergency delivery of the Equalizer in the event the facility should be breached by extra-dimensional assassins.

Every floor was being equipped with a yellow emergency button behind a glass case that would release the chemical into the air and set off an alarm. Since Monq's to-do list was perpetually long and growing, he had to make choices. At the moment, implementing the security measure was his top priority.

Stagsnare Dimension

Archer was aware that Number Seventeen had volunteered for reeducation and Rothesay was giddy about putting the successful candidate through his process, which would turn an average man into an assassin without conscience, who would react to any order without question or delay. Rothesay used a combination of hypnosis, drugs, sleep deprivation, and drill.

By the time Number Seventeen left in the transport, the person he had been was gone as if he'd never existed. It was a premature death. His body was still walking around, but his point of view had been shoved aside and replaced by the most potent sociopathy, carefully calculated to be just the right stuff for a stone cold killer.

The ruthless travesty of the whole thing made Archer ask himself for the thousandth time if it wouldn't be better to be decent people who were oppressed than to be the oppressors who came to power by murder and held that power with a soulless philosophy.

Jaik, his lead lab assistant, was talking. It pulled Archer out of the dark introspection.

"I'm sorry. What?"

"I said, 'What are you doing with those mice? What's that you're injecting them with?'"

"Oh. It's just a little hobby project. Nothing

I'm ready to divulge. I want to get a little further along with it. If it works out, it may be a paper."

That satisfied Jaik, who turned away with a head nod, and went back to his own work.

Rothesay had increased the number scheduled for the third attempt from twelve to twenty. So Number Seventeen arrived in Loti Dimension with a biolocator programmed with twenty life signatures, each matching one of the proposed members of the second mission, and orders to kill. The third assassination team's departure would initiate shortly after his return with a report of one hundred percent success. Nothing less would do.

The transport deposited him on the edge of an aromatic landfill near London, but he didn't care. He wasn't sightseeing or on vacation. Seventeen smiled to himself when he checked his device and saw that thirteen of the twenty on his list were living in the U.K.

No feelings were associated with tracking the targets. Every synapse in his brain that fired a compunction response to harming others had been disabled. Thanks to Rothesay's sophisticated techniques, Number Seventeen was a killing machine who responded to command exactly the way a battery operated toy responds to its remote signal.

There was no social imprint left to interfere with a directive, no individuality, no imprint of social mores or morality. The universe had been distilled down to nothing more than a goal that was perverse, to be achieved by an abomination that was evil.

The closest one of the targets was living nearby in Threehalfpenny Wood. He would start there.

Over the following two weeks, there was a cluster of unexplained murders in the United Kingdom. The Ministry of Defense Police took over investigation because no two of the crimes occurred in the same local enforcement area. They were widespread and appeared to be totally unrelated. None of the victims knew each other and no common link was found other than the fact that they were all dispatched by identical method.

The thirteen men had all been sleeping in their own beds. The perpetrator had placed a pillow over the face of each before firing multiple shots to the head. In one case the victim lived alone. In another the victim's young wife had been out late at a bachelorette party and discovered the body when she returned home. In five cases, the victim's wife or girlfriend never heard anything and awakened to the sight of a grisly and violent death. It was a safe assumption that the gun had a sophisticated form of silencer because even heavy sleepers wouldn't sleep through multiple gunshots otherwise.

The other six were sleeping with partners who had been lighter sleepers. Unfortunately for them, the killer was set against leaving witnesses.

All told, the U.K. damage was twenty one dead and nineteen orphaned.

It took the Ministry some time, sending evidence to various labs and experts, to confirm for certain that the bullets were not a match for any that had been manufactured. Anywhere. While that might conceivably be explained away, as a personal project of a gun enthusiast, what couldn't be explained was the alloy used in the composition. One of the metals simply didn't exist in the Catalog of Elements. That was a fact that wouldn't be reported.

The two investigators who had been assigned the case were having coffee in a London office when a Scotland Yard detective knocked on the open door jamb.

"I believe you will be interested in this."

He placed a report between them. During the past week, when the rampage had stopped in the U.K., there had been six other identical events elsewhere. One in Sweden, one in Morocco, one in Canada, and three in the United States. It was a pattern, but it wasn't like any serial killing pattern in record.

Nineteen of the twenty names on the list were eliminated by the alien assassin. The twentieth had already expired, verified in person by Number Seventeen, who took a photo of the mausoleum drawer plaque where the remains were entombed.

It was a successful mission by any standard. In addition to terminating all living targets, he had taken a biolocator reading on Elora Laiken every day for twenty-six days in a row. Her location had not changed.

As much as the people who were closest to Storm hated to admit it, after two weeks, they had to get back to work and leave the search in the hands of species who could actually, well, search. They had obligations to other personnel and to The Order itself. So, much as Ram, Elora, and Glen hated to continue going through the motions of life without Storm, there really wasn't a choice.

The Hunter Division stationed at Jefferson Unit was transferred leaving a skeleton crew that basically consisted of Z Team, that was if you were counting active duty knights. Ram and Elora were on the premises, but retired knights weren't officially counted as part of an installation's defense system.

Fennimore was in residence because he was using accrued vacation time to delay separation from Elsbeth. Elora speculated to Ram that they were probably trying to decide whether or not they could live without each other and whether or not they wanted to try.

Dozens of support people were transferred, farmed out to other facilities because they simply weren't going to need as many staff, particularly medical.

By the time the dust settled, what was left was minimal staff for the infirmary, Research, meaning Monq and his research team and lab technicians, enough kitchen corps to cover the reduced numbers, Maintenance which was janitorial and housekeeping, and, of course, the trainees and their instructors.

A system of drills aimed at the trainees had been devised and implemented because the kids were the biggest concern. Second sons had been the focus of The Order's work for centuries and that probably wasn't going to change until the last vampire was either dead or reintroduced to life as a human. Even though the safety of the boys was priority, no one was worried. The chances of J.U. being attacked were miniscule. It was just a matter of better safe than sorry.

The first day after the exodus, Elora went down to breakfast with Helm, planning to meet Ram after his shift in the search war room. She found it a little sad to see the once-bustling Hub practically deserted. It was even echoing.

Like Ram knew what she was thinking, he said, "Thin's change. Right?" She nodded, grudgingly. "Acceptin' that is part of maturity."

"Okay. I was with you right up until the part where *you* started talking about maturity."

He grinned. "Suggestin' I'm no' full grown, are ye?"

She laughed. "You are not luring me into a sex-laden dialogue until I've had my morning chocolate."

"Aye. Cocoa is a grand start to a tête-à-tête."

A shadow came over her face. "There are some changes I won't accept."

Ram knew she was talking about the fact that Storm was still missing. "Oh, aye, my girl. Some changes we will *never* be acceptin'."

Storm had helped Rammel study to go undercover as a bartender at Notte Fuoco in New York, he'd thought he hadn't paid much attention, but he'd picked up more than he thought. It only took one day to get the hang of running Hal's place the way he liked it. Hal must have had his share of truly lousy employees because he wouldn't stop telling Storm that he was lucky to have owned the door he walked through. ·

The first night Storm took his tips and set them next to the cash register for Hal.

"Hey, what's this?"

"I think it's, um, tips."

"Well, then, this is yours, not mine."

When Storm hesitated, Hal said, "That advance I gave you was against pay. Not tips."

His tip money wasn't going to pave the way to a penthouse, but it enabled him to get some sweats, a jacket, running shoes. Stuff like that.

So life took on a routine of working and waiting to be found. Storm took orders, made drinks, washed glasses, carried stock, emptied trash, swept, mopped, wiped down the bar, washed and dried the bar linens and quickly learned to feel at home in a white apron that tied around his waist. And he was glad for anything that could distract his mind from missing home, even if for just a few minutes at a time.

The worst time was crawling into bed alone at night. He missed Litha like a physical ache. Knowing that she was just as worried and scared, well, that didn't help at all. He knew she'd be tearing up the passes looking for him. He also knew that Rosie was probably continuing to grow like a weed, even though he held on to the irrational hope that he'd return to find everything the same.

The only thing he could think of to do, that might help, was to stay visible as much as he could. His gut instinct told him that he'd be easier to find if he was out in the open. He had no reason to believe that was true, but if there was a chance…

He hoped like Hades that sooner or later someone would look for him in the right place.

So, when he wasn't working or sleeping, he walked around the city or took a trolley to Golden Gate Park where he divided his time between reading, and running to keep in shape. The incline of the hills made a great workout and he needed the burn.

The books Hal had left behind in the studio apartment, when he'd lived there himself, were not what Storm would have expected. Dickens, Descartes, Spinoza, James Hilton, Bram Stoker. An eclectic mix revealed a guy who was deeper and more complicated than his manner suggested, giving support to the adage that appearances can be deceiving.

After Storm closed up at night, he took a shower just to wash off the energy of the lost souls who made up the Halcyon patronage. Then, before going to bed, he would spend some time at the dinette writing out his story for Hal in longhand. He left the document under his pillow during the day thinking that, if he disappeared, it would be found. Hopefully by Hal. If it was the only thing the guy wanted, it was the least Storm could do in return for the extraordinary kindness and generosity that had been extended to him.

One night, customers long gone, Storm had closed up and polished off the checklist except for one last thing – taking out the trash.

Opening the alley door, the first thing he noticed was that a night fog had come rolling off the bay. The mists hovered and swirled and gave the illusion of life to the night air. The second thing he noticed was a pricking of his senses that sent him straight into high alert. He braced for the adrenalin rush that always followed.

There was no mistaking the reaction. He'd experienced it too many times not to know exactly what it meant. Vampire.

In the dim light coming from the street at the end of the alley, a dark figure was pressing a woman against a dirty wall. If Storm had been anybody else, he might have taken the two for lovers, but that scene was disturbingly familiar and he knew what he was looking at. Predator and prey.

He was on the verge of choosing a course of action when movement at the other end of the alley drew his attention.

Walking abreast, four figures emerged from the fog. To Storm, possibly because he was on alert, they seemed to be moving in slow motion, the athletic grace of dancers coupled with the lethal purpose of predatory machines. *Knights.* It was beautiful. Watching them silently stalk toward him, he felt a wave of pride wash over him. It stood his follicles on end and set his molecules vibrating, but he didn't have time to indulge in emotion.

The vampire raised his head and looked to his left. When he saw the glory of Black Swan knights coming for him looking like they were empowered with the authority and righteousness of the gods, he dropped his victim, intending to flee the alley.

As fortune would have it, someone had broken down a wood pallet and left it in the dumpster. Storm reached over and snapped off a dagger-sized shard of the splintered wood. When the vamp turned to run away from the knights, he ran straight into the practiced aim of a vampire slayer who was far, far from home. With shock evident in his colorless eyes, he looked down at the blunt end of a wooden shiv sticking out of his chest.

Storm locked gazes with the vamp as he died, and muttered, "I know it's not your fault. But it's not hers either. This is the only kind of cure I've got with me. Better luck in your next life." And with that, the body crumpled to the concrete.

After glancing at the knights, he walked across the alley and placed two fingers against the woman's neck. When they reached him, Storm looked up into their curious faces and shook his head to indicate that she was past saving. He stood and looked at the four, one by one, then said, "Gentlemen. If you'll excuse me."

The stunned foursome exchanged looks and, before Storm disappeared into the bar, one of them managed to say, "Hold on, brother. We've got a couple of questions."

Storm stopped and seemed to be considering. After a few beats, he opened the alley door and held it ajar.

"It's a long story. I'll buy you a drink if you want."

One of the knights swept his gaze over his three teammates as he took out an intelliphone and touched a virtual button on the screen. "Go ahead. I'll call for cleanup. If he's buying, I'll take a Jack Neat."

Halcyon Dimension.

Angel loved racing season. He could have used a bookie or found a convenient off-track betting establishment behind a Chinese apothecary, but then he'd be cheating himself out of the full-bodied experience.

Yes. He liked to gamble on horses, but he also liked the atmosphere of the track: sounds, sights, and even smells.

So four times a week he took his Jaguar F-Type for a twenty minute drive on 80, across the bay, past Berkeley to Golden Gate Fields. He had suffered a streak of losses and was in big to his "financier", but if that thought tried to nag at him, he pushed it down so it wouldn't interfere with his enjoyment of the day or his ability to choose the lucky pony.

At the end of the day, he got in his beautiful car and drove west. Unlike the heady anticipation of going to the races, the kind that he had experienced earlier in the day, there was nothing to block out personal confrontation with the situation. He was worse off. Not better. He knew that, sooner or later, he was going to have to be a big boy and face it.

He parked the Jag in his secure garage space. That security cost him almost as much as he paid for his apartment, but it was worth it. Everything about his life was eclectic. He lived in a high rise with a beautiful view and it would have been Trump expensive if it wasn't for the fact that it was located in a questionable neighborhood.

Angel could have gone home for a drink alone, but decided on going to his neighborhood bar to drink alone there. It was just getting dark, early to be drinking, especially without dinner, but whatever. Walking up the block he noticed that the neon sign was winking.

Somebody was sitting at his table. Well, maybe it didn't have his name engraved on a reserved sign, but it was where he liked to sit. So he took one of those corner booths that was designed for five people. By the time he had slid over the red leather, the bar owner was standing there ready to take his order.

"Hey, Hal."

"Evening, Mr. Storm. What'll it be?"

"Usual."

"You got it."

As soon as Hal moved away, Angel took out a little black cigar and lit it with an old-fashioned fluid lighter. He liked the look and feel of a *real* lighter and even enjoyed the smell of the chemical catching flame. There weren't a lot of bars left in San Francisco that allowed smoking. *Pussies.* As he pulled smoke into his mouth, he thanked the gods that Halcyon wasn't one of those.

Hal set Angel's drink in front of him. "Start a tab?"

"Yeah. Thanks."

An hour later, Angel put out the little black smoke, settled up with cash and left Hal's bar. Maybe he'd go home and watch reruns on the Jukebox network. Why not? Millions of ordinary people obviously loved to watch TV about guys like him who bottomed out in deadly serious shit with seriously deadly bad guys. Maybe he'd turn that around and watch optimistic shows about funny and functional families on Juke.

Maybe he'd go to a club and look for somebody who wanted to be his girlfriend for an hour. What he ought to be doing was looking for a poker game so he could balance out some of his losses. But that behavior wouldn't qualify as self-sabotage.

He hadn't walked five steps away from the entrance to the bar before Baph's men grabbed him.

"Well, there he is. Pretty as a dark angel. Hello, Storm." Baph was wearing the expensive overcoat that he always wore, winter or summer, and a smile that could only be described as chilling.

"Dick."

The guy's name was Richard. Angel called him Dick just to dick with him, but privately, that was in his own head, he thought of him as "Baph", short for Baphomet, because he bore an uncanny resemblance to the ancient infamous engraving. Angel didn't know what species the guy was, but he put the goat in goatee. In addition to notable facial hair, he had vertical slits for pupils, horns and was probably sporting a sizable pair of breasts under all that outerwear.

Angel would bet on it, but even he had to admit that wasn't saying much. After all his poor management of the betting impulse was what had brought him to that moment.

Baph's tone was sugar sweet. Too sweet. "Let's go over here and have a little dialogue." Following the direction his eyes went when he said, 'over here', Angel deduced that 'here' meant the alley. He thought about trying to run for it, but the two goons anticipated that move and grabbed him first. He had a matched pair of thug accessories, one on each side forcibly escorting him to the far side of the dumpster, past the reach of street lights.

"You know I like you more than most of my addicts. And not just because you're so pretty. So it's going to hurt me to hurt you and that makes me even angrier than if I didn't have feelings for you."

"You have feelings for me?" When there was no reply, Angel said, "Look, uh, Richard…"

Baph sneered. "So it's Richard now, is it? Shut it, junkie."

"Junkie?"

"You object to the term? The monkey on your back doesn't care whether your Jones is chemicals or horses. Do we agree you owe me money?"

"Yes."

"It's unfortunate that you're choosing to spend your time in low class bars nursing hooch when you could be doing something productive. Like winning enough money to pay your debts. What do you think I ought to do about that?"

"Give me another week?"

Baph laughed without making any noise. "Sure. Sure. Another week. No problem. But I think it needs to be an incentivized week. Seems painfully clear you're lacking motivation. So we're going to give you something painful to remember when you're making choices during your week's reprieve. Maybe it's your looks that's your downfall. I can fix that for you."

Baph reached into the overcoat and withdrew a surgical-sharp instrument that seemed to match his reputation for liking to deliver his own messages. Personally. When Angel realized that the situation was serious and coming to a head, he started struggling to get out of the hold the gumbahs had on him.

It was then that the miracle occurred.

Angel was jerked free of the hold the two miscreants had on him just before they were privileged to have their heads knocked together by an angel. It was as close as either would ever come to communion with one. Meanwhile, the demon, Deliverance, grabbed the intended victim, whom he believed to be his son-in-law, and vanished with him.

Kellareal and Deliverance had happened upon Angel Storm at the same time. After a half hour debate they agreed to call it a tie. Next they fought over who would get to deliver Storm to Litha.

"How did you get to be friends with my daughter anyway?"

"I was watching her. I followed her into a pass. She sensed she had a tail and doubled back on me."

"Something about your phraseology suggests to me that you may be a fan of film noir."

"I am a fan of film noir."

Deliverance stared at Kellareal for a minute. "Why were you watching Litha?"

Kellareal smirked at the demon. "Like you don't know."

"Pretend I don't and tell me."

"The Council wants her watched because she has enough power to go *Carrie* on the whole world."

"Oh, that."

"Yes, that."

"And you were 'tailing' her?" The incubus punctuated the air with quote fingers when he said tailing. "Since when are angels in the biz of following demons?"

"Like I said, she's special. You know it. And I'm one of them."

"Them?"

"An emissaric seraphim."

"That supposed to mean something to me?"

Kellareal looked at Deliverance like he was an imbecile. "Perhaps not. The point is that I was given the task of keeping tabs on your girl and we ended up being friendly."

Deliverance could not hide his distaste at that possibility.

"Back to the issue at hand. I'm her father and his father-in-law. I was present when he wandered off and caused all this trouble and I should be the one to put him back where he goes."

"Actually, since you're the one who lost him and caused all this trouble, you're the *last* creature we should entrust with his safe return."

When the demon could see that no argument was getting him anywhere, he finally said, "Please. I need the win."

"Did you say please?"

"I did. And you heard me."

"Say it again."

Deliverance wanted to launch himself at the black-eyed blonde and take him to the ground, but he held his temper. "Please."

To Kellareal, getting the demon to beg was as good as a win. With a smile full of smug, he acquiesced, which left Deliverance with two thoughts about the emissaric seraphim: first, that Kell was surprisingly decent for an angelic chap and, second, that the angel was a sucker for not insisting on negotiating a better deal than two utterances of the word 'please'.

It took less than four minutes to get to the vineyard and Deliverance chuckled all the way. He also made sure he had a death grip on Storm.

Litha was going to be so happy and so surprised. The demon sensed what part of the house she was in and dropped the lunker in the master bedroom right outside her bathroom door. He knocked softly.

"Litha. It's Dad. I have a surprise. And don't say I never did anything for you."

Without waiting for a response, he popped out, feeling triumphant and thinking he deserved a femme feast in celebration.

Angel couldn't begin to process what had happened. One minute he was in an alley about to be cut, the next he had his arms full of a soft, curvy woman who had flung herself at him and then grabbed on, demanding kisses like her life depended on it.

He knew Baph was wonky. Maybe there were

odd ideas about punishment wherever he was from. Or maybe the piece was like a last meal. Either way, he was partaking.

Litha had been coming out of the shower wearing a towel. It had disappeared seconds after she rushed that big body and collided with the one person who could put her world back on its axis and make it start spinning in the right direction again.

She stripped him out of his pants and boots, but couldn't wait longer than that to get him inside her. The threat of being without him forever had ramped her desire into a tight spiral. So she left him in his tight-fitting tee and nothing else. She wished she had six hands so she could touch him everywhere at once. On one level she was in the middle of a prelude to the most feverish fuck of her life. On another level she was checking to make sure he was okay.

He interrupted both her preoccupations by grabbing her up and dropping her onto the bed seconds before she felt his weight settle. It felt good. It felt familiar. It also felt… different somehow.

The sex was rough compared to what she was used to, but she didn't care about that. When Storm fought, he fought hard, holding nothing back. In general, he approached life with a similar intensity, but his bedroom manner was characteristically different. He had a preference for lengthy foreplay and slow, tender, sweet, sincere lovemaking. The pounding into her body was almost brutal. She ignored the distant look on his face and chalked up the hurried humping to the same desperate feelings of separation and uncertainty she'd been suffering.

He yelled out an orgasm and collapsed on top of her. It wasn't like Storm to be oblivious to whether or not she'd been properly pleasured, but they'd both been through a lot. And she was so glad to have him there.

"Welcome back." She smiled into his mouth. "I'm going to need another shower. Why don't you join me? Let's get clean together then I'll feed you and you can tell me everything."

She pushed at him to get his weight off her. When he rolled off to the side, she rose from the bed and headed back toward the bath.

He turned his head to watch her saunter away and felt a sizable appreciation for the sight of her curvy backside. Yeah. Sizable and growing larger between his legs. Again. So soon.

Normally Angel didn't do play and stay, but he was up for a repeat with Green Eyes. He got up to follow her. She'd invited him into the shower and he didn't need to be asked twice.

Litha turned and smiled just in time to see him grab the shoulders of his tee with both hands, jerk it over his head, and drop it on the floor.

Her smile faded when her eyes drifted downward to the elegant and intricate dragon tattoo that started at his left pec, ran around his ribcage and ended out of sight at his shoulder blade.

"You got a tattoo?"

"Yeah. Like it? It's not exactly new."

"Not new? What do you mean 'not new'?"

Angel cocked his head at her look of confusion. "I've had it since I was nineteen."

"Nineteen?"

He smirked at the question as he prowled toward her.

"What's with the question, sweet tits? You're starting to sound like a parrot."

Litha's brain circuits scrambled to put the puzzle pieces together and she didn't like the picture she was getting. "What's my name?"

He stalked toward her. "Names aren't really my thing, cutie pie."

"Oh gods." Her knees felt weak and she might have been a little lightheaded for a second.

Storm would never call her something so ridiculous. He knew how she felt about stupid pet names, especially those that involved pastry or produce: cupcake, pumpkin, peaches, pie.

Her look of horror kept pace with her growing realization that the man whose semen was currently seeping down her thighs, was not her husband. She emitted a sound that was a cross between a cough, a sob, and strangulation, then grabbed a bath sheet off a hook within reach and hurriedly drew it around her. The imposter responded by sculpting Storm's face into a wicked smile that her spouse simply did not have in his range of expressions.

"Aw, baby, don't cover up now. I like the view."

While he grabbed a corner of the towel and began playfully pulling it away from her, she grasped the black diamond pendant and squeezed. If Deliverance thought he was in trouble before...

When Litha's dad appeared a moment later, Angel jumped and yelped a little.

Deliverance looked at the unashamedly naked

Storm and smiled. "Having fun yet?"

Litha gathered her bath sheet around her with as much dignity as she could muster, circumstances being what they were, and hissed at her father.

"You know, you would think that, with a name like Deliverance, you could manage to *deliver* the right Storm."

The demon jerked his head at a naked, confused version of Storm. "It's not him?"

She shook her head. "*Definitely* not."

Deliverance openly sniffed the air then knowingly looked at his daughter.

She hated the scarlet blush that she knew was creeping up her neck toward her face, darkening the already pink effect of the beard burn his stubble had left on her cheeks. But she didn't hate the color of humiliation nearly as much as she hated her dad at that moment. If she had ever been more irate, she couldn't remember when. Pair that with righteous indignation and she was summoning every scrap of remaining patience to make her voice even enough so that she didn't sound every bit as crazy as she felt at the moment.

"Get. Him. Out. Of. Here."

"Where do you want me to take him?"

Litha turned to face the wall and put one hand out in front of her against the tile for support. "Just get him into some pants and wait in the kitchen."

"Okay."

He had the gall to sound dejected. Turning to the unwanted version of Storm, the demon raised his eyebrows.

"You heard her. Cover it up and follow me."

When Angel didn't move, Deliverance snapped his fingers and waved his hand in front of the guy's face. "If you're waiting for me to dress you, that's not...," he stopped and looked at Litha's tense posture, "that's *probably* not going to happen. Pants on and come with me."

Looking a little dazed, Angel pulled on his pants and shirt and grabbed his boots on the way past, casting a look over his shoulder at Litha as he left. He followed Deliverance down the hallway to the kitchen where the demon leaned against a counter with his arms crossed and glared at the confused transplant like the whole thing was his fault.

Good-Looking-Angry-Man might not have anything to say, but Angel had questions.

"Where is this? Who are you? Who is she? How did I get here?" His eyes darted around the kitchen. "Never mind. Scratch all that and let me make it simple. What the fuck is going on here?"

Good-Looking-Angry-Man made no move to gesture or speak. Angel decided he would give it as long as it took to pull his boots on. When time was up and there was no answer forthcoming, he stood and glanced toward the back door.

"Fine. Then I'm out of here. See ya."

"Sit down."

It wasn't an invitation. It wasn't a command. It sounded more like a foregone conclusion, as if Deliverance had never experienced not getting his way and couldn't even conceive of the possibility.

"Why? It was a sweet bag, but I'm done with her and you don't seem to have any answers soooo..."

If Angel Storm had understood that he was

talking to a powerful, eight-hundred-year-old elemental that some called demon, and that the "bagging" to which he referred was said demon's daughter, he might have been more concerned about the flash of irritation he saw in those black eyes.

"Done with her?"

Deliverance's tone was incredulous. No creature in the cosmos would dare talk about Litha with such an absence of respect. He didn't consciously call a fire ball to his hand. His emotional reaction just brought it on involuntarily. It would have felt marvelous to laugh while the contemptuous underling incinerated, but he didn't want to see any more hurt or shame or disappointment on his little girl's face. And he didn't want to be scolded anymore either. So he willed the hot flame to change to cool blue and then spit out.

"What the hell?" Angel's eyes had gone wide when Deliverance produced fire from nothing.

"Sit and shut it or you may find *I'm* the hell humans like to use to scare children."

Angel Storm wasn't fond of following orders, but decided to make a prudent exception in that case. He sat. And shut it.

For a long time, Litha stood in the bath not moving, just trying to wrap her brain around what had happened and process. That meant a few tears and a lot of curses. She felt betrayed by her own body. It wasn't a willing infidelity. It couldn't have been willing if she'd thought dragon man was her husband, but in final analysis, how much of a difference did that make? She'd taken another man inside her and the shame of it made her nauseous.

Storm. He was out there somewhere probably scared he couldn't find his way back, while   some look-alike loser was getting off in their bed.

She took a hot shower, scrubbing her skin until it was raw and red. The whole time she was having to work hard at beating back a feeling of queasiness. All that scouring didn't make her feel better, but not doing it would have made her feel so much worse.

When she couldn't stall any longer, she pulled on some old soft jeans and a long sleeve tee. Litha sat on the edge of the bed and called Elora. Mercifully she picked up on the second ring.

"I need you. In fact I need both of you. Can you square away some babysitting for a couple of hours?"

Elora had been sprinkling some raspberry vinaigrette onto a salad. She didn't have aspirations or desire to be a great cook and she didn't prepare food often, but sometimes she liked to eat in with her little family - just herself and her two boys. She stopped tossing and grew serious.

"Of course. What do you need?"

Litha sighed. "I need a meeting. You, Ram, and Glen. Your apartment in twenty minutes. Rosie's been with Glen for the last four hours. She can come if he wants to bring her."

"Okay. Litha. Tell me what's wrong?"

"It's just too much to explain on the phone."

When Litha joined her guests in the kitchen, she was holding a pair of handcuffs lined with purple sheepskin.

"Which one of us are you planning to use those on?" Storm's doppelganger sounded like he was hopeful that it was a joke.

Her eyes grazed over him before she leveled her father with a look.

"I'm going to Ram's and Elora's. Give me a ten minute head start and then bring… him to the *inside* of their apartment. I don't want anyone to see him." They heard an audible clink when her palm slapped the counter. When she removed her hand, there was a key sitting on the shiny black slate. Holding the cuffs toward Deliverance, she said, "You will use these. When you arrive with our guest, I'll unlock the cuffs."

Deliverance knew he had made an even bigger mess of his mess, but couldn't help being who he was. So, picking up the cuffs, he said, "And you just happened to have these lying around because..."

"It was an inside joke between my husband and me. You remember my husband? THE ONE YOU LOST!"

"Jumping Jehosophat, Litha..." The sparks that flew from her eyes could have been a trick of the light. Those that spit from her fingertips were audible pops and very, very real. Like Kellareal, he thought it was best that she didn't know that – between the mastery of magick and her demon blood – his daughter was one of the most powerful creatures in the universe. If she was mad to the point of involuntary sparking, he was paying attention.

"Okay. Everyone stay calm."

When she turned her attention to a wide-eyed

Angel, he stood up and said, "Thanks for the memories. I'll just be going."

Deliverance put his hand out and halted the exit. "You'll be going when I say you're going. Meanwhile, just relax. Nobody's hurting you."

Angel cursed under his breath.

Ram and Elora were standing in their kitchen staring at each other, wondering what could be going on, when there was a polite knock at the door. Elora glanced at her pretty salad that was already starting to wilt and look as sad as week-old flowers.

Rammel opened the door and stepped aside to welcome Litha.

"I've only got ten minutes before Deliverance gets here. And, before I forget, I told him to come directly to your living room. I hope that's okay."

Elora looked concerned. "You want to sit down? Are you hungry?"

"No. And no. Let me get this out."

Ram and Elora looked at each other and nodded toward Litha. "Of course. We're listening."

Litha explained what had transpired, omitting the highly personal parts, naturally.

Ram's phone buzzed on the counter. He picked it up and talked quietly.

"Glen's on his way with Rosie. He got held up on the way out the door."

"Okay. Let's go in here and sit down." Elora motioned toward the living room and Litha nodded.

Deliverance popped in with Angel in tow. Blackie took one look at the fake Storm and starting growling. He was working himself into a crescendo when Elora called him off. As his alpha, he deferred to her, but made it clear he wasn't happy about it. And he didn't take his eyes off the man with the shifty eyes and the untrustworthy smell.

Litha watched Ram's and Elora's reactions and said, "It's not him."

Elora eyed Angel up and down. "You're sure?"

Litha laughed at that, but there was no humor in it, just bitterness. "No room for doubt."

"Wow."

As soon as Litha unlocked the cuffs, Elora picked them up and looked at them.

"Ingenious, Litha. Your idea?"

Litha's mouth pressed into a firm line that gave her a determined expression. "We're not losing anybody else."

"I'm assuming we're gathered to talk about what to do about this?"

Litha nodded.

Ram looked at Deliverance. "What's so hard? Just put the fucker back where you got him. And next time, be more careful. Great Paddy! I can no' believe I am havin' to say this to you. How many times can one demon be makin' a fuckwad mess of thin's?"

While Ram was dressing down the demon, Elora opened the door for Glen.

"Daddy!" Rosie rushed toward Angel with her arms thrown open expecting him to pick her up and swing her around while covering her face with kisses.

"ROSIE! STOP!"

An average child that age probably wouldn't have stopped at the commanding tone, but Rosie was born with her parents' memories and experience. She stopped and turned to look at her mother with eyes that momentarily looked too big for her face.

Litha pulled her little girl close, then said quietly, "It's not Daddy, sweetheart. It's just a stranger who looks like him."

Litha looked up in time to catch Angel's shocked expression and see his eyes go straight to Rosie.

Elora took Rosie by the hand and led her into the kitchen. On the way past Angel, Rosie looked up at him like he was responsible for disappointing her in the worst way.

"Come on. I've got your favorite macaroons." The kitchen and living room were only separated by a bar so Elora could see and hear everything. She picked Rosie up and set her on the kitchen counter next to her. "How's my girl?"

"I want my daddy back."

"Yeah. I'm with you, kidling. We all want your daddy back. And we're working on it."

Ram resumed his line of thinking. "So, again, what's the problem with just droppin' him off wherever the dimwit picked him up?"

Deliverance jerked his attention to the elf and narrowed his eyes in warning. Angel slid toward an empty corner chair and eased down as inconspicuously as possible, thinking he might as well get comfortable.

"Hold on." Anyone present could have looked at Glen and known the wheels were turning. He was wearing his studious, real genius look. "It may not be so simple."

"'Tis simple. Just put the fucker back."

Rosie, still sitting on the kitchen counter, giggled and whispered to Elora, "He said a bad word."

Elora smiled. "Darling, we must be patient with your Uncle Rammel. He doesn't know any better." Rosie grinned and nodded like it was a conspiracy. "I need to go talk to the others. Do you want to stay here or go to Elsbeth's?"

"Stay."

"Do you want some books to read?" Rosie shook her head. "Okay, then. Down you go on three. One. Two. Three." On three, Rosie jumped and Elora eased her safely to the ground. It was one of their games.

"That would be rash," Glen said. "This could be a gods' sent solution to one of our problems and I think we should work with it."

"What do you mean?" Ram looked up in the middle of the question when Elora came back into the room.

"We were all thinking, and when I say all, I mean everybody who works for The Order was thinking that this whole interdimensional interface - made possible with assistance by Elementals…" He nodded toward the demon. "…was the most important thing that's ever happened in the The Order's history. Next to the vampire cure that is.

"So we're all revved up, ready to solve a thousand cold cases, and redefine our understanding of… everything. If somebody leaks that it's possible to get lost in the passes, no one in their right mind will ever venture a ride again. We don't want to upend the possibilities before we have a chance to work out the kinks. The potential is too big."

"What has that to do with the phony?" Ram asked.

"Well, if we could train him to impersonate Storm until the real Storm can be found…" In sync Ram, Elora, and Litha looked at Angel. "No one would ever be the wiser." He looked over at Elora's dog. "No one except Blackie."

It was two minutes to closing and Storm was finishing the mop up when three customers came in.

"Sorry. We're closed."

The one with the goatee in the hat and the overcoat came closer until Storm could see that his pupils were shaped wrong, vertical slits. The guy pulled up a chair and took off his hat like he was going to stay a while. The fact that he had horns underneath that hat did nothing to alleviate the creep factor.

"Very funny, Angel." The newcomer looked around the bar before his eyes came to rest on the mop still in Storm's big hands. "Oh how the mighty have fallen." He gestured toward the door with his chin and one of his human associates dropped the security bar, locking them in.

Storm was calm. "Name's not Angel. You've got the wrong guy and, like I said, we're closed. So if you would just…"

The guy who had locked the door had circled around behind Storm.

"So that's how you want to play it. The old it-ain't-me."

Storm didn't know what sort of creature it was, but there was something about it that was vaguely familiar, like he'd seen a painting or drawing.

"Look, clearly you have mistaken me for someone else. Since I'm not that someone, say goodnight and leave before one or all of you end up hurt. I'll even throw in some peanuts for the road. Who doesn't love late night snacks?"

There was no reaction from the creature as silence drug on for some time. "You know I never realized you were entertaining." He looked at his associates. "Peanuts!" When he chuckled, they laughed with appreciation. "I appreciate your concern for my well-being, Angel."

"I don't know if you're hard of hearing or just low, but either way it looks like I'm not getting rid of you until you state your business. So, say what you have to say then get out."

"Disrespectful, Angel. Call me by my name."

Storm's eyebrows rose. "Last time, I'm not who you're looking for and... I. Do. Not. Know. Your. Name."

"So," the guy steepled his fingers the way Sol always did, "it's like amnesia. Is that it?" When Storm said nothing, the creature said, "Richard Shade, but you can call me Mr. Shade."

"Mr. Shade?" Storm didn't even try to hide his incredulity. "Sorry. Just not a comics fan, but I'll agree to call you Dick if you'll just get to it."

"It's a little too late for talk."

"Has this Angel caused you harm?"

"Alright, gorgeous, I'll play. *This* Angel owes me a lot of money."

"For what?"

"Gambling debts."

"Somebody who looks like me."

Shade leaned closer and pinned Storm with a level look. "*Exactly* like you."

"How much?"

"*Exactly* like you."

Storm rolled his eyes. "How much does he owe you?"

"Seventy-five thousand."

Storm whistled. "What did he do with it?"

"Horses."

"He bought horses?"

Shade smiled and spoke with mock patience. "Bet. The. Track."

"Oh." Storm was thinking about his circumstances and about what it meant to have a counterpart in another dimension, one who, perhaps, hadn't gotten the opportunities he had, hadn't met the same people. "Let's say I was willing to talk about settling this guy's debt. Would you be willing to negotiate?"

Shade looked at his thugs and nodded. The men closed in on Storm with hostile vibes and aggressive postures. One of them was punched in the solar plexus with the mop handle and collapsed like a paper tiger, a blue one who couldn't breathe. The other took a chop to the neck and fell unconscious. Neither of Shade's professionals ever laid a finger on Storm. Even more impressive, Storm had not moved from where he stood flat footed nor had he taken his eyes away from Richard Shade, who was then studying him with much greater interest.

Bringing street thugs to a hand-to-hand showdown with Storm wasn't really sportsmanlike. After all, his Black Swan training had been topped off with Elora's special sauce, an elegant and superior style of weaponless martial art that was indigenous to her home world and flawless in its execution, easily repudiating any defense against it.

"You want to talk now?"

"I've got to admit that you are intriguing. You don't talk like the man who borrowed from me. Repeatedly. And gamblers don't usually come with the sort of self-discipline required to develop those moves."

"Again, and let me say I'm getting tired of repeating, I'm not your guy. I don't owe you money, but I might be willing to negotiate a compromise on repayment."

"If you're not the guy, why would you do that?"

Storm smirked. "You're not interested in motive. You're interested in money."

"Can't a businessman be curious?"

Storm tapped his watch. The thugs were groaning and starting to get up. "You want them to go for Round Two with me?"

Shade looked them over and shook his head. "Seems like a waste of time. What's your offer?"

"Twenty cents on the dollar. Get me in an honest poker game on a Monday night and stake me."

The creature made an unidentifiable sound, but Storm thought he may have cleared his throat. "If

I've heard you right, and I believe I have, you have offered to settle a gambling debt by procuring an extended line of credit. For gambling."

Storm's expression didn't change. He continued to look Shade directly in the eyes blatantly and unashamedly. "In your world I'm sure that's unorthodox, but if you put me in an honest game, I'll win."

It wasn't a boast. Storm couldn't lose at poker unless he wanted to. He'd played the Thursday night game at J.U. for years and could have won every hand. But the truth of it was that he found the inexplicable ability freakish and disturbing and didn't want anyone to know.

So he considered it a social pastime. He won just enough to seem average, never enough to raise the slightest suspicion. If anyone at Jefferson had been considered a shark, it was Ram.

"Well, Mr. I'm-Not-Angel-I-Just-Look-Exactly-Like-Him, I'm sure that offer would be thought unorthodox in any world. Call me crazy, but I think I like you. At least I like this version of you better than the one who's been taking out loans for the past two years.

"I'll get you into an *honest* game, but I'll only front you the money if you put that fancy car up as collateral."

"I don't have a car." Storm blinked as he rethought that. "That I know of."

Shade spoke slowly, like Storm was retarded. "Would you like me to show you where it is?"

"Okay, let's put it this way. Whatever car you think is mine, wherever you think it is, consider it pledged as collateral."

"Well said." Shade put out his hand to shake. Inside Storm recoiled at the nasty look of pointed yellow fingernails, but made himself shake hands without changing expression.

"Only on a Monday night. It's my night off."

"I'll be in touch."

Deliverance left the little gathering, to continue his search for the right Storm, while the others continued to mull over the logistics needed to pull off a *Prisoner of Zenda* sting operation. With everybody Storm knew as targets of an incredible con game.

The first step, convincing Angel Storm that he was in another dimension, proved to be a bigger challenge than any one of them would have guessed. Having been on his own since age fourteen, he was skeptical of stories that weren't readily verifiable by his own senses or those that didn't fall within his personal experience of the world.

After an hour of taking turns trying to convince him, Litha, who had been silent throughout the discussion and glaring at Angel, probably because he wasn't her Storm, stood up and walked over to where the handcuffs had been left on the kitchen bar.

"Oh for gods' sake. Come here."

Angel looked suspicious. "Why?"

"I'm going to prove it to you the only way I know how."

"And how's that?"

"I'm going to give you a quick tour through the passes. We're going to look in on some other experiences of reality that will leave no doubt in your mind. Then we're going to come back here and get on with the serious business of trying to turn you into a passable copy of my husband."

He thought about it for a few seconds, then stood up and held out his wrist. When he stood up, Blackie came to all four feet in one motion. He didn't growl. He didn't bark. But his ruff was standing up and he did manage to communicate that one wrong move would result in a throat torn out.

Litha snapped the cuff on while Angel stared at the dog. Then they were gone.

Elora turned to Rosie. "You hungry?"

Rosie nodded enthusiastically. "I can get dinner."

"What do you mean?"

"I know where the Hub is."

Elora chuckled. "I'll bet you do, but…"

Rosie smiled and vanished. Elora gasped and leaped up from the sofa. "Rosie! Rosie! Shit!"

"It's okay," Glen said with complete aplomb. "She does this sometimes."

"What do you mean she does this sometimes and it's okay? This is NOT okay, Glen!"

Glen shrugged. "No need to get hysterical. She'll be back in a minute."

"Don't you dare tell me not to get hysterical. WHERE IS SHE?"

"She said she could get dinner. My guess is that she's downstairs in the Hub having them make up some club sandwiches. Probably with fruit cups

157

and Twinkies if they have them. She might have gone to the Mess kitchen, but probably not. She likes the peeps at the Hub and they treat her like a mascot."

Elora looked panic-stricken.

"Would you like me to go down and find her?" Ram asked.

Elora stormed toward the door. "I'll find her myself."

"Take your phone," Ram said. "I'll call if she turns up here first."

She found Rosie sitting on a stool at the Hub, talking to a girl named Brendle, who was setting two sacks in front of Rosie. Brendle looked up. "Oh, hey. We were just trying to figure out how she was going to carry both these bags. Now you can take them."

Rosie smiled at Brendle angelically.

Elora grabbed the sacks. "Thank you." She leaned close to Rosie. "You're in *big* trouble, young lady." She froze. She could not believe that she was so shaken she'd actually uttered the phrase 'young lady'. She wanted to cut her own tongue out.

"Are you mad at me, Auntie?"

Elora looked down into those big eyes and her heart melted. That precious baby was missing her father. That was enough negative emotion for a child to handle.

"No, Rosie. Your auntie was just scared. I love you so much and, when you disappeared, it almost made my heart stop. Please don't do that anymore until you're all grown up."

Rosie cocked her head at Elora. "I'm grown up. I'm just in a little body."

"Just the same, will you ride the elevator back

with me?"

"Sure." Rosie jumped down from the stool and began skipping toward the elevators.

When Litha returned with Angel, he looked even more discombobulated than Elora had felt when Rosie had popped out.

Litha unlocked the cuffs and said offhandedly, "I think he believes us now. What's next?"

"Dinner on your little girl," Elora said.

Litha frowned. "What do you mean?"

After hearing the details of the incident, Litha turned to Glen. "Why haven't you mentioned this?"

"Because I thought you had enough going on. We set up some rules about where she can go and how long she can be gone. No harm can come to her, you know. I mean think about it. How is anybody going to catch her unless she wants them to?"

All the adults looked at Rosie at once. She smiled around the orange slice she was eating.

They talked for a while longer about the plan, then Glen did a review.

"We're going to start the make-over tomorrow. We'll meet downstairs in Sol's conference room at nine. As for what happens until then…" He looked at Angel. Then he looked at Litha. "We're going to need to keep appearances normal. He has to go home with you. Sorry."

Images of Angel and his tattoo standing naked in her bedroom flitted across her mind and she shuddered involuntarily.

"So we're agreed?" Glen asked.

"I'm not." Everybody turned to look at Angel. "Give me one reason why I should want to learn to pretend I'm this guy who you all think is such hot stuff. One minute I'm minding my own business, *about to be maimed and mutilated*, and the next I'm in the middle of a…"

He stopped short and glanced at Litha, who promptly turned bright red, either from embarrassment or fury. It was impossible to say, but Elora noticed the reaction. Let the speculation land where it may.

"…of a strange situation, in a strange place, with you people. So what, exactly, is my motivation to cooperate with this makeover?"

Ram spoke up. "You make a very good point. Certainly you're here through no fault of your own. From your point of view I'm sure it seems unfortunate that fate delivered you to us. As to your question about motivation, I'm happy to provide you with insight into why it would be in your best interest to work with us.

"In a far corner of the deepest sublevel of this building is a chain link kennel where a ferocious beast used to be kept." Blackie's head came up, ears pointed forward, and he looked at Ram like he understood what was being said. "'Tis quite secure, I assure you. Escape would no' be possible. If you would rather be spendin' the next however-long as a prisoner there, while we wait for my friend's return, that can be arranged.

"If you decide to comply with our demands, you will no' give us any trouble nor will you attempt to leave. Be assured that your hostess, her father, and any of his kinsmen can track and return you within minutes. Should you force us to prove that, you will earn yourself an unpleasant and unnecessary twenty-four hours in the kennel."

Angel smirked. "You won't do that."

Ram raised an eyebrow. "I will no'?"

"You've spent the past three hours talking about what to do with me and why. Where do you think I was while you were doing that? I'll tell you. I was sitting right here listening. You're not going to put the almighty Storm in a kennel in the same building where you're trying to convince people nothing has changed."

Ram appraised him for a couple of beats. "Sharp as a tack you are! Another good point. And you're right. Thank you for bringin' it to my attention."

Ram pulled out his intelliphone and started fiddling with it. When he found what he was looking for he slid his thumb over the selection and put the phone to his ear while everyone in the room watched to see what would happen next.

"I need a secure Hurricane kennel built tomorrow mornin'. Somethin' for an extra large dog that would hold even if he was angry 'bout havin' visitors." Pause. "Yes." Pause. "Perhaps you could move it to the top of your list. Money is no' an issue, but I will be needin' it done in the mornin'." Pause. "Yes. Close by." Pause. "I'm handin' the phone off, but keep this number. I'll be your contact and payment." Pause. "Hang on."

He handed the phone to Litha. While Ram stared at Angel, they both listened to Litha give her

Victoria Danann

address and tell the fence company to construct the kennel inside the garage. Yes. She would leave the garage door open the next day. She handed the phone back to Ram.

"I'm sendin' you the email to invoice." Pause. "Yes. I will pay as soon as it comes through." He hung up and looked at Angel. "Are we understandin' one another then?"

Angel glowered in a way that let Ram know they weren't likely to be buddies. Ever. But he managed a temperamental nod.

"Again, you will no' be givin' Mrs. Storm any trouble 'tween now and the morn. This is me bein' calm and collected. You do no' want to see my hot blooded side."

Elora leaned over and gave Ram a breathy whisper. "*I* want to see your hot blooded side."

In better times, that would have gotten a laugh and a wet kiss from Ram. All things considered, the smile she got in return would do.

When everyone was gone and Helm had been returned. Ram and Elora ate cold sandwiches on toasted bread that had been good hours before and talked about the challenges of trying to turn one person into somebody else, especially one taciturn and surly person who was not in the least enthusiastic about a makeover.

"There may be a dozen lookalikes out there. I don't know. I guess there could be a hundred. Or a thousand," Elora said.

"But there's only one Storm." He finished her sentence.

Elora met Ram's somber eyes. "Yeah."

At the vineyard, Litha left Angel waiting in the kitchen while she made a few preparations. When she returned, she had some ground rules to lay down.

"You can stay in the guest room. I've put some clothes in the closet and some toiletries in the bath. Do not set foot in my room or Rosie's. You have the freedom of the house. You can feed yourself, watch TV, or whatever, but you can't go outside until you have the skills necessary to double as my husband – in case someone we know should come by.

"Tomorrow morning my father will be back here to transport you to Jefferson Unit. Be ready to go at nine. It's going to be a busy day for you. Questions?"

"Yes. What do you want me to call you?"

"What I want is for you to never speak in my presence again. What I must tolerate, for now, is what Storm calls me, which is Litha. Now, if there are no more questions…"

"Okay." She turned to leave, but his voice stopped her. "I won't tell your friends."

Litha's entire body tensed, knowing what he was referring to. She hesitated at the doorway for a moment, but didn't respond.

Rosie looked up into her mom's eyes when Litha leaned down to tuck her in. "Can I sleep with you tonight?"

Litha sat down on the edge of the big girl bed and reached to brush a lock of wavy dark hair away from Rosie's face.

"It's weird having a strange man in the house

isn't it?" Rosie nodded. "Especially when he looks so much like Daddy." Rosie nodded again. "I feel the same way and I'd really like to have some company in that great big bed tonight."

Rosie looked so relieved that Litha felt a tug on her heartstrings.

"He looks like Daddy, but he's not like Daddy."

"I know, sweetheart. Nobody is."

The next morning Litha dropped Rosie off with the monks and headed to Jefferson Unit. She hadn't checked her phone for messages and didn't see the text reminder from Ram to leave the garage door open, so she had to make a trip back home. She stopped at the Hub for a second coffee before taking the elevator down to Sol's conference room. Taking hot coffee into a pass was an invitation to catastrophe. So she waited until she was out of the passes for a second cup.

All parties from the night before were assembled and ready to go. Barrock had been given the day off so they could talk freely without having to worry about a young ear pressed to the closed doors.

The smart boards were in use, since the search for Storm was still on, but Glen had old fashioned pens and notepads for any who wanted them and hadn't brought their own device.

Deliverance arrived with his passenger right on time and Litha unlocked the cuffs.

Glen sat Angel at the end of the table furthest away from the door and addressed the opening comment to him. "I've taken precautions about interaction with personnel this morning, but just in case, until further notice do not engage anyone other than the people you see in this room. If someone talks to you, just smile and nod when appropriate. We'll take care of the rest."

Angel nodded absently. He was preoccupied looking at the poster size photos of Storm that were hung all around the room.

Glen continued. "I don't know what you go by wherever you came from, but while you're here, your name is Storm."

"I go by Angel."

At that, Litha looked up, as did Elora and Ram, almost as if they were actually considering for the first time that he was more than a cardboard cutout of Storm.

They were thinking his fate had been to be in the wrong place at the wrong time. They knew they were using him, felt bad about it – to varying degrees, but that wasn't going to stop any of them from proceeding.

He was thinking that the moment of his kidnapping could not possibly have been more opportune or timely and that he was lucky to land where he was. But that was a bit of info he'd be keeping to himself.

"Well, this may suck for you, but like I said, your name is Storm until we return you to life in…" Glen looked at Deliverance.

"Halcyon."

"…Halcyon Dimension."

Angel perked up. "Halcyon? That's the name

of my neighborhood bar."

Glen looked unimpressed. "Good to know. Now the first order of business…"

Glen's attention was drawn to the door opening and filling up with a formidable figure carrying a duffle over his shoulder. "Somebody order pizza?"

"Bubba!" Elora jumped up and rushed to give him a hug.

Kay dropped the duffel in time to get both arms around her. "Lump. You better not ever call me that in front of my sisters or they'll pound you. They think they're the only ones entitled."

"Well, they're wrong about that, but I get it. I wouldn't let anybody else call me Lump."

Kay laughed softly and gave Elora a squeeze. His eyes swept the room and came to rest on Deliverance. "Who's that?"

Ram looked at Deliverance and it dawned on him that a situation was in the making. "Uh oh."

Elora tightened her arms around Kay, turning the hug into a form of restraint. "Kay. Don't go flying off. That's Litha's father. He's working for us now."

With a growl Kay shoved Elora aside, something she wouldn't have thought possible.

"You!" Kay's eyes were taking on that feral look that was the harbinger of a berserker rage.

Elora and Ram both stepped in front of Kay to try and divert his attention.

"Paddy's Curse, Elora. Who called Kay?"

"I did. He deserves to know that his partner is missing."

"Yeah? Remember what Simon's office

looked like after Hurricane Kay blew through?"

"Can we argue about this later? Kay! This is not helping. We can't find Storm without that demon."

As Kay turned toward Elora, the berserker seemed to recede a little, but they were far from home free.

"What?"

"You've got to work out your differences and work together."

Kay gaped at Elora. "Work together?" Apparently that idea was so mind boggling that it brought Kay's human side fully back to the forefront. "That can't be a serious request."

Kay's focus went right back to Deliverance, who stood waiting calmly and dispassionately with his arms crossed over his chest.

"You kidnapped my girl!"

"You killed my father. My kin wanted a retribution killing. I think you got off easy."

"Got off easy? Got off easy?" He repeated that like his brain was so scrambled by the incredulity of that statement that it got stuck on a loop. "You pinched her!"

The room was quiet as a tomb while everyone held their breath waiting to see what Deliverance would say to that.

Elora pulled at Kay to try to divert his attention to her. "Kay. Look at the chain of events. I'm not pretending to know how all the puzzle pieces fit together, but Katrina's kidnapping led to Litha and Deliverance finding each other. Right now, she's kinda miffed at him, but overall I'm thinking that was a good thing. That led to Katrina insisting that Litha be her maid of honor and that led to one of the most romantic moments in history. Also a good thing." Elora glanced at Litha and saw that her face had softened and her eyes were misty. "I know that Storm's the philosopher, but it just seems like there was a little meant-to-be in there. Don't you think?"

When Kay reviewed the incident through a filter of reason, he had to admit that Katrina had been frightened but not harmed. Not really.

While Kay was mulling it over, Litha turned to the demon and said quietly, "Dad. I need you to work with us on this."

He looked at Litha for a few beats, then shrugged his shoulders and returned his attention to Kay. "Okay. You can pinch me back."

One thing that could be said about Deliverance. He was not predictable.

The offer of a retaliation pinch seemed to completely take the wind out of Kay's sails. And, as much as Kay might despise the incubus for the scare he'd been put through, he didn't think pinching would make him feel any better about the thing. He glared at Deliverance.

"First, you took my girl. Now you've lost my partner. When I look at you, I see bad news walking. I will leave you alone, but just stay the hell away from me."

"Fair enough. Your loss," Deliverance said cheerfully just before he winked at Litha and popped out.

Glen flopped into a chair. "Who wants cookies?"

Ram raised his hand. "I do."

Kay gave Ram a shoulder bump greeting. "Sorry about that."

"Pffft. We've all come to be quite fond of your high strung, extra sensitive side."

"Still funny, Rammel."

Glen stood up with a mouth full of chocolate chip cookie. "Okay, B Team. Enough with the reunions and high drama. Hugs all around and then let's get back to it. We've got work to do."

Kay looked at Ram and pointed at Glen as if to say, "What is that about?"

Ram grinned and shook his head. "The long of it is, 'tis a story. The short of it is that the kid's in charge."

"Of Jefferson Unit?" Kay gave Glen a thorough once over. The astonished tone in his question might have been insulting to anyone besides Glen. But he knew the situation was astonishment-worthy. So he just smiled as he munched down an enormous chocochip cookie. "Want milk with that?"

Back to Ram, Kay said, "I can't have been away that long. Where's Sol?"

"On a sexy vacay with our very own Farnsworth. Whom he's marryin'."

Kay looked dubious. "Now I know you're shitting me."

"On your own time, gentlemen. Take a seat if you will," Glen interrupted. "What we need to accomplish today is twofold. We need to assess our subject, identify bullet points, and assign duties. Let's take it one category at a time. We'll start with his body.

"Storm. If you would be so kind as to stand up and remove your shirt."

"What?"

"Take off the tee." Angel made no move to comply. "Is there a problem?"

"Yes. There's a problem. I'm not auditioning for pinup."

"That's okay because no one here is interested in photos."

He got to his feet slowly and hesitated before pulling his shirt over his head. Standing there being ogled he felt vulnerable and self-conscious to a degree he didn't know was possible. The collective murmurs of disapproval had him blushing and turning shy.

"Great Paddy, man. Where is your pride?"

"It's a good thing he's not auditioning for pinup," Kay snickered to Ram.

"What are we going to do about the ink?" Elora asked Glen without taking her eyes away from the dragon tattoo.

"Make sure he keeps a shirt on."

Glen cleared his throat. "Thank you, ah, Storm. That told us what we need to know. Please feel free to get dressed."

"He's ten pounds over and belly dancers have better def," said Kay. "I'll bet he can't even run an eight minute mile." Ram and Elora nodded in unison. "I'll take on getting him in shape."

Angel pulled on his tee and started to sit down.

"Not so fast." Elora was up and moving toward the end of the table. She pushed his chair out of the way with her foot to clear some room, then asked, "Ever done any fighting?"

"Like in a bar?"

Elora heaved a sigh. "I'll take that as a 'no'. Alright. I'm going to try to slap your chin. Not hard. I won't hurt you. I just want to get a look at your reflexes and counters."

She flicked out a jab that glanced off his jaw. It was over before Angel knew she'd moved.

Walking back to her chair she said, "My fourteen-year-olds could permanently disable him in two seconds. I'll take martial arts." Then under her breath, so only Ram could hear she said, "For all the good it'll do," as she sat back down.

"Okay. Moving right along. I'll take Black Swan history and make sure he knows who we are, what we are, what we've done, and what we're doing." He looked at Ram, Kay, and Elora. "I'll throw in some B Team fun facts, but the three of you will probably want to fill in the color. Also, as friends, you will catch it and bring it to his attention when he does or says something that is un-Storm-like." They nodded.

"Litha, same thing. I want you to work on the subtleties. You don't need to schedule extra time. You can do it at the vineyard over dinner or whatever. Facial expression, body language, tone of voice, verbal inflexion. Correct anything that's off.

"If we don't get it right, people will start to be uneasy. They may not know *what* is wrong, just that *something* is wrong. I also want you to work with him on people he knows. I'll help you pull together photos and fill in names, dates, and so forth."

Half to himself, he said, "It's a stroke of good luck that the Hunter Division was just transferred out or we'd be in trouble trying to recreate the relationship he had with every one of those knights.

"Sir Hawking. You're known for being good with stories and that's what I want you to do. Give Litha a few days to work with him on people and then I want you to make up scenarios and role play with him."

Ram nodded. "Sure."

Glen looked at his watch. "Questions before we get started?"

Elora spoke up. "We need a place for Kay to stay."

Glen grinned. "Not a problem. With almost all the knights shipped out, we've got a lot of vacancies. Anybody else?" He paused. When no one else spoke, he said, "Let's get started on a schedule."

They decided that Kay would be first up in the personal coach lineup. So he left the conference room with Angel in tow muttering something that may have included the words "ass" and "flabby".

All parties involved in the construction of the proposed elaborate ruse knew that it wasn't the clone's fault, but it was impossible to not resent somebody walking around with Storm's face, when every one of them was grieving the absence of the real Storm.

Before Litha left to take her own search assignment for the day, she and Glen went over a list of the people Storm would need to get up to speed on. Elora went to her morning class on hand-to-hand with the younger boys and planned to work Angel in between that and her afternoon class.

Glen wrote himself into the schedule "training lunch" every day. It was multitasking. They both had to stop and eat. Glen could discuss the history of Black Swan, and Storm's unique place in it, while he was eating his midday meal in the conference room, as he'd been doing ever since Storm had gone missing.

Ram, Elora, and Kay were pleased with that arrangement because they could lunch together in quiet camaraderie without the unwanted shadow.

Two and a half hours later, Kay dropped his charge off at Glen's. Angel's hair was wet and he was wearing scrubs.

"Why's he wearing scrubs?" Glen asked.

"Because he worked up a sweat and nobody brought him a change. This is the only thing we could find to put him in."

"Umm. Good thinking."

"Glad you approve."

"Come back after lunch and I'll have your temporary quarters ready."

"Okay. So…" Kay looked around. "How's it feel to fill his shoes?"

Glen shook his head. "I respected him before. Now I think he's a god."

Kay smiled and clapped Glen on the shoulder. "The place hasn't fallen down around your ears. That means you must be doing okay."

When Kay left, Angel, who had been ignored to the point where he was starting to question his visibility said to Glen, "You know I *can* talk."

"What's that?"

"If you'd asked me why I was wearing scrubs, I could have told you myself."

Glen stopped and looked at Angel, really looked, for the first time. "My apologies. What would you like for lunch?"

Angel was amused by the breadth of that open ended question. "Twelve ounces of New York Strip, medium rare, with Béarnaise sauce, broccolini still crisp, two poached tomato halves, and French fries. Oh and dessert. Apple pie with cheddar cheese melted on top."

Angel wore the barest suggestion of amusement while he waited for Glen to tell him he was being ridiculous. Instead, Glen picked up the phone and repeated the order word for word adding, "Two of those. I'll also have a Coke."

He looked at Angel with eyebrows raised.

"Water."

"And one of those big square bottles of water with the tropical flowers on front. I'll be in my office. Leave the trays in the conference room and call me when it's here." Pause. "Yes." Pause. "Yes." Pause. "That's right. Okay. Thanks.

"Let's go in my office. We need to keep you out of sight until you're ready to interact."

The office was only a few feet away. Glen motioned for Angel to enter first and then closed the door behind him. As he sat down behind the large desk, he said, "How was the workout?"

"Hard."

Glen smiled. "You work out regularly?"

Angel rolled one shoulder like he was testing to see if it still worked. "I walk a block and a half to the garage where my car is parked. Sometimes I slow dance with women."

Glen looked at Angel like he was waiting for him to get to the part where he described actual exercise.

"That's about it. No point in overexerting. I have better uses for that energy."

Glen cocked his head. "Like what?"

Angel grinned. "Wine, women, song, and, in my case horses."

"You like riding horses."

Angel barked out a laugh. "No, kid. I like to *bet* on horses."

"Oh. So what work do you do?"

"Work?"

"What do you do for a living?"

"Are you listening? I said, I play ponies."

"You mean you're a professional gambler?"

"Yes. That's it exactly. A professional gambler."

Glen stared at him trying to imagine how Storm's cross-dimensional counterpart could possibly end up as a professional gambler. It was mind boggling.

"Are you married?"

"Again! Wine, *women*, and song. Not many wives would appreciate my lifestyle."

"No doubt that's true."

"I have a question for you. How did somebody your age end up wearing the Pope hat to this party?"

"You mean why do I appear to be in charge?"

"Are you suggesting that you're not in

charge?"

"I'm suggesting that, while I'm filling in for the guy who really runs the place, we're always sixty seconds away from chaos, bedlam, and/or pandemonium. Storm was overseeing to make sure nothing got away from me, which was a comfort I can tell you. He was my security blanket. Now he's not here. As you know.

"As to how I came to be the last one sitting behind this desk, it's a long story and we've got work to do on you today.

"We're going to start with simple stuff like what we are and why the other people you've met care so much about the guy you look like."

After lunch Elora came by for Angel.

"Do not speak to anyone on the way to the sparring room. If somebody stops us and presses the issue, I'll say you have laryngitis. Got it?"

Angel shook his head. "Look. Maybe your Storm is stupid, but I'm not. I believe I can think my way through a simple instruction like keep your mouth shut, without having you be such a condescending…" He wisely decided the prudent thing would be to leave that sentence unfinished.

Elora's teeth pressed together, but she let the attitude go. After all, it wasn't as if he had volunteered to work for The Order as the rest of them had. "Good. Let's go."

When they got off the elevator at Sublevel 3, the open session time in the fitness center for all personnel who were not hunters or trainees had just ended. That meant they had to pass several women on the way to the sparring room. Angel flirted up every one of them on the way by and every one of them did a double take followed by a look of surprise. When they reached the sparring room, Elora practically shoved him inside.

She looked pissed. "I really needed to include, 'And don't flirt with women who are not Storm's wife' in my instructions?"

He smirked. "I didn't bang anybody, did I? What difference does it make?"

"The difference it makes is that Storm is serious minded. He wasn't into random flirting when he was single! And that goes triple for now that he's not! Didn't you notice how shocked those girls looked?"

Angel shrugged his shoulders and rolled his eyes, which just looked ridiculous on Storm.

"Serious minded. Didn't flirt even when he was single. Sounds like a douche to me."

Before he could say, "Oops," Angel found himself slammed against a wall with the Lady Laiken's one-handed iron grip around his throat.

"You're not even worthy of saying his name out loud. Let me tell you something about the guy you will never hold a candle to. I don't think anybody else in the history of Black Swan could have made a respectable team with an alien woman, a hotheaded fun lover, and a berserker to work with. He's a great man. And you? You're just the stuffing in an animated Storm costume."

Angel sneered at that. *Ball bustin' bitch*. But he felt something inside his chest squirm uncomfortably and the muscles in his jaw flexed painfully. For a split second he wondered what it would be like to have people care that much about him, what it would be like to be admired and respected and... loved.

She released him, looking disgusted and like she'd rather be anywhere else.

When Angel was deposited at the vineyard that night, Elora's words were still eating at him. *You're just the stuffing in a Storm costume.* He was tired in body and spirit and mostly just wanted to be left alone. He took his plate to the living room and ate watching TV instead of in the kitchen with Litha and Rosie.

After Rosie was bathed and ready for bed, she went into the living room to say goodnight to the guy who looked a little like her daddy. Litha was bone tired, but still had every day chores to do. She was busy putting laundry away when she heard Angel yell out.

She ran down the hallway to find him on his feet cursing a blue streak.

Litha grabbed Rosie up. "What is the matter with you? This is a child."

He gaped. "That is *not* a child! Children don't burn you when you reach out to pull their hair." Litha narrowed her eyes and her nostrils flared. "Playfully! Pull their hair *playfully*!"

"I was just gonna say good night," Rosie said to Litha in her own defense.

"Yeah. Me, too. I reached out to tug at the end of her hair and she burned the living daylights out of me."

"Let me see." He showed it to Litha. Rosie's little handprint appeared in a bright red perfect outline on his forearm. "Okay. Come with me."

He followed them into the kitchen. Litha pulled out a barstool and told him to sit while she got ice and aloe out of the cabinet, but he watched Rosie the whole time.

"What is she?" he asked.

"Special," was all Litha said.

"Yeah. I can see that."

"I'm sorry." Rosie offered Angel an olive branch, more with big eyes than words.

"You didn't do anything wrong, Rosie," Litha assured her. "You should always follow your instincts if you think someone might hurt you."

Angel was indignant and gaping. "What are you teaching her?!? No wonder she's a little demon seed!" He was looking for a fight at that point and expected his comment to inflame, but instead, Rosie beamed at him and her mother was unfazed.

"What I'm teaching my child is none of your business."

"It is when it raises third degree welts on my skin. There *is* somebody in this room who didn't do anything wrong." He looked at Rosie. "And it's me!"

Rosie giggled at him, which sort of felt like the last straw to a tired and distraught accidental traveler.

"Look. I don't want to be here. I want to go back where I belong." As soon as the words left his lips he knew it was a lie, one of the biggest he'd ever told.

That's the last thing I want.

"Well, you're stuck with us for now," Litha said quietly as she smoothed aloe on his burn and secured an ice pack over it.

Angel went to bed right after, every single muscle aching, many he hadn't known he possessed. The big guy was merciless. Kay. Stupid name for a man. He pushed Angel like he was training for a prize fight with billion dollar stakes. And there was no doubt in Angel's mind that Kay was enjoying his pain. It might not be so bad if he didn't know he was going to be expected to get up the next day and do it again.

Stuck with us for now. That was when, in the moments before he was claimed by sleep, the thought occurred to Angel that maybe he didn't have to go back to his debts, to Baph's knife, and the nobody who gave a fuck if he lived or died. Correction. There probably were some who would prefer he died.

Maybe the other Storm wouldn't be back and, maybe, if he actually applied himself and acted like he gave a shit, he could step into the sweet life this other Storm had lucked into. *And the regard of all these people who think he shits liquid gold.*

Right after Litha put Rosie down for the night, the doorbell rang. She looked through the glass and saw that it was her mother-in-law. While a range of curse words had a play day in her head, Litha called out, "Just a minute", through the door. She ran down the hallway to the guest room and knocked.

Angel was in bed. He was still awake with a reading light on, bare chested, just wearing pajama bottoms. He was also too tired to get up, so he and his dragon tattoo stayed right where they were. "Yeah?"

She opened the door. "My mother-in-law is here. I need you to stay quiet and stay out of sight."

"Unless you can hear my snoring from down the hall, that won't be a problem."

Litha shut the door and ran back to let Storm's mom in. When she opened the door, the older woman said, "I'm sorry to come so late, but you're never here and I was getting worried."

"And you haven't seen the baby in a while." She got a smile and a nod in response. "Come in. Let's open a bottle of the good Chardonnay and have a talk."

Litha suggested they sit in the living room and promised to be right back. She poured two glasses.

As she offered her mother-in-law one of them, Litha said, "Evangeline".

Storm's mother went by Eva, but Litha thought her name was too beautiful and romantic to abbreviate. It was also gratifying that Eva smiled just a little whenever she heard her given name.

"We need to have a heart-to-heart." Eva looked concerned, but nodded. "Storm and I both have some secrets." Eva grew very still. "As it happens our secrets are related to your secrets."

Litha watched Eva's reaction carefully. She broke eye contact with Litha then her eyes wandered downward to her wine which she suddenly seemed to find fascinating. She took a sip and waited.

"Before I go further, I must have your promise on Storm's life that you will never tell what you hear tonight."

Eva looked worried. "Yes. Of course. What's wrong, Litha?"

"I'm not joking. Not anyone. Ever. For any reason."

"I promise."

Litha took in a deep breath. "You know that Storm is…"

"Special," Eva interrupted as she stood abruptly. "He's special. I shouldn't have come so late. I need to go." She bent to set her wine glass on the table and started to gather her purse.

"Eva. I know you don't want to talk about this, but you can't see Rosie again until it's settled. I'm not being arbitrary or mean. There are really good reasons."

Storm's mother sucked in a ragged breath like she'd been slapped. Litha wished she could spare the woman the conversation because she looked like a wound had just been opened. It was clear that it was difficult, but she sat back down and reached for the wine glass. It was clear she wanted to see Rosie more than she wanted to keep her skeletons in the closet.

"I'm so glad you decided to stay. I'm not here to judge or blame. And you can feel safe because I can't betray your secret. Not without doing the same thing to my family." Eva looked curious and seemed to relax just a little. "I know your husband isn't Storm's father."

Eva blinked rapidly, but it didn't stop her eyes from filling to overflowing. She reached for her purse and withdrew a delicate monogrammed white handkerchief. That, in itself, amazed Litha because she didn't think those were even being made anymore. As Eva lifted the corner of the hanky to her tear duct, she said, "Does Storm know?"

Litha hadn't known Storm's mother long enough to love her, but she certainly liked her and wished that she could spare her that discomfort. "Yes. He does," she said quietly.

Eva's face didn't crumple. She drew her shoulders back as if she was trying to bolster emotional strength with physical support.

"The thing is," Litha continued, "my father is like Storm's father. And that means your granddaughter is even *more* special."

Eva's eyes widened a little and Litha saw that she was starting to prepare herself for anything. "How?"

"Birdie?" A little voice said from the hallway.

Both women turned to see a beautiful little girl in a white nightgown standing in the archway that served as a living room partition. One look at Rosie answered Eva's question about 'how' special. She had Litha's unusual eyes and wild curly hair, but the rest of her was pure Storm. Eva saw a feminine version of the child her son had been: his nose, his mouth, his chin, his expression of concern. She was so overcome with both shock and emotion that she let out a little hiccup of a sob.

Rosie instantly trotted over and climbed into her grandmother's lap. "What's wrong, Birdie?"

Eva covered fast and brilliantly. "I've just missed not seeing you. That's all." Eva circled her arms around Rosie and laughed through her tears. "How did you know I wanted you to call me Birdie?"

"Because you said so when I was a baby. You said that's what you called your Gran and it would be nice to be Birdie."

Eva looked at Litha. "So where's Storm?"

"For half his life you've known that there are some questions he can't answer."

She smiled. "Yes. He's special."

Litha grinned. "He certainly is." She looked at Rosie. "We both think so." She looked back at Eva. "But now I see he didn't get his specialness from just his father."

Later, when Litha opened the door to bid her guest good night, Eva turned and said, "Did you know that Storm is my favorite?"

"I suspected as much, but that secret is just as safe with me."

"Thank you, Litha. Isn't Elora Rose just… perfection?"

Litha laughed. "We think so."

At noon the next day, Angel continued his game of ordering something for lunch that he didn't think the kitchen would be able to produce. But when it arrived, instead of eating, he kept falling asleep while Glen was talking. Glen decided to let it go because he knew Kay and Elora were being merciless in their training. He smiled to himself suspecting that, maybe subconsciously, they needed to prove that no clone could measure up.

After a few days he was staying awake

through lunch and seemed to be halfway interested in Glen's briefing on B Team and Storm's relationships with the other knights.

He'd also reached an accord with Rosie, who by then resembled a nine-year-old.

Glen gave Angel a homework assignment. He was supposed to read the account of the founding of The Order of the Black Swan. That night after dinner, Rosie asked Angel if he would read her a story before bedtime.

He started to say no, but then saw an opportunity to multitask. He had to read the thing anyway. He might as well get credit for being a syrup-hearted suck up and read it out loud to the kid. Another upside was that, after boring her beyond belief, she'd never ask him to read to her again.

Litha was well aware of the subject matter and knew the content would be highly inappropriate for any *other* nine-year-old, but Rosie wasn't like anybody else.

"Rosie, that story is about vampire and part of it is very, very sad. Are you sure that's the kind of story you want to hear tonight?"

Her little head jerked toward Angel. She studied his eyes like she could see right through him, then turned back to her mother and nodded. "I do want to hear it."

So Angel settled on the living room sofa and began. "In the year 1458 there was a Count who lived happily with his wife…" As the story progressed, Rosie had come closer and closer until she was leaning against his arm. There was a part of him that knew he needed to shrug her off and make her move for his own protection. There was a part of him that knew that, if he let her stay there cuddled up against his arm, he was going to feel something and be sorry for it.

So he let her stay and she opened a crack in the wall around his heart.

When he said, "I guess that's it," she looked up at him with big searching eyes.

"My daddy is a vampire hunter," she said.

"I know," he replied almost in a whisper.

"You could be like Daddy." She looked so sincere, so intelligent, and so intense for a little girl.

"I don't know about that, sweetheart."

Sweetheart? Where did that come from?

After Rosie went to bed, Angel sat at the kitchen table with Litha. Every night she covered the table with photos and gave him various facts about Storm's relationship with different people he might encounter. Litha didn't remember the exact day or time of the shift, but at some point, Angel had stopped sighing, rolling his eyes, studying his fingernails, and acting like a kid who'd been sent to detention. He had begun to show an interest, had applied himself, studied the details, asked questions and no longer acted resentful when she corrected him about a mannerism or posture or the way he phrased something.

"That's enough for tonight. I think you're at the point where we can turn Ram loose on you?"

"Oh boy."

In spite of herself, Litha chuckled at that. "Sir Hawking was a little intimidating during your last exchange with him, but believe me, he has another side."

She rose from the table to finish cleaning up from dinner. Angel sat and watched her. There must have been some women like her in his life at some point. From what he remembered of his mother, she was warm and loving, but there hadn't been anyone like that since he'd left home. For the first time he asked himself why he hadn't stayed in contact with her. For the first time he wondered if his disappearance had caused her worry. *Gods of glory. Am I an asshole?*

Litha was sexy, but not because she wore provocative clothes and not because she tried to strike poses or be coquettish. She was sexy because, when she spoke she sounded genuine and sincere. Her mannerisms were not calculated in terms of provocation, but flowed effortlessly as an extension of her personality. When she loved, she was unconsciously and unpretentiously graceful and feminine. In other words, she was grounded in authenticity. A real woman. The best kind. And Angel found her more fascinating every day.

She was beautiful, but not because she wore a lot of makeup. She was beautiful because her eyes were so deep a green they were exotic, other worldly really. Her hair was wild and seemed to suit her perfectly. It was outrageously curly, but not frizzy.

He knew she hated him because of the sex, but she'd made an effort to be patient with him about learning all the details of someone else's life: the names, who they were to Storm, how he *really* felt about them, and so on. She'd been polite and courteous enough that sometimes he could fool himself into thinking he was a real house guest.

He liked having dinner with Litha and Rosie at the end of the day. For one thing, it was kind of cool to see the kid grow into somebody else every single day. Rosie talked about her adventures and Litha asked questions. When her mother was searching for Storm, which was most of the time, Rosie's grandmother came to the villa and stayed with her, or she went to the monastery and spent time with the monks, or she went to Jefferson Unit and was passed around between Elora, Ram, and Glen – depending on who was available.

Litha hated missing out on spending time with her, but Rosie was clearly enjoying the arrangement. There was no missing the fact that her favorite subject was Glen.

Sometimes they asked Angel about his day. And that was…nice. He knew he was starting to like it too much and he knew that everything about that was fucked up. Even he couldn't be stupid enough and masochistic enough to get too comfortable or fall in love with a life that didn't belong to him.

It wasn't just Litha and Rosie. His body was starting to feel like it belonged to somebody else. He was getting strong. And cleaned out. It was amazing what a few vegetables and a lack of alcohol could do. Between the toxins flushing away and Kay's bouts of brutality that he passed off as "workouts", Angel's gut had turned rock hard and defined itself into distinct hills and valleys.

Kay had stopped treating him like something that Roto Rooter pulled out of the drain. Even though he still loved to say things like, "*My* partner would not quit at that many pullups if he was magically transformed into an eighty-year-old woman who had never worked out a day in her life."

Then there was Elora. He had to admit that, on the rare occasion he managed to do something right and get a smile out of her, it was oddly gratifying. She didn't coddle him, or even cheerlead, but she never failed to acknowledge any small accomplishment and, in his eyes, that meant she was fair.

If he landed a punch or a kick, she'd laugh and say, "So you got something going on in there after all, huh? Let's see if you can do that again." Every positive citation was a victory.

He knew he was in big trouble when he started to like getting up in the morning because, any minute now, the real Storm might show up. Then he'd be back in a dirty life in a dirty alley about to get sliced up by a monster and the worst part of that was that he deserved it.

The Black Swan people? They'd be so glad to see that guy, they probably wouldn't even say goodbye. He'd be nothing more than old news and he'd end up where old news goes to biodegrade without them ever giving him another thought.

From Litha's point of view, there was no upside to living with Angel. It would have been bad enough having a stranger in the house changing the energy and the dynamics, privy to every detail of their lives. But this stranger, who looked just like Storm made her heart hurt even more. It was taking its toll in the way she felt tired all the time. It was taking its toll in the dark circles she saw under her eyes in the mirror. And the guilt about neglecting Rosie topped off the grief so that she was always on the edge of crumpling.

She missed him in a way that was a physical ache and worried all the time about how he fared. The worry was justified. She'd traveled the passes enough to know that not every dimension would be welcoming to a stray human/part demon. A voice brought her out of her thoughts.

"I know you're sad all the time."

She stopped what she was doing and turned to look at Angel. "Yes," was all she said.

"What was it like when…?"

"What was it like before he was gone?"

Litha walked over and sat down at the table.

"You know Storm was recruited when he was fourteen." Angel nodded. "So he finished growing up in a culture that was all male and very military. That's just one of the reasons why it melts my heart that he's so good with our little girl." She smiled. "He does dishes without complaining.

"We both wanted this place." She looked around. "I mean *this* exact place. We both grew up around here and both set our dreams on owning this vineyard one day. We found that out about each other when we were working for The Order in Edinburgh. It was enough to make you believe in kismet.

"I guess I'm rambling.

"So, your question was, what's it like being married to Storm? It's the very best kind of easy. I think that's how you know you're with the right person, at the right time, in the right place. At least that's what 'right' means to me. Love shouldn't be hard. Or maybe I've just been lucky.

"I fell in love with him the first time I saw him."

"Did he feel the same?"

"No." She shook her head, looked at her hands in her lap, and laughed softly. "The first time he saw me, he looked right over me like I wasn't even there. I'd been struck by lightning, as sure as if he was a god, but I was just an invisible mortal.

"It wasn't all that easy to get a chance with him. He'd been hurt, recently, and he was like a grouchy old bear who just wanted to be left alone to nurse his wounds. If you looked at him wrong, he'd growl and strike out." She looked away and her expression was wistful. "But he came around.

"Shocked me and a whole bunch of other people. We were at Kay's wedding. He was best man." She looked at Angel. "They're partners, you know. I was Katrina's maid of honor because she was so grateful to me for taking her place as hostage to a demon. It turned out not to be sacrificial or altruistic because the demon was my dad." She rolled her eyes as if to say, "You've met him and you know how he is."

"After the ceremony was over, Storm and I were supposed to follow the bride and groom down the aisle. We'd rehearsed it the night before. I moved to take his arm, but he stayed right where he was and, more or less, demanded that I marry him on the spot.

"He's the most splendid man ever conceived. All I could do was stand there and think how lucky I was." A tear spilled out of her eye and she flicked it away. "I couldn't even make my voice work to say yes even though that's what I was screaming on the inside. My mouth was moving, but I couldn't get any sound to come out."

Before he could slap it down and sit on it, Angel had wished he was that guy. He knew nothing could be more stupid or self-destructive than falling in love with the wife of the guy he was impersonating. *Christ.*

"What about you?"

"What?"

"Who's missing you? Wife, girlfriend, mom?"

"Nobody."

"Nobody?"

The surprise on her face was replaced with pity and just as quickly that was replaced with a silent question.

"I want it that way." He shrugged it off and made his features perfectly passive.

Litha's eyes searched his face like she was really seeing him for the first time.

So that he could be absolutely certain of his privacy, Glen sent Barrock on an errand and closed the door to Sol's study before he placed the call to Simon. As he listened to the ring, he double checked his watch. It was before noon at Jefferson Unit, well inside the work day at Edinburgh.

"Director Tvelgar's office."

"Margaret. This is Glen. How are you?"

"Very well, Glendennon. How about your young self?"

Glen smiled that Margaret, who was well into her eighties, managed to slip a bit of age bias into her greeting. Very slick.

"Passable. I'd like to speak with the man if I can slip past the dragon at the gate."

"Ach! Fresh as ever, Mr. Catch. And what shall the *dragon* be tellin' the Director about your business with himself?"

Glen chuckled. "I'm sure you'd like to know, Margaret, but this is Sovereign to Sovereign business."

"Careful of the altitude. It can be chilly at such lofty climes."

"Believe me, Margaret, I'm freezing my tail off, but until the rightful Sovereign returns to the throne, all I can do is hang on and try to emulate the man who belongs in this chair."

It was Margaret's turn to chuckle. "'Tis downright frightenin' how quick you are, Mr. Catch. Hold on."

After a few seconds, Simon picked up.

"Glen. How goes it in the Colonies?"

"I don't know, sir. I'm calling from the United States of America."

"Ha! If you're joking, it can't be all bad."

"I suppose it isn't *all* bad, but it's bad enough."

"Oh."

With as much brevity as possible while still giving the Director the respect he deserved, Glen offered a briefing and status report. When he paused for a reaction, there was silence.

"Sir?"

"So, let me be certain I understand correctly, Catch. Nemamiah went on vacation with his girlfriend leaving you in charge with Storm overseeing. Then Storm was lost in a rift between dimensions and is gods know where. Meanwhile, the idiot demon was told to fetch and came back with an alternate version of Sir Storm, whom you and his inner circle have been attempting to pass off as our Storm. All that means that you've been running Jefferson Unit alone while, at the same time, running interference to keep anyone from discovering that Sir Storm is not himself. Literally."

"The only exception I would make to that summary is that there's just something very wrong about referring to Farnsworth as someone's girlfriend."

"Hmmm. Well, Catch, I always knew you had potential, but I must admit you amaze me. You've not just handled this admirably. You've done as well as any seasoned administrator might have given these circumstances. Probably better than most. Just one question."

"Yes, sir?"

"Why the devil didn't you call Nemamiah and tell him?"

"Because, sir, it was my understanding that this is the first vacation the Sovereign has taken. Ever. And piecing together bits of what Sir Storm has said, I believe he deserves a vacation."

"I see. You're one of a kind, Catch. No doubt about it. So you've called for help?"

"In a way. I'm calling for a favor. I'd like to borrow someone from Headquarters. I've been thinking, when I was in Edinburgh – because I was privy to the agendas of most of the various departments – I was able to surmise the overall goals and interests of The Order. If you don't mind me saying so."

"That's perfectly alright. Go on."

"It has occurred to me that this situation might be a one-time opportunity to study an alternate version of a person, the parallels and differences I mean. This Storm and our Storm were born with the same identical bodies, but the expression of personality as adults is quite dissimilar.

"This would be better than the nature versus nurture twin studies. It's a study so pure there's no need to control for error or variance."

"Go on."

"I'd like to try and gain his cooperation in establishing his biography, which could then be compared to Storm's. And I think I have a plan about the best way to do that. I'm not sure it's entirely ethical, but I'm very sure it would produce flawless results."

"What's your plan?"

"Aelsong Hawking. If I could borrow her, I could pass her off as an Order historian who specializes in the collection of biographies."

"I see what you mean regarding the ethics of the thing. Having someone interviewed by a psychic as gifted as Ms. Hawking without knowing they were talking to a living lie detector… Without touching the question of ethics, it's devious to be sure."

"I know. And Song is ideally suited for the task. She's up to speed in the sense that she knows the *real* Storm. I mean *our* Storm. This one is just as real, I suppose. Like her brother, she's talented, loyal, and pragmatic. We can trust her."

"Indeed. I agree that this is an opportunity that may never come again. We must learn what we can, while we can."

"Yes, sir."

"The project to which she is currently assigned is one that could easily be set aside for something as unique and important as what you propose. Make arrangements to quarter her. She'll be there tomorrow. Margaret will let you know exactly when."

"Thank you, sir."

"Keep up the good work, boy. The Order is fortunate to have you. I hope you don't have my job in your sights. I wasn't planning to retire just yet."

"High praise, sir. Thank you, but no, I've had enough of administrative duty. Between the two of us, it's harder than it looks."

Simon laughed softly. "That can be said about most things in life, Mr. Catch."

"Yes, sir."

"Carry on."

"Yes, sir."

Two days later, Angel reported for his regular lunch session with Glen in Sol's conference room. He set his gym bag down by the door and took a seat in his usual place to wait for Glen. He was deciding what he would have for lunch when Glen swung through the door as he was ending a call and closing his phone.

"How are you today, Storm?"

"I suppose I can't complain."

"You could, but it wouldn't do you any good." Glen laughed at his own joke, but Storm didn't find it quite as amusing. "There's someone I'd like you to meet."

Angel responded only by raising an eyebrow to suggest a sentiment of, "What now?"

When the door opened, Aelsong's eyes locked on Angel's straightaway. She breezed in wearing the same fetching blonde curls as her brother, but longer, and a blue silk dress that made the blue of her eyes so arresting it would be impossible to look away. The silk moved around her body with such fluidity that it gave the illusion that she'd been hit with a fan like one of those hair commercials. The incongruity of the fact that she wore big clunky fur lined ankle boots only seemed to add to the appeal. Being a man who knew how to appreciate fast horses and beautiful girls, Angel sat up and temporarily lost interest in anything that wasn't Song.

"This is Aelsong Hawking. She's Ram's sister in case you didn't already notice the resemblance. Song. This is Storm."

The dress and the woman came to rest directly across the table from Angel. She extended her hand. He knew he needed to rise, but forgot that he first needed to push his chair back. His ass came to a hard crash in the chair a second after launch. The upward momentum was reversed when his lap hit the table edge. She laughed softly without seeming impolite while he tried again with an embarrassed smile and ears turning beet red. Any red-blooded female would be flattered.

"How do you do, Mr. Storm?"

"Ah, well."

"That's not what you told *me*!" Glen chided while Angel cut him a dirty look. "Right. That's neither here nor there. And, clearly, this is a no-joke zone.

"First order of business is to order lunch. Then we can talk about why Song is here. Storm, what will you have today?"

"I was thinking club sandwich."

"No pheasant a la orange? No Suite of Sea? Or Strawberries Romanoff?" Glen asked.

Angel shook his head. "Club sandwich."

Song looked delighted. "Storm loves club sandwiches! Practically lives on them."

Angel looked at her with renewed interest. "You know him?"

"Oh, aye. He's been fast friends with my brother since they were teenagers. Visited our home in Ireland many times. When he was no' comin' along, Rammel talked about him often."

"Aelsong, what will you have for lunch?"

She looked at Glen then smiled at Angel. "I must be susceptible to suggestion. Now I'm findin' myself in the mood for a club sandwich." She looked at Angel. "Are we havin' that with chips?"

We? "I was thinking French fries."

She smiled. "Oh, aye, I forget that here chips are called French fries. Aye. 'Tis what I'll be havin' as well."

Somehow, when she said the word "here", she

left the impression that she was making the best of roughing it in the wilderness.

While Glen called the kitchen, Song turned to Angel.

"All thin's considered, you appear to be doin' well. I really can no' imagine bein' in your position. Surrounded by people you do no' know who want you to mimic someone you ne'er met? I'd find it confusin' and terrifyin'."

"Yeah. It's confusing at times, but so far, the only things terrifying are the workout regime Kay has me on and the fighting thing with Mrs. Hawking."

Aelsong laughed. "She lets you call her that?"

Angel thought about it. "I guess I've never tried." His contemplative look was replaced by an evil smile. "Why? Does she not like to be called that?"

"You did no' hear that from me, Sir Storm."

That was the first time anyone had referred to Angel as Sir Storm. He felt his body jerk, not enough so that anyone would notice. The tiny movement would have been imperceptible to an observer. But he felt it. No mistaking a profound visceral reaction to the idea of being called "Sir" Storm. There was something about the addition of that title, made up of three little letters, that struck a spark in his soul as surely as the turn of an internal ignition.

Perhaps the catalyst was the dedication that shown through in Kay's punishing drive toward physical perfection, or Elora's relentless insistence on a skill set committed to muscle memory so that thought wasn't required for performance, or the underlying passion and unmistakable pride that Glen imparted in his lessons about the history of The Order of the Black Swan, or the way Ram was so ferociously protective of his teammate's family. Maybe it was all of those things or maybe there was something innate in Angel that lay dormant waiting for the right moment, the right stimulus, to awaken the seed of exceptionalism.

"Tough is it?"

"What?" Angel was brought back from his odd reaction by her voice.

"The workouts with Kay. The fights with Elora. You said terrifyin'."

"It's not as bad now as it was at first. Now the hardest part is always hearing about the paragon I'm supposed to be impersonating. To listen to his friends, you'd think he can walk on water while doing his taxes and composing a symphony."

Song laughed again. "Oh. So they've been tellin' you he's all that, have they?"

"Perfection personified. He broke the perfection mold. He's the smartest, strongest, most righteous son-of-a-bitch to ever be born. Oh, and let's not forget, he does dishes, too." Angel rolled his eyes.

She laughed. "You forgot handsomest."

"I didn't forget. Just exercising some humility – since I look just like him. Supposedly."

Song's eyes drifted around the room at the poster-size photos. "Aye. He is beautiful and 'tis no point denyin' it." Her eyes slid to Angel. "And, just so you know, there's no 'supposedly' about it. You *do* look *just* like him. I once got into a lo' of trouble with Elora for calling him the dark and broodin' one. She does no' put up with any teasin' where he's concerned."

Angel smiled. "Dark and brooding?" Song nodded and smiled. "So there is a flaw."

"No one's flawless." Angel smiled. "Although, to be fair, he does come close."

She chuckled when Angel's face fell and his shoulders slumped dramatically.

Glen closed his phone and sat down at the head of the table. "Now, let's talk about why Aelsong's been invited to our lunch date."

Angel couldn't really say no to telling his life story with those big blue eyes staring at him hopefully. If he was willing to allow Elora to torture him under the pretense of learning to fight, he could certainly stand to look at Ram's sister while he talked about himself and hear the lyrical lilt of her accent. She wasn't Litha. But she sure was cute.

"I'd like to ask you a question and I hope you won't take it the wrong way."

"Certainly." She seemed at ease and not the least guarded about the prospect of an unknown question.

"Everyone else around here has been more or less acting like they've just come from a funeral. You seem, um, cheerful. Did you not like Storm?"

"Oh, aye. I like him just fine. I simply have a philosophy about expectin' the best outcomes. 'Tis a lot less wear and tear than the alternative."

"An optimist. It matches your, uh, persona."

"Thank you!"

"You're welcome."

As the days wore on, Angel became so good at impersonating Storm that sometimes nobody corrected him for an entire day. They were all starting to relax around him and accept him, which made him feel better than it should have. He couldn't figure out why he cared what they thought one way or the other. Of course he knew why he cared what Litha and Rosie thought, but he kept that to himself.

Of all of them, Rosie had been the first to accept him. She knew he wasn't her Daddy, but she liked him and acted like she cared about him.

Just ten days after he'd read her the story of Jungbluth and der Recke, Rosie was the equivalent of fourteen. It was a Sunday afternoon and Angel had finished his workout with Kay - always an adventure in brutality. He'd also completed private tutelage on Black Swan from the boy genius and the daily smack down from the Lady Laiken.

He was making a smoothie when Rosie came into the kitchen.

"I'm going to play chess with Glen."

She was wearing a cute outfit with a skirt that was a little on the short end of the spectrum. The blood drained from his face when he thought about Rosie going out in public dressed like that.

"You're not going dressed like that. Go change."

"Why?"

"Why? Because…"

When he imagined some asshole doing to Rosie what he had done to that girl who stopped him outside the club men's room, he became enraged. The idea of someone hurting Rosie made him want to exterminate every male on the planet just to insure such a thing could never happen. That's when realization struck. That girl had been somebody's daughter. She might have been young and rash, gullible and naïve, maybe even stupid, but she didn't deserve what she got from him just because she was wearing a short skirt and wanted a second helping of fuck from him. Standing there in Storm's kitchen looking at this little girl who might have been his own, he wanted to kick his own ass until he bled out in a long and painful way. *Public service indeed.* He was a public enemy.

He finally decided to go with, "Because I said so."

She stared at him for a few beats and then laughed. "I'm going. See you later."

"Rosie! I'm not kidding around."

She blew him a kiss and was gone.

Litha came home a few minutes later to find him fuming.

"What's the matter with you?"

"Your daughter left here practically *not* wearing a skirt."

Litha blinked. "You mean it was short?"

"It wasn't short, Litha. It was practically non-existent!"

Every muscle in Angel's face was tense, his voice was definitely elevated and he was definitely aggravated.

"And you're upset about it because…" He crossed his arms over his chest and scowled. Litha's face and voice softened. "Do you have protective feelings about Rosie?" She asked quietly. "It's okay if you do. You've been watching her grow up even if it's been only two weeks. It's been an amazing experience. Hasn't it?"

Some of Angel's anger seemed to melt away hearing Litha call what they'd witnessed a shared experience.

"I... just don't want to see her get hurt."

"Rosie can't get hurt. You should know that." Her eyes went to the burn mark on his arm that was fading, but still visible.

"I don't mean hurt that way."

Litha smiled knowingly. "Okay. Let's make hotdogs."

"What? What does…?"

"Storm loves hotdogs. I wouldn't let him have them very often because I'm the food police, but I feel like being close to him tonight. So let's eat chili and cheese and gods-only-know toxins and die early. What do you say?"

He looked like he was thinking it over. "Dying early? Sounds like a plan. I'm in."

Litha and Angel called it a three napkin dinner. They were wiping dripping chili and cheese away with every bite when they heard a door slam in the house. They both stopped eating and looked at each other.

Litha was surprised to hear Angel say, "Stay here."

"No. I'm sure it's Rosie and, if she's slamming the door, it means that maybe she needs somebody to talk to."

Angel hesitated. "Let's verify. If it's Rosie, I'll leave you alone."

"Deal."

Litha knocked on the door. "Rosie? You there? Can I come in?" There was silence for a few seconds and then foot stomping on the suspended hardwood floor.

Rosie jerked the door open, turned around, and stomped back to her bed. Litha glanced at Angel then stepped in and closed the door behind her.

"What happened?"

She'd never even seen Rosie out of sorts, much less angry and about to cry.

"He left before our game was finished."

"Oh. Well. that's not so bad, is it?"

"He had a date, Mom!"

"Baby, you can finish your game anytime." Rosie glared at her mother until Litha caught the drift. "Oh."

Rosie threw her hands up and then threw herself on her bed. "I hate him!"

Litha stood motionless, trying to make sense of her own life. Less than a month ago, the teenager in front of her, apparently caught in the grip of full blown woman-child angst, was an infant no longer than her arm from shoulder to wrist. And it was shaping up to look like carrying her parents' memories wasn't going to save her from teen hormones or from the experiences that stir those hormones into tantrums. Apparently every soul has to walk that valley alone, demon or not.

"Rosie, you know Glen is too old for you."

Rosie made a garbled noise and an

exasperated gesture. "For how long?" She looked at her watch. "Three hours?!?"

Litha had to concede that her daughter would be Glen's age in less than two weeks. "A little bit of an exaggeration, but I get your point. The thing is you're not old enough for Glen today. And, when you are, you need to be prepared for the possibility that the people we want don't always want us back."

A tear slipped down Rosie's cheek and broke Litha's heart. "Is this supposed to be helping?" she asked quietly.

"Well. Yes. I hope so."

"He's mine."

Litha smiled sadly. "Rosie, he's not yours just because you say so. You know I think the world of Glen and your dad is very fond of him. Someday, if you end up with someone like that, I'm going to feel like the luckiest mother-in-law ever. But you can't claim another person like calling dibs. It just doesn't work like that. Well, it doesn't work that way for us. For elves and a few others, but not us."

"Why not?"

"Because every coin has two sides. If you could claim Glen, whether he agreed to it or not, then someone could claim you whether you agreed or not."

Rosie looked at her mother with liquid emerald eyes. "But I *know* he's mine. What do I do?"

Litha thought about it for a minute. "How did you leave things with Glen?"

"I tumped the chess board and scattered the pieces all over the room. Then I called him a cocksucker and left."

"Rosie!"

"What?"

"You did not call him that."

"Yes I did."

"Where did you ever… never mind. Darling, you cannot use language like that. It's just not acceptable."

Rosie narrowed her eyes at her mother.

"You found a memory where your dad called somebody that, didn't you?" Rosie nodded and narrowed her eyes even more. "And me, too," Litha said with resignation. Rosie nodded again. "Well, that didn't make it right and certainly you don't have many such memories."

Rosie narrowed her eyes again to which Litha said, "Your father?" Again, Rosie nodded.

"Okay, enough about that. You threw chess pieces, called him a name… Did you yell at him?"

"Yeah." She said it like, "Well, duh!"

"So you threw chess pieces, shouted that he is, well, you know, then came back here and slammed the door."

"Yes."

"Alright. I'll tell you what we're going to do. You're going to lay low for about a week. Then we're going to find out if Glen is interested, but only if you make a deal with me first that, if he's not, you'll let it go."

Rosie chewed her bottom lip. She had enough demon blood to understand that deals are sacred. She also had enough witch blood to know she could probably manipulate Glen's will with a commanding/compelling spell, even though the great-grandmother who visited her in dreams would have a fit if she did and even though she knew in her heart it wouldn't make Glen love her the way she wanted and needed him to love her. She pulled in a big breath, blew it out, and said, "Okay. What's the plan? Does it involve shopping?"

Litha laughed. "That's a ridiculous question. The way you grow, every day involves shopping."

"I know. I mean *special* shopping."

"No. Now listen."

"All yours."

"We're going to get Auntie's help. If you continue to mature at the rate you have been, in seven days you'll be eighteen. I'll get Elora to go to Glen and mention that you're ready for what they used to call 'coming out', you know, ready to date. Then she'll ask if he has any friends we might set you up with.

"We'll see what happens then. What do you think?"

"I think it's brilliant if it works. I think it sucks it major if it doesn't."

"Where did you hear a phrase like 'sucks it major'?"

Rosie chuckled. "Where do you think?"

Litha's eyes flared and she put her hand over her mouth. "We probably need some ground rules concerning what you 'remember'."

As she stared into those red rimmed eyes that were so like her own, Litha couldn't help but think about how bizarre it was to have a daughter who appeared to be going on fifteen. She was barely prepared to be mother to an infant, much less that. How she wished Storm was there to share the experience; good, bad, and bizarre.

Storm.

While Glen was in the shower, he was thinking about the way things had been left with Rosie and feeling unsettled about it. He couldn't have guessed that telling her he had to cut the chess game short and get ready for a date would cause her to explode into a full-on snit. The most baffling thing was what she'd said. "You mean a date with somebody else?"

Somebody else! What the fuck?

Yes. He was going on a date with somebody else. Did she think he was a pedophile?

Sure she was fun to spend time with. What other girl, of any age, could beat him at chess? No need to spend a lot of time chewing on that question. The answer was easy. None.

What other girl, of any age, would think *everything* about him was wonderful? Again. Easy answer. None.

Actually, he thought everything about her was wonderful, too. But she was fourteen for crap's sake! And what was he supposed to do with that? If her father knew that Glen had any kind of non-babysitting thoughts about his daughter, Glen might as well be a dead man walking. But if Storm hadn't disappeared, Glen wouldn't have spent so much time with Rosie while Litha searched. And searched. And searched some more.

On the one hand he'd thought Rosie was kind of cute standing there like a fire-breathing dragon with eyes shooting sparks. He almost chuckled out loud. What stopped him was the impression that he'd hurt her feelings and that was what wasn't sitting well.

It was Rosie, after all. She was sort of his. His to take care of is what he meant.

She'd just poofed away with that look of betrayal on her cute little face. No goodbye. No talk to you soon. He was accustomed to seeing Rosie look at him with adoration. Not like she'd just been slapped.

He was thinking he might as well call and cancel the date that had caused all the uproar. He wasn't going to pass for good company in the mood he was in. Which was what? *Shitty.* That's right. He was in a shitty mood.

He should call Rosie and apologize, say he was a fucking thoughtless rude asshole and ask her to please come back and finish the game.

Yeah. He should do that, but he wouldn't because he was afraid she'd say no and he didn't think he could stand it if she was really that mad. *So how does that work, Glen? You want to be a Black Swan knight and you're afraid to call a tweeny girl because she might reject you? Fucking head case.*

Litha had met with Song at Jefferson Unit a few times to flesh out notes about Angel. The meetings weren't exactly clandestine, but they were deliberately unbeknownst to him.

In the process of comparison, a picture of what matched and what didn't began to emerge. Apparently everything had been the same until the two versions of Storm were fourteen. After that Angel compromised most of what he reported to Aelsong. She easily read in his mind that he didn't want her to know the truth about his lifestyle, the choices he'd made and, for the first time, he felt pricks of shame about what he'd done with his life. He didn't want to measure himself against the invisible persona that loomed over every aspect of his existence every second of every day, but it would have been impossible not to. Sir Storm was on everyone's mind, in everyone's heart, and on everyone's lips.

Over the years Aelsong had developed the ability to 'read' with a poker face. She never gave away that she recognized a lie in the telling.

When she finished her project, she handed over the results, and left for Ireland to help prepare for her mum's big birthday party.

Since Team Makeover was requiring less and less of Angel's time, Elora took up the slack and increased his exposure to weaponry, mostly modern.

"Storm is the one who teaches guns. He's an unbelievable marksman. That means the same ability is surely lying dormant in you, just asking to be waked up. You ready?"

"Not particularly, but I have time on my hands. So, you got something you want to show me, I'll stand still and listen."

On a big sigh and a little instruction from Elora Laiken, Angel opened a window to a world of talent he hadn't known he possessed. In his world, guns were only owned by governments and well-

Victoria Danann

connected criminal elements. Being caught with a firearm carried such a hefty prison sentence that most found the risk unacceptable. The last thing that Angel could have imagined was that he would be good with a gun.

All was quiet with Jefferson Unit operating at thirty percent capacity. It seemed even quieter with Kay gone home for the weekend to see Katrina and Ram gone to Ireland for his mother's birthday, which was more or less a command attendance.

Elora was invited, of course, but thought the trip by air was needlessly long for someone Helm's age and the alternatives, either taking him through the passes or leaving him behind, were unthinkable.

She'd told Ram, "Any activity that could end with fleeing from five French-speaking and immortal adolescent vampire – or fill in the blank – is not an authorized activity for Helm."

"And when are you thinkin' he will be old enough?"

Elora gave Ram her dead serious face. "This little boy will *never* be tall enough for that ride."

Ram said he had a strong preference for traveling to Ireland the old school way, on a company jet, "rather than bein' handcuffed to the kinky asshole of a demon".

Elora replied, "I can't really judge him harshly for wanting to use your body for pleasure. I want to use your body for pleasure most of the time."

Ram perked up, looking interested. "Like now?"

Elora opened her mouth to say something in the come-hither family when Helm started crying as if on cue. Both parents' shoulders slumped simultaneously.

"Can you hold that thought for half an hour?" She moved toward the baby, but continued talking. "Don't worry about Deliverance. He'll do what Litha asks and the quicker you get to Ireland and back, the less time we'll be without you."

Ram sighed heavily. "I'd feel better if I had a deterrent. Somethin' like wolfsbane." He brightened. "Demonsbane! Do you think they have some in the basement at Edinburgh?"

Elora laughed. "I don't know if there even is such a thing as demonsbane. You can ask, but even if it exists and they had some, they probably wouldn't give it to you." She shook her head. "You know the worst thing he's going to do to you is squeeze your ass. Women have been dealing with that kind of unwanted attention since the big bang."

Ram turned his mega-kilowatt smile on her. "You know I just realized there's a sexual reference to 'big bang'."

She laughed in spite of not wanting to encourage him. "You're hopeless, but I don't like to see you worried so I'll talk to Litha and ask her to make sure Deliverance knows you're hands off."

"Promise?"

She lowered her lids and smiled in response. "Would that be an opportunity I hear presenting itself? Soooooo. What will you do for me?" she asked as she finished fastening a fresh diaper for Helm.

"A deal is it now? I'm thinkin' Litha is a bad influence on you." Ram lunged and growled against her neck. "Will be lovin' you past the end of time."

"Oh, well, all right then."

Glen didn't see Rosie for nine days. Not because he didn't try. He called and left messages asking her to come see him or, if not that, to call back. She didn't reply to any voicemail, but finally, after four days, sent a single text that simply read, "Busy."

He sent other texts trying to tempt her with her favorite things.

We could get ice cream from the Hub and eat it at the duck pond. Or, *I could give you another chance to beat me at Y Box. You pick the game.*

She didn't even bother to respond.

Glen had weathered post puberty as a kid who was confident, cute, sweet, funny and easy to be with. Girls responded positively to the package and they did it in a unanimous sort of way. It seemed those particular characteristics were universally desired and appreciated.

In late adolescence the cute, sweet, funny kid took that inherent werewolf confidence and upgraded to irresistible hawtness paired with just enough bad boy vibe to get a nocturnal fantasy rating off the charts. That combination meant that he was used to being in demand and being pursued.

Not only was he unaccustomed to being told no, but he found out that he also didn't like it. At all. And, it seemed, he *especially* didn't like it coming from Rosie.

If he'd had the option of popping across the continental U.S. in a matter of minutes, he would have done exactly that. He would have banged on her door and demanded to have it out, but she was holding all those cards, which made the aggravation even more grating.

He was struggling to keep perspective so that the whole thing didn't distract him from the business of running J.U. That was the very last thing he needed. Even before that incident, he had believed he was barely holding down the fort.

Yeah. That's me! Look Mom, I'm holding down Fort Dixon.

He would have stopped and laughed at his own joke, but he was just too mad at Rosie to find anything that amusing. Not even himself.

By the time Elora came to him with the question about setting Rosie up on dates, he was bona fide combustible.

"What?!?"

Elora took note of the fact that normally laid-back Glen definitely wasn't himself. He was out of sorts to say the least.

"I said, 'Rosie's mother and I wonder if you know any nice boys your age that you might set Rosie up with," Elora repeated, ignoring the ballistic emoting. "We think she's ready to put a toe in the waters of the wonderful world of dating."

"Are you out of your mind?"

Elora's eyebrows shot up to her hairline. "I don't think so."

"Litha is in on this?" he accused.

"Yes. She thinks it's a good idea."

"What is WRONG with you people?"

Elora's confidence in her wicked matchmaking skill was growing in direct proportion to the level of fluster and frustration Glen was demonstrating.

"Nothing's wrong with us, Glen. You're the one who's yelling. Where's that signature cool that makes the girls throw panties? Whatever it is, maybe I can help. Do you need somebody to talk to?"

"Okay. How about this? NO! I don't know anybody who wants to date children. If I did, I'd set them on fire myself. AND NOBODY IS THROWING PANTIES!"

"Come to dinner tonight. I have the little table in the wine room reserved. It'll be nice and private. Just the four of us. We can talk about it. Maybe clear up some of your misgivings."

"Four of us?"

"You, Litha, me, and Rosie."

Glen's head jerked up. "Rosie's coming?"

"Why, yes. Of course."

"I accept. What time?"

"What's good for you? Eight thirty?"

"I will be there. If she thinks that I won't have anything to say just because her mother is there, she's going to…"

"Yes?"

He thought better of finishing that sentence. He realized he must really be losing it if he came that close to telecasting a take-down ahead of time.

"Never mind."

"Is something wrong? If it's Jefferson Unit

biz, maybe I can help. You know I will if I can."

When Glen looked at Elora, it was plain that he was miserable. His eyes were almost pleading for some kind of relief from an invisible source of torture. "You can't help."

"Okay, then. If you're sure."

"Sure."

"See you tonight."

"Yeah."

Elora was sure that no matchmaking conspirator had ever walked away from putting out a feeler with a greater feeling of satisfaction. She could hardly wait to get out of sight and hearing distance – werewolf hearing distance – so that she could call Litha and make a report. Love between her two favorite new adults seemed like a farfetched fairy tale, but many stranger things had happened in and around the interests of Black Swan.

Glen arrived for dinner at exactly eight thirty. Litha and Elora were waiting with warm smiles and a nice Chardonnay, which he thought was a sissy drink, but didn't say no. The single dinner table set in the middle of the wine room was intended for special occasions that required more atmosphere and privacy than could be found in the Mess, even though it was elegant by any standards.

The mother and adopted aunt motioned for Glen to sit. He seemed unusually restless and looked around nervously, like he was expecting an ambush. Litha poured a glass of white and handed it to Glen.

"Thank you. So, where's Rosie? Did you

decide it's past her bedtime?"

Litha smiled indulgently. "Don't tell Child Protective Services, but I let her go to bed when she pleases."

"Really," Glen said with an overtone of accusation. "Shocking, but not surprising."

"Why, Glen, are you judging my parenting style harshly?" Litha asked.

He set the glass down after taking a sip and seemed to be considering his response as he sucked air through his teeth. "She's your daughter and I'm sure it's not easy raising her with Storm away. It's not my place to judge."

"Very diplomatic and cautious of you." Litha studied Glen for a minute. "She'll be here shortly. She just needed another minute to finish what she was doing."

Glen snorted. "Video game or TV show?"

"No. I think it had something to do with hair, but since we have a minute to ourselves, I'd like to ask personally if you know some nice boys your own age who could be trusted to gently introduce Rosie to the mine-field of dating. Her circumstances have been so unusual that she hasn't had the opportunities most girls have to interact with boys growing up. I think she needs to be eased in, don't you?"

"As I told your cohort…" Glen glanced at Elora.

"Cohort?" Elora interrupted, registering her protest to the implication with an amused twinkle.

He ignored that and proceeded as if she hadn't spoken. "…everybody I know who might be up for blind dating would be expecting someone who is…"

"Sorry I'm late. Oh good. You didn't start without me." Rosie had popped in behind Glen.

He turned in his chair thinking he would give her a piece of his mind for the way she'd behaved the past week, but when she came into view, he did a double take and was dumbstruck. Rosie had aged physically to just about the same age as Glen.

Her hair had grown so that it fell around her shoulders. The sheer weight of those raven tresses pulled a lot of the curl out and left her hair thick, wavy and glossier than he remembered. The girlish eyes that had glittered when she took his knight with her bishop now looked almost identical to Litha's. She was wearing a dark emerald green silk dress that draped her body sensuously without being overtly provocative. It made her eyes look… *captivating*. She had grown to about the same height as Elora, which meant she got the tall gene from her dad and her figure had curved into an hourglass shape that made Glen swallow hard as the sweep of his eyes took her in.

Her breasts, full and rounded, had captured his gaze so that he didn't seem to be able to look away. Rosie looked down at her chest like she was afraid something was on the front of her dress. "What's wrong? Did I spill?"

Glen snapped out of it enough to stand.

"Hi, Glen," she said brightly while taking a seat. He was flummoxed that she said hello as if everything between them was copacetic and totally cool. "I'm starved. What are we having?"

"I hadn't thought about it," Litha said. "Glen, what do you feel like?"

Glen was staring at Rosie with his lips parted. It wasn't a full on gape, but it was a statement that he'd ventured way outside his comfort zone. Almost in slow motion, like some part of his brain registered from deep in a well that Litha was speaking to him, he brought his attention to her.

"Food. Ah. No. I… It's Rosie's evening. Let her decide."

"Oh. That's sweet, Glen." That one half dimple always left Glen wondering if he'd really seen it when she smiled a certain way.

It was a miracle that he'd been able to put together a coherent sentence and speak it out loud. He deserved credit for that. What he didn't deserve was to be accused of being sweet.

Sweet?

Glen didn't want Rosie thinking he was sweet. Sweet was for kittens, pink hearts, glace and other outrageously sugary substances. Sweet couldn't run Jefferson Unit in the absence of both Sovereign Nemamiah and the next best thing – her father. Sweet wouldn't be put in charge of a life or death operation to rescue the Lady Laiken.

Glendennon Catch was not "sweet" and he resented the implication. Sweet was not the word he wanted to hear her use to describe him. He wanted to watch her look at him while the perfection that was her bow-shaped mouth smiled and said words like heroic, sexy, badass or irresistibly delicious.

So he opted for acting out, slumped back in his chair, tried to look bored and said, "Whatever."

"Let's find out what Crisp has to say about what's going on in the kitchen tonight. So, Glen,"

Rosie started in a conversational tone so polished it sounded like she'd been to finishing school. "How much longer will you be running the show here? Is Sol ever coming back?"

"Next week."

"Well, I'll bet you can't wait to get back to doing whatever you were doing before."

"Whatever I was doing before? Seriously?"

Rosie's face fell when she heard that his tone was clearly offended. "Well, I didn't know you before, you know."

That seemed to bring the conversation to an abrupt halt. Rosie and Glen stared at each other. Litha and Elora sat quietly across from one another, witnessing the exchange and occasionally glancing at each other in wordless communication.

Glen seemed to be becoming more surly and sullen by the second. Elora pushed back her chair and stood. "I think I'll go see what's keeping Crisp."

As suddenly as Glen had lost his voice, he found it. He leveled a focus on Rosie she'd never seen before and she had to resist squirming under the intensity of it.

He stood as he threw his napkin down on the table without taking his eyes off Rosie. "Do you think I might have a word with you? In private?"

She glanced at Elora, who winked, and then at her mother, who was completely noncommittal. Seeing that she was on her own, Rosie nodded to Glen and pushed her chair back.

He held the door to the courtyard open so that she could pass first. On her way by she opened her mouth to say something, but he stopped her by holding up a finger. He put his hand against the small of her back and guided her to a door on the opposite side of the fountain. It opened to an empty meeting room, the one where the French vampire had first appeared in pursuit of Rosie's mother.

The only light in the room was coming from the garden lights and filtered through the windowed walls. Glen closed that door behind him and turned to face her. His eyes ran up and down her body slowly in a conspicuous way. It made Rosie feel self-conscious enough to have to resist curling up into a protective ball. The fact that she felt like he did it deliberately to unsettle her also sparked her anger.

"So you've changed?"

What she was dying to know was, *do you like what you see?* What she said was, "You can always be counted on for sharp insight, Glen."

He smirked. "Sarcasm is a different look for you, too, sweet Rosie. So, you're wanting me to set you up to go out. What did you have in mind? Dinner? Movie? Fanny fucking?"

Surprise flitted across her features, but she quickly regained her composure and lifted her chin defiantly. "I hadn't thought about the details. What do you recommend?"

"This is *such* bullshit!" His expression hardened as he loosened the hold on his feelings. He didn't raise his voice, but his tone said he wanted to throttle her as did his body language when he took a step toward her. "You want to tell me why you froze me out?"

Rosie didn't know exactly what to expect from the reunion, but she wasn't prepared to deal with the force of angry energy that was emanating from Glen.

She didn't back away, but shrugged prettily and looked at her nails like she was bored and would prefer to be elsewhere. Everything about that reaction stoked the fury Glen was trying to tamp down. She glanced up and noticed his nostrils flared in reaction. He was fuming.

"You hurt my feelings."

"I hurt your feelings." He restated that with the exact same inflection. "You froze me out and refused to talk to me for over a week because I hurt your feelings."

She stopped avoiding looking at him. She met his gaze with her eyes and matched his intensity with her own. "Bad!"

He gritted his teeth. "Bad?" He shook his head and knitted his brow like he had no idea what to do with that word.

"You hurt my feelings *badly*."

"What are you talking about, Rosie? How could it hurt your feelings badly that I cut a chess game short?"

"Ugh! Not because you wanted to pause the game. Because you were going out on a date! Gods!"

Glen stared at her like she was alien while trying to process that. He took in the resolute set of her mouth and the flush of the truth-telling embarrassment that colored her cheeks. And he waited for those eyes that had sparked a lightning flash of anger, when she thought he was being dense, to lift up and meet his again.

While he looked at the girl who stood in front

of him, who was so strange and so familiar all at the same time, he ran through a range of possibilities. At the end of that mental exercise he decided to go with one of the ideas expressed in Newtonian physics. The simplest explanation is usually the correct one, even if it seems farfetched.

"You were jealous." His face softened as he lowered his chin and said it evenly with a little hint of wonder, while a little bit of mad was seeping away.

She gave him a look like she thought he was slow. A look that said, *Just now coming to the party?*

"Yeah." She confessed it with exquisite simplicity, no artifice, no feminine ritual of subterfuge or manipulation. "I was *so* jealous that I contemplated putting a hex on the skank even though doing that would bring shame to the witch side of my family for generations."

The corners of his lips twitched. "How do you know she was a skank?"

Her eyes flashed when she looked up again, letting him know she didn't share his amusement.

"This whole conversation is causing me to think that rumors of your genius are greatly exaggerated. You know that?"

His grin turned into a satisfied smile. "I didn't go." He ducked just a little to force her to look at him eye to eye.

"You didn't go." Understanding dawned. "You didn't go on that date?"

He shook his head no.

"Why not?"

"Because the whole thing had upset you, which resulted in me being upset, too. I tried to call you and say I was sorry."

"Oh," she whispered.

As the shape of forming that word lingered on her beautiful lips, Glen was finding it hard to think about the conversation instead of the burn in his chest and the twitching in his cock.

"Why didn't you return my calls?" She looked down at the floor. "There's no stopping now. If you're laying it out there, let's lay it *all* out there."

"You may not like it."

"I may not. Let's hear it. Then I'll let you know."

She studied his face for a minute like she was trying to decide whether to press forward or retreat.

"At first my feelings were really hurt."

He took another small step into her space that brought him close enough to feel the heat of her aura and catch her scent, which was hard to place. It was almost like it was wafting on currents, not lingering quite long enough to be conclusively identified. It seemed to be alternating between rainstorm and the pungent, erotic smell of Dragon's Blood resin set on fire.

"And then?" he asked softly.

"Then?"

"*After* your feelings were hurt."

"Then I was hurt *and* mad."

His lips twitched. "Why were you mad, Rosie?" He couldn't help noticing that she closed her eyes when he said her name. "Tell me," he breathed, leaning into her.

"I couldn't stand the idea of another woman being with you."

"Another woman?" She glanced up to see him grinning at her.

"Are you making fun of me?"

He wasn't making fun of her. Exactly. But he wiped the grin away because there was no point in being deliberately antagonistic. Though he wouldn't mind experiencing the sight of her spitfire again and the rush of being in the presence of its power, he knew that wasn't the right time to bring it out.

"Why don't you want me to be with another woman, Rosie?"

"Because you're mine." Matter of fact. Death and taxes. The sun comes up in the east, goes down in the west. So far as she was concerned, he was a foregone conclusion. Like destiny.

"I'm yours?" His mouth curved into a genuine smile. "So how did you see this going? Your plan was to cut me off and ignore me for nearly two weeks, get me so frustrated that I was ready to strangle you, then show up here all voluptuous curves and pouty lips, asking me to set you up with some *nice boys*."

'Nice boys' was dripping with sarcasm and ridicule. Rosie couldn't decide if the offense he'd clearly taken at that notion was because he didn't know any or because he thought the idea of nice boys was pansy.

He pressed on without waiting to see if she took his meaning. "Did you think the idea of you with somebody else might make me jealous?"

She pulled back, looked away again, and muttered, "I guess. Maybe. Something like that."

"Hmm. Well. As plans go, I guess it was okay." Her eyes met his. The uncertainty seemed to have been replaced with a hint of hopefulness. "Who came up with it?"

"My mother."

He barked out a laugh. "Litha did?" Rosie nodded. "Scary. And Elora got in on it, too. Fuck. A guy doesn't stand a chance around this place."

Even in profile, he could see that brought her brows closer together. He could see that she was too inexperienced to understand that his declaration meant he was waving a white flag of surrender.

He put his fingers under her jaw and turned her face toward him. What he saw there was uncertainty and the fear of loss. By all the gods, she was double jeopardy. Hot. *And* cute.

"Rosie." He said her name quietly, just the way she always dreamed he would. "I'm a nice boy. Can I be your first kiss?"

He didn't wait for a response, but leaned in and gently brushed his lips over hers. Her lips were luscious, begging to be swollen from lovemaking, and they tasted every bit as delectable as they looked. But still, the kiss was beyond awkward.

Glen repositioned himself in front of her and took her face in both his hands. As he continued giving her light kisses, one right after another, she began to respond to pressure and suction, mirroring what he was doing. As soon as she started to get the hang of it, he deepened the kiss and, when he did, she immediately moved closer – pressing the softness of her young body into his. The resulting sensations made a clean cut through his connection to rational thought. Intimate contact with Rosie was so arousing it defied description. Something about her ratcheted every nerve ending into overdrive.

Elora was talking as the door opened before her eyes found them in the semi-darkness. "Hey, you two. We need to give Crisp our dinner order. Oh." They looked up at Elora just before she hurriedly backed away. "Sorry." She closed the door and was gone.

Glen had broken the kiss as soon as his brain registered the interruption. After Elora had come and gone, he looked back at Rosie whose eyes had a glaze of haziness. And he was sure it was the sexiest thing he'd ever seen.

"Glen. I wish..."

"What?" She didn't answer. "Tell me. What do you wish?"

"I wish I was *your* first kiss."

His jaw went slack and he felt what little bit of resistance he had melt away with that dreamy look in her eyes. *All the gods.*

"Sweet... Rosie, it might as well have been my first kiss. Believe me. You're not like anything else in the world."

Litha looked at Elora with a question on her face, as the auntie slid back into her chair. "Well, mom, our little girl is sprouting womanly wings as I speak."

Litha didn't know whether to cry or clink glasses with Elora. "I'm not old enough for a kid who's wing-sprouting. I wish Storm was here."

Elora reached over and took Litha's hand. "Me, too. I can't stand to think about the fact that he wasn't here to…" Elora decided to try and lighten the mood before it turned into a tissue contest. "I wish he was back in this dimension where he's supposed to be, but I can't go along with wishing he was *here*. If he saw what I just saw, I suspect he'd have a few choice words, and maybe a beat down, for our Glen."

Litha stared at Elora for a few seconds and then laughed. "Which one of us do you think should be the one to give Glen the badass speech on Storm's behalf?"

"You decide. I could threaten to give him the beat down Storm would lobby for. You could threaten to scorch his ass. He's kind of grown comfortable ignoring threats coming from me. So he might pay more attention if it comes from you."

"Seriously, should I be worried? She's innocent. Physically at least. And Glen is…"

"…a teenage player. Yeah. I know. He's too smart to not know that Rosie isn't a date night throw away. First, he's a good kid."

"We could do worse, huh?"

"Don't get me started. He's the best. Second, he knows Storm's coming home. If that's not an incentive to make good choices, then Glen isn't as smart as we're all giving him credit for.

"And, don't forget that *we* did start this.

"What if Glen had set her up? Of all the scenarios for Rosie being introduced to male-female interactions, this is practically a controlled environment, an ideal outcome."

Litha nodded and held up her glass. "To Glen."

"To Glen," Elora agreed and they clinked

glasses.

It took some doing for Shade to set up a worthwhile game on a Monday night. When the details were finalized, he gave Storm two days' notice. On Monday night, the car arrived to pick him up and drive him to the game location in the Tenderloin, not the best address in San Francisco. Shade was waiting in the backseat. Apparently he thought Storm needed an escort.

They rode in silence. When the car pulled over, Storm turned toward Shade and held out his hand expecting cash. Instead, the creature said, "I'll be accompanying both you and my investment. Spectators don't make you nervous. Right?"

One of Storm's shoulders lifted in a half-hearted ambiguous shrug. "Suit yourself."

"After you."

Storm exited the car, looked around, and waited on the sidewalk for directions as to where they were headed. A block behind them a black Hemmy stopped and parked.

When Storm had mentioned the upcoming game to the knights, they'd exchanged glances and decided later, amongst themselves, that on Monday night they would be happening to patrol the area around wherever the event was to be held. After all, one place was as likely to turn up a biter as another. So they might as well.

They watched Storm, the loan beast, and his goons enter a hotel that should have been imploded decades earlier. As soon as they were out of sight, the knights followed. They'd done enough research on Richard Shade to anticipate that Storm might need some capable backup at some point in the evening. When they asked around, they learned that Shade was infamous for striking bargains and then changing the terms at a whim on authority of the muscle that accompanied him everywhere he went.

Yes. The hunters had believed Storm's story for three very good reasons. First, the organization they worked for was all about the strange, bizarre, and the hard to accept or reconcile with reality. Second, there was eye witness evidence. All four saw him take out a vamp with a practiced ease and efficiency that had veteran Black Swan knight written all over it. And, third, he knew too much about The Order to be anything other than what he claimed to be.

Storm hadn't asked for back up, but he wasn't the sort who would. In the minds of the knights, that served as further proof that he was one of them, even if he was an alien.

So looking as inconspicuous as possible, they eased down the street separately toward the door where Storm and his escorts had entered the dilapidated building.

It was just after nine o'clock when the game began in a room behind the hotel lobby. It had no door, but was still considered private because that hotel didn't get uninvited visitors.

One of the team of slayers slipped in and confirmed that the game was underway, making a quick visual assessment of the number of players and spectators. Shade and friends were sitting out of the way, along the wall, but close enough that Storm would be mindful of their presence.

Six hours later, when Storm was up seventy-eight thousand dollars, he left the game. Shade said nothing. He and the two lackeys followed Storm out of the building.

Once on the sidewalk, Storm handed over seventy-five thousand.

"There you go. Paid in full, a debt I never owed, but taking your word that somebody did."

Shade's voice was low and gravelly. "Get in the car, Storm. I don't conduct business on sidewalks."

"There's no business to conduct. I just paid you off. We're done. I'm no longer obligated to ride in a vehicle with you, trying not to choke on whatever that smell is. I'll find my own way back. Then… don't want to see you again. Hope we're clear."

Shade's smile turned menacing. "We're done when I say we're done. The original debt was seventy-five. Interest has accrued since then. I'm going to need another fifty to clear."

Storm smiled, looked at the ground for a split second, and shook his head at the deserted surrounding neighborhood.

"Gave you a chance to do this the easy way. You're money ahead. It's all good. If I were you, I'd count my blessings with my dollars and be on my way. I don't care how you sort it out in your own mind. But. We. Are. Done. If you push for another outcome, you won't like the results and you have my word on that."

Storm turned to leave. Shade nodded at the goons who started to reach inside coats for handheld firearms. The guns never cleared lapels before they were in the possession of Black Swan hunters whose presence had not been detected by any of them other than Storm.

"We'll just take these."

When Sir Randeskin got close to Shade, he turned to Storm. "What exactly is that?"

Storm shrugged. "Dogged if I know, brother."

Randeskin never took his eyes from Shade, while Sir Blitheness patted him down. Blitheness removed a dagger in a jeweled scabbard. It was beautiful. Looked like a ceremonial weapon that belonged in a museum. He passed it over to Randeskin who whistled as he admired it and withdrew the blade. He took his time examining the artistic intricacy of the etchings on both sides before laying the razor-sharp edge against Shade's throat.

"What is that smell? Ugh. All the gods." Randeskin coughed in Shade's face. "Look. We may not know what you are, but we know who you are, where you live, where you do business, and with whom. This man…" his head moved in Storm's direction, "…is connected in ways you can't begin to fathom."

"What do you want?" Shade gritted between his teeth.

A little more pressure was applied to the knife, driving the point home, so to speak.

"What we want is for this to be as easy as getting your acknowledgement that the thing is settled and your promise that Storm won't be hearing from you again. But, since we know we can't count on you to stand by your agreements, we're forced to put our faith in your sense of self-preservation.

"So it's like this. If you ever see this man again, run the other way. Because if he ever sees *you* again, you and this very fine knife are going to get much closer than ever before. And it's so pretty, I'd hate to see it get rusty because of being buried in something wet. Likewise, if anything happens to him – *anything* – get your affairs in order fast because you can count your remaining hours on your fingers."

When Randeskin released Shade, he shoved him toward the waiting car at the same time. He stumbled back, but was caught by one of the thugs before he went down to the pavement.

"We'll hold onto the weapons for now."

Shade's eyes went to the dagger still in Randeskin's hand and his face darkened. "That dagger is…"

He didn't get a chance to finish the protest before he was interrupted. Looking at the knife appreciatively, Randeskin said, "The dagger will be taken care of. Mark my words or the same will be said about you."

Shade's eyes flashed with hatred. He stopped long enough to give Storm a good hard look before getting in the car. Storm gave him a slight smile and a little wave goodbye that was so out of place it came off looking like an affront.

The five knights stood in the dim light of a few partially lit neon signs and watched the car's tail lights until they turned off two blocks away. Storm turned his attention to the knights.

"Thank you kindly, gentlemen. You know where you can always come for a free Jack and a strange tale." They laughed. "Any chance I can push my luck for a ride home?"

"We just gave the biters a six hour holiday, which means our quota is suffering. Still got three hours of night. Come on patrol with us."

The offer made Storm's gums itch. He never would have imagined that he'd miss hunting, but on occasion, when he didn't run from the truth of the darkness in himself, there it was. His shadow side missed everything about it, maybe even the ugly parts. If he ever got back to his own world, he would have to give that the thought it deserved.

"Would be an honor," he said. "Lead on."

They clapped him on the back and regarded him with a wholehearted camaraderie that was as welcome as it was unexpected.

Archer had made some very fine and very handy improvements to the inter-dimensional transport. One of the niftiest was the fact that the device could be reprogrammed to calculate a new destination intra-dimension.

The Ralengclan team arrived in Loti Dimension and used a handheld biolocation device to find the Laiwynn. When they discovered that they needed to be on the inside of a secure military base, they set new coordinates for the transport to deliver them next to the building where she was located.

They slipped into Fort Dixon under cover of

night and emerged next to the Jefferson Unit building. Archer had sent a twenty-first man whose only job was to stay with the transport. He would close the portal, making the transport and himself virtually invisible, and reopen every forty minutes starting one hour from count.

Each of the twenty wore black and carried a pack with an assortment of tools and weaponry.

After a quick on-the-spot analysis, the team leader, a guy named Farouche, turned to his second.

"Easiest way to breach a building *and* maintain an element of surprise?"

"Not sure, sir."

"The roof. We need to get in through the roof. There's only one other exterior entrance. Secure, but flawed. Electronic mechanism. I need it disabled so that it can't be opened from the inside without a blow torch or a genius."

Browers, second in command, assigned that duty, then turned and said something to the guy carrying the grappling gear. He dropped his pack and retrieved the four prong titanium hook with one hundred feet of cable – way more than was needed to scale a four story building – and the boost, the launch weapon that would silently fire the hook and pulley like a missile without raising either alert or interest.

"If luck is with us, this very boring building will have a good size lip just begging to be hooked."

Indeed, there was a nice size lip to catch and hold the hook. The architects wouldn't have thought about that as a design flaw.

Two Whister pilots were on call, playing cards in the pilots' shed as was their habit.

One held his free hand up in a motion to silence the other. "You hear something?"

The second pilot listened intently for a few seconds. "No. All's quiet."

So they turned the music back up and resumed their game.

The first guy in line was harnessed. When the remote triggered the pulley, he flew to the roof so fast it almost looked like he'd been launched like a human rocket. Within twelve minutes twenty Ralengclan were on the roof awaiting orders from Farouche. His attention had been drawn to the lights and music coming from the pilots' shed and to the two who were playing cards and laughing about singing along to some bizarre tune.

Farouche pulled a knife and motioned to Browers, who did the same.

The Whister pilots had less than two seconds to register surprise before deep slices were carved into their necks, instantly severing both carotid arteries and jugular veins. When the pilots were released, they slumped forward over the table where they'd spent so much time on call.

The front door was secured. No one was leaving the building unless they could get to the roof and that was a trap. Nowhere to go from there with both pilots dead.

Browers pulled the scrambler out of his pocket, but wanted to delay enabling until necessary. As soon as all communications devices were disrupted the occupants of the building would be made aware that something was up.

The entire fourth floor was dedicated to

knight's quarters. There were three banks of elevators. One was centrally located with three cars. The east and west end stations had two cars. All three locations had adjacent stairwells, but the only access to the Whister pad on the roof was from the fourth floor, central elevators stairwell.

Elora had used one of the two east elevators – the only one that was working - to return home from dinner. It seemed lots of stuff was breaking down since the maintenance staff had been pruned by the transfers.

Helm had fallen asleep in his stroller. Blackie sat waiting patiently, nose almost touching the seam in the middle where the doors opened and closed. The dog had gone into a crouch and was growling before the doors opened wide enough for Elora to see the problem. She moved to the center of the car and saw men in night camo uniforms pouring out of the central stairwell, coming from the Whister pad on the roof.

At that point, they were about two hundred feet away.

Her first thought was that it was some sort of drill and that she hadn't been advised. That idea was quickly overruled when one of them seemed to identify her on sight and pointed something that resembled a weapon in her direction. That, and the fact that strange men, whom she didn't recognize, who were definitely not supposed to be on the Whister pad, were racing up the hallway in her direction, brought her to a quick, but accurate conclusion. Jefferson Unit was under attack by Ralengclan. No matter how "silly" that might be.

She grabbed Blackie's collar to keep him from lunging forward, pushed the CLOSE DOORS button, and set the destination for Sublevel 1. Some of the intruders had stopped to kneel, shoulder automatic weapons and aim. At her. And Helm! And Blackie.

The doors closed before any of them were hit, but it felt like time was standing still while she waited for the elevator car to descend. She heard five pings from above. Bullets hitting the outer doors of the elevator on the floor she'd just left.

She scooped Helm out of his stroller setting him astraddle the shelf where her waist met her hip, and got ready to move as soon as the doors opened. The elevator wasn't fast, but it was a lot faster than the time it would take to descend five floors in the stairwell. Even assuming commando-level fitness.

As soon as the doors opened, she pulled the emergency stop button to decommission that elevator. One down.

Running straight for the closest alarm that Monq had installed, she broke the glass with her elbow and pushed the big yellow button to set off the gas, then braced to be stripped of enhanced abilities. *Get ready to be an average elf.*

Initiating Monq's Equalizer released the gas, but also set off the alarm, which was ten times louder than it needed to be and sounded like a giant goose was honking once every three seconds. With frayed nerves and juices flowing, all she needed was the irritation of a sound like that.

While she still had speed to call on, she raced down the hall to the media center which also contained the intercom equipment. At that point she didn't know that the Ralengclan had scrambled communication signals, rendering cells, wireless, and cybernet useless. She was going for the intercom because it was the most efficient way to communicate an emergency to Jefferson Unit occupants. The fact that it was the *only* form of communication still operational, since it was entirely independent of externalities, was good luck.

The intercom system was WYSIWG. The wired mic was built into its own base and sat in a base in the middle of a table. She picked it up and started to speak into it, but got nothing. Pulling away, she found an ON switch on the back and tried again.

"This is NOT a drill. Repeat. This is NOT a drill. We are under attack. All non-essential personnel, stay in your quarters. All others report to your stations. And Monq! Shut off that FUCKING noise NOW!"

Elora dropped the mic and ran for the hallway to the west end stairwell. Helm was crying so loud he was practically screaming because of the sound of the alarm and she didn't blame him. She felt like doing the same thing herself.

Before she reached the west end stairs, two things happened. The alarm stopped. *By all the gods, living and dead, thank you, Monq.* And the hallway filled up with twenty-three teenaged trainees who had just descended two floors from their quarters on the second story. Quickly.

That was two bits of good news. First, the fact that the boys were there meant that the west end stairs were clear for Elora to get to Sublevel 2. Second, after the alarm went off, Helm stopped crying.

The bad news was that she had nearly two dozen kids standing in front of her, none of them bullet proof and none of them where they were supposed to be – safe in their quarters behind locked doors.

"Do you not understand what all those drills were for?" The trainees could see that Elora was furious, but they were unfazed. And, come to think of it, not the least panicked by the fact that Jefferson was under attack. Elora's odd response was to observe that Black Swan recruiters obviously knew what they were doing.

Kris Falcon crossed his arms over his chest and raised his chin. "We know what drills are for."

"Never mind. Come with me."

Helm had grown heavy and so had her own center of gravity. She glanced at her watch and quickly did the math in her head. Three hours and seventeen minutes meant the effects would wear off at half past midnight.

The good news was that she had to assume the Ralengclan didn't have any more advantage than highly trained, super fit *male* commandos would in any dimension.

She stood at the top of the stairs descending to Sublevel 2 and gestured for the kids to go down before her, keeping a watchful eye on the elevators and the hallways.

"Hurry. Wait for me in the armory. Go. Go. Go."

Sublevel 2 contained the research labs, Monq's suite, training simulators, firing ranges, and, most importantly, weapons. It would typically be quiet and deserted on a week night after dinner, with Monq being the only one who was quartered there. On that particular night, however, Deliverance hadn't come to take Angel to the vineyard. Angel had waited around for a while after dinner and finally decided he might as well get some target practice in.

Just like Elora had suspected, he was a natural with guns and liked shooting so much that it was recreational for him.

When the alarm went off, he reasoned that sooner or later people would make their way to the armory. So that's where he was waiting when Z Team rushed in.

"Hey," he said.

The four of them gave him strange looks. The one with the tat tails curling up his neck said, "Hey? He's not even looking at us like something he just scraped off his boot."

People could accuse Angel of a lot of things, but being slow wasn't one of them. He figured that if Storm had a deal with these guys, he'd better preserve the deteriorated state of relations. So, he said, "My mistake. Thought you were somebody else."

When Elora and the kids broke in, they found the four knights who had been left to defend Jefferson Unit and one knight-in-pretense. Her eyes took in the scene and locked on Angel. "What are you doing here?"

"I *was* doing target practice."

Zed Company had the full complement stash opened up, all cabinets and the vault that required top security clearance to open the combination, and were outfitting themselves like it was a world war. Monq ran in looking unsettled.

Elora moved toward him. She held Helm out to him, but Monq shook his head. "Take him!" Monq shook his head again. "Monq! We've got two jobs here. Fighting or babysitting. Which one do you want?"

After one second of consideration, Monq reached for Helm, whose displeasure with the new arrangement was equal to Monq's if not greater.

Glyphs spoke up. "You kids need to get cover and stay out of our way. We've got work to do."

Falcon looked at Glyphs. His body language screamed defiance. "We don't take orders from you. We take orders from her." He jerked his chin toward Elora.

"Yeah?" Glyphs looked at Elora and sneered. "Well, you'd better stay out of our way, too, Red."

Elora gaped at him, wondering if she'd imagined the lip curl, but didn't have time to deliver a lecture about the courteous and respectful regard knights are expected to extend to one another. She called after Z Team as they were leaving the room. "Don't be in the wrong place at the wrong time because we're sealing passageways."

They didn't acknowledge hearing her in any way.

She turned back to Monq.

"Okay. Take Helm and all these kids to Fire Testing. Get inside and lock up. It will act like a bunker until we either get rid of the threat or help comes. Go right now."

Monq motioned to the vault. "The new stuff is top shelf on the right in little bubble size vacuums.

You've got to be extremely careful with it. They look like poppers, same size and shape. And they perform the same way except that, instead of making a big pop, each one will take out everything in an area of about fifteen feet. Make sure you're twenty feet away just in case. Throw it hard. The vacuum case will break open and the popper will detonate."

"So it requires somebody with a pitcher's arm."

Monq started to say, "Or you," then remembered her extras were temporarily sidelined.

"Monq. Your mission is that baby. Do you understand?"

He nodded and turned to go. "Come on, boys."

They didn't move.

Elora stopped arming herself when she realized the kids weren't moving. "This is SO not the time for rebellious acting out. Go with Monq!"

Bo spoke up. "All respect, ma'am. We're Black Swan. That means we may not be knights, but we're not hiding either. If you want to call that 'acting out', then so be it."

"Monq. Go on. I'll deal with this."

Elora talked to Bo while she was making weapons choices and shoving things into a pack. When she was satisfied, she handed the pack off to Angel. She knew he was good with guns and packed accordingly.

"Here. See what goodies Santa brought you and figure out a way to make yourself useful."

"Yeah. Batch me up one of those goodie bags, too, mama."

Elora wheeled around to see Fennimore. She grinned. "You're a sight."

"Why, thank you, darlin'."

"You got our girl locked down?"

"She has sworn on our unborn children to stay put and keep the door locked. No matter what."

"One less worry."

"It is. I'll go with him." Fenn's eyes slid to Angel, whom he believed to be Storm. "We'll sort out the east end."

Elora jerked her eyes to Angel who nodded as if to say, "Don't worry. I got this." Then he opened his mouth and said, "Don't worry. We got this."

She nodded and handed them a pack with the C9. "This is the new stuff. Just one will seal a passage, safe distance twenty feet. Whichever one of you has the strongest, most accurate arm, throw them like poppers and make sure you're clear.

"These are the same aliens who came for me in Ireland." She gave Storm a look to let him know it was a shared memory. Then she said to Fennimore, "They're wearing black. They're trained, but not like us. I'm their objective."

"How many are there?"

"Don't know. I had to get the baby out of harm's way and couldn't stay to count."

"Okay. What's the plan?"

"Two prong ambushes. We're going to try to lure them to S3, seal them in and shut off heat and air from the main controls on S1."

"How are you gonna do that, Elora?" Fennimore looked dubious.

"I'm going to get on the intercom and tell

them to come and get me. They probably won't be dumb enough to send everybody down there, but they *will* send some.

"So here's what I want you to do. Get down there first and blow every elevator from the inside. I don't know, maybe you can throw the popper just before the doors are closing?" Angel and Fennimore just looked at each other. "We need all seven out of commission. Don't leave *any* operating. Then seal off the east and west stairwells so that their only route is by way of the Hub stairs. Give me a time frame?"

Fennimore looked at Elora hard while he was concentrating on calculations. She could almost see his brain circuitry busy running scenarios. "I think we can do it in fifteen minutes."

"I'll give you twenty including time to get above S3 and out of sight. When you think that all the rats that are going to eat have taken the bait, blow the stairwell."

Angel said, "Suffocation. Not exactly a warrior's death fantasy."

Elora grinned. "It'll take a while, but... yeah."

"What's the other part?"

"After we've culled the eager beavers, I'll get back on the mic and tell them I've moved to the Courtpark." She handed Fennimore a pack. "Make sure there are no civilians in the stairwells before you light 'em up." She paused. "Z Team's out there. Rogue."

Fennimore pressed his lips together. "Just what I'd expect."

"Twenty minutes."

He took his pack and strapped an automatic

over his shoulder. "You take care or Storm and I will be answering to that crazy ass elf."

Her eyes darted to Angel and back to Fennimore. She smiled. "See you later. And, Fenn, if it's the other side, you tell that elf that…" She misted up and didn't finish.

Fennimore put his big hand on her shoulder and shook his head. "Tell him yourself."

"Harder. Wait. Oh. Ow. Ow. Ow. Ow." Rosie stopped and looked at Glen with concern. He said, "No, baby. More pressure on the penis, but easy with the balls."

"Oh."

Rosie could have accessed her parents' memories and learned a few things about sex. Instantly. But she felt like she owed them privacy where some things were concerned. So she'd decided to figure it out on her own, trial and error, like everybody else, and Glen didn't seem to mind. It was one area of her life where she wanted *all* her experience to be her own.

If he was a kiss and tell sort, he would have said that Rosie was a fast learner, eager to please, and so greedy in bed that she was relentless.

Beautiful.

Glen sat with his back against the headboard on the verge of being stroked to permanent nirvana. Rosie's eyes were lit with wonder, which was a huge turn on. Having her in his bed was a huge turn on. Knowing he was the first to ever touch her was a huge turn on. The fact that she believed she could claim him just by calling dibs, strange as that was, it was also a huge turn on. Really, everything about Rosie from her voice to her smile to her touch had him walking around hard when he needed to have his mind on running Jefferson Unit instead of in his pants. Or hers.

There was so much to do that any time he took for himself felt like slacking, but that didn't mean he was *always* going to say no. Who in his ever fucking right mind could say no to Rosie?

Making time for her was a little like a respite in heaven. He was watching her closely as she watched her own hand slide up and down on his cock. He was sure he'd never seen anything more erotic than the expression on her face. There was something about being the object of somebody else's fascination that jumped his excitement level off the scale. Rosie was full of firsts and records for Glen. Sweetest kiss. Hardest come. Most perfect fit. He should start a list.

Guided by instinct alone, Rosie was leaning forward like she was thinking about touching the tip of her tongue to the slit where precum was glistening. Glen held his breath while every muscle in his body went rigid with agonizing anticipation. As if in slow motion he saw her tongue peak out and reach toward the engorged head, coming closer, closer …

Then bam! Deliverance was standing by the side of the bed occupying the empty space that had been there a moment earlier. "Hey kids."

Glen's body jerked involuntarily like he was seizing. He stared at the demon wide-eyed. While his brain tried to process what just happened, his dick deflated to flaccid faster than a balloon with a pin stuck in it.

Rosie, on the other hand, was perfectly calm still holding his, now limp, penis in her hand. She looked up and said, "Grandy. What are you doing here?" as if she'd just run into him at the donut shop.

Glen had opened his mouth to say something along the lines of, "WTF!" when Deliverance answered.

"We may have a line on your pop, precious."

Rosie dropped Glen's cock like a hot potato. It slumped over onto his stomach looking sad. It isn't every day a guy teaching the art of the hand job gets interrupted by the girl's grandfather. Fortunately for Glen, Rosie's Grandy had no puritanical notions about sex. None. He took no more notice than he would have if he'd found them together eating ice cream and feeding ducks.

"I don't want your mother to get her hopes up and be disappointed. I was thinking maybe you should check this one out and sign off. We don't want to end up with a menagerie of stray Storms to feed."

Rosie stood up with no apparent self-consciousness about her beautiful body and started to get dressed in a hurry. Being part werewolf, Glen wasn't as shy about nudity as most, but having Rosie's grandfather stand over him caused him to pull the covers over himself.

"Good thinking, Gran. Take me there." She stopped. "Hold on." She went into the bathroom and was doing something with her hair.

"What are you doing?"

She poked her head out. "If it is him, I want to

look okay."

Glen turned to Deliverance. "Would you mind surrendering the room so I can get dressed with a little privacy? In my *own* bedroom?"

Deliverance shook his head and turned his back muttering something like, "Humans and their weird ideas. How's this?"

Glen jumped into his jeans and pulled a tee shirt over his head just as Rosie was coming out of the bathroom. He put his hands on her arms. "You've never looked better. If it is him, he's going to be blown away."

She offered a little smile, but he could tell she was nervous. "What if it *is* him?" she whispered.

Glen grinned, "Rosie, going to meet your dad? It's the biggest thing that's ever going to happen to you. When he gets back, we're all going to celebrate together." *Right after he tears me a new one.* He kissed her. "Get back to me. One way or the other."

She nodded, gave him a peck on the lips, walked toward Deliverance, and they were gone.

At the same time they vanished, the giant goose honking alarm went off. At first Glen thought that Deliverance and Rosie popping out had set it off because the timing couldn't have been more perfect. He scrambled into boots and ran out the door not caring about the bed head.

He was delayed by a few instructors who were quartered on the same floor as the boys and had to convince them to get back into their apartments and stay there. By the time he was free, he was just plain lucky to pick one of the stairwells that was clear. He made it to Sublevel 2 and almost plowed over

Fennimore and Angel on their way out of the armory.

"Slow down, rookie. We're carrying explosives," Fenn said.

"Sorry."

Elora looked up when she saw Glen. "Well, that's unanimous. All twenty-four. Glen, this operation is militarized until the threat has passed. I need you to turn command over to me."

Glen didn't hesitate. "It's yours."

Elora looked at the rest of the boys. "Are you going to do what I say?"

Falcon said, "Not if it involves waiting this out in cupboards."

She stared at the resolve on Falcon's face for about three seconds.

"Glen, give them weapons and as many clips as they can stuff in pockets. They're all familiar with the Centerfires. Give Falcon a SIG. Give Jvorsten a Braum.

"DO NOT SHOOT EACH OTHER OR I *WILL* GROUND YOU. PERSONALLY.

"Glen, Monq is bunkered in Fire Testing with Helm. I need you to take Blackie and put him in there. I knew he wouldn't go with Monq so I didn't even try it. He can't be in a closed building with live fire. What the…?" Glen turned around to see a stream of civilians standing out in the hall. "For crying out loud, people. Can't anybody in this operation just do what they're told?!?

"Glen, give me your belt."

He didn't hesitate to take off his belt and give it to her. While she was talking she was looping it through Blackie's collar, to rig a makeshift leash.

"Form a detail. Take six other trainees. Get these people and this dog to Fire Testing and lock it down." She handed the leash to Glen. "Put them in there and seal the door. If you have to." She gave him a look. *"Carefully."*

She gave him a small square of C5 and he nodded.

"And," she pulled him close and whispered, "If you can get some of these younger boys to get inside with them, do it. Rally point is the Hub. If you come across those Z Team bastards, tell them I'm in command and, if they don't submit to my authority, I'm hauling their carcasses to Edinburgh Trials when this is over."

"You got it. Be careful."

"Yep."

Glen took Bo and Blackie and five of the younger boys and instructed them to bring the civvies. "Listen up folks. Stay tight and no dawdling. Bo and I bring up the rear."

Glen sent two of the fourteen-year-olds ahead, weapons drawn, to make sure the way was clear and told the three thirteen-year-olds to keep the people moving.

Elora felt a rumbling vibration in the floor and figured Angel and Fennimore must have found purchase on one of the targets. "I could use a little good news," she muttered to herself.

"Lady Laiken?"

She turned to see seventeen too-young faces looking at her expectantly. Each wore a resolute expression and she knew she had no hope of getting them to stand down. Looking them over, she noted the irrefutable evidence that Black Swan knights might be influenced and tempered, but they were not made. They were born.

"You're in, but only if you wear vests and helmets." There was some grumbling about the helmets. "Grouse all you want. Those are my terms. Non-negotiable.

"Six knights and seven trainees are deployed. We're support. Work together. Grab as many weapons as you can carry, but only the ones that you have T4 clearance to use. Throw everything that's not nailed down into the vault before I reseal it.

"Multitasking. Hear me talk while you suit up and secure the room. We have to split up and work in teams and that means we'll be out of contact once we leave this level. We basically have to go guerilla on the intruders.

"I want to be very clear about this. These men are here for me. To assassinate me. If you go down to S3 and wait it out, I think you'll be okay. It's not your fight."

The boys were very quiet and didn't look happy. Kris Falcon finally said, "Teachers think we don't pay attention, but we do. If they're here for one of us, then it's our fight. You're one of us, aren't you?"

She smiled. "Indeed I am. At this moment, proud to say so." She stood on one of the benches in the middle of the room and raised her voice.

"I wish I could be with each and every one of you, each and every minute, but that would just put you in more danger. The best I can do is tell you to pick a partner you can trust. Stay out of the aliens' sight. If you have a shot that you can take without endangering yourself or any of us, take it. If you don't have a clear shot, stay under cover and wait until you do. They may be wearing Shieldo. Aim for the head or the groin." She noticed the boys wince when she said the word 'groin'. "No time to be squeamish, people. You can disable a man fast with an expando in the dick and keep him alive for questioning. The Order has a lot invested in you. Don't squander that investment.

"Remember, they're here for me. That means stay far, far away from me at all times.

"Before you go, I need someone who can get to the intercom undetected. Like through the A/C ducts. Have we got anybody like that?"

"Spaz can do it," Wakey said.

"Spaz?"

Wakey smiled sheepishly. "It's, um, what we call Chorzak. He does it all the time."

Someone pushed the little fourteen-year-old forward.

"Does what all the time?"

"Crawls around and listens to what's going on. He knows *everything*."

The implication of what "everything" entailed was clear in the boy's undertone. Elora jerked her head toward Spaz. He had the decency to blush, but at the same time, couldn't completely suppress a smile.

"Shame on you, um, you don't mind being called Spaz?"

"No ma'am."

"Alright, well, shame on you, Spaz. That is *very* un-knightlike behavior."

"Yes, ma'am."

"When this is over, I'm going to see to it that Monq outfits the ducts with a mild electric current."

"Yes, ma'am."

"*Always* leave yourself an escape. Rally point at the Hub. If you can't get there, then stay away. Primary goal is to stay alive. Everything else is secondary. Go."

The room cleared in a hurry. She felt another rumble under her feet.

"Spaz." She stumbled on the word because she was having trouble getting past calling him that. "I need you to get to the media room. Get on the mic and say this. 'I just saw Elora Laiken heading for the bottom level.' You got that?" He nodded. "If you can't get to media, or if the area is busy, go to Plan B. There's always something else we can do and you need to live to spy another day."

He gave a boyish smile and a little salute. He climbed up on the lockers and took the A/C panel off with expert speed. She watched his tennis shoes disappear into the duct. When she turned around, there were still two kids standing there. Kris and Wakey.

Her eyes went to the vault. There were no more vests or helmets.

"Shieldos and helmets are gone. We need to get you to someplace safe and fast."

"That's not on our agenda," Wakey said.

"Pardon?"

"We're shadowing you."

Elora's face softened and her heart just melted as she looked between the two of them. "Thanks for the offer, guys, but nobody can be anywhere near me until this is over. Being next to me right now? It's more than dangerous. It's practically suicide, especially without equipment.

"Let's try to get to S1. When we're there, we split up. Got me?"

Kris answered just to show solidarity with Wakey. "We understand you, but we're not doing that. We're staying with you. The Order can afford to lose us. We're trainees. You're another story."

"What happened to, 'I take orders from her?'"

When Kris Falcon ducked his head and grinned, it changed his face dramatically.

What a little heartbreaker he's going to be. If I can keep him alive.

They heard the sounds of live fire coming from one of the stairwells, followed by another rumble underfoot. "All out of debate time."

Elora pulled her snub nose Cuefire, the one that Storm had picked out for her, and started for the stairwell with Falcon and Wakenmann close behind.

Storm had a couple of hours before he needed to be at the bar. He was walking around China Town, looking at odd things in windows that were supposedly edible. He stopped in front of the Hoang Jewelry. There was a jade necklace in the window that caught his attention. It was a darker, richer green than any he'd ever seen. So close to the color of his witch's eyes. Not emeralds, but close.

He noticed movement and looked up to see a tiny, smiling woman motioning for him to come in. His typical response to proprietors' invitations to shop was to shake his head, smile politely, and keep walking. And that's what he did. He walked for about ten feet, then turned around and went straight into the store.

He pointed at the necklace in the window. "That one. How much?"

The little woman pulled it from the display and motioned for him to hold out his hand. She draped the necklace over his hand and forearm and then turned over the price tag so he could read it. The petite merchant smiled and half-bowed as she watched Storm's reaction to the feel of the cool smooth stones on his skin. It was as if the piece wanted to attach itself mystically. And he had to have it. Two thousand four hundred fifty.

Storm laughed out loud. By the time they added taxes it would come close to the extra he'd won at poker. Easy come. Easy go.

"Hold it for me." He handed it to her. "I'll be back in twenty minutes."

He left the store smiling and jogged back to the bar to get the money. Impulsive buys were so out of character for Storm that the purchase of the necklace would be a first for him, if he went through with it. But there wasn't *really* a question in his mind. He was going to go through with it.

That was the first time in a long time that he didn't feel like he was spinning wheels. He was showing the Fates that he was so positive he was going home that he was buying his wife a souvenir from another dimension. He was going to buy that necklace and, by gods, he was going to see Litha wear it. He could picture how it would look lying on that scrumptious skin she inherited from the sex demon. In his fantasy, he could imagine the green of the jade complementing her eyes so that they looked like the green lava pools she said she would take him to see.

So he tore through the bar, grabbed his money from its hiding place, and jogged back to the jeweler. The petite Asian woman smiled and bowed as she encased the necklace in a black velvet box and fastened the clasp. She put it in in a gold bag, tied a shuck string, and told him to be sure and come again.

She'd been standing on the other side of the street for a while. She watched him go into the jewelry store and was waiting for him to come out. For all she knew there were countless versions of Storm in similar realities to Loti Dimension, but that was irrelevant. She didn't need to play twenty questions to know that the man inside that jewelry store was her father. All the minutes and hours that she'd wished for that moment that would put her family back together again. Then it was at hand and all she could do was stand there trying to decide what she would say to him.

Hi. I know you don't recognize me, but I'm the daughter who should be learning to roll over in her crib. How are you?

Storm left enjoying the feel of the weight in his hand and, for the first time since he had been lost, he felt found. He was going home.

He lifted his head and looked across the street.

It felt like something was pulling his attention, but there was nothing out of the ordinary. The sidewalks were teeming with people hurrying back to offices after lunch. Nothing special. No reason for that fine honed instinct of his to engage, just a crowd of people awash in a riot of diversity.

Then he did see something out of the ordinary- one person, a girl, who wasn't carried along with the pedestrian current. She was standing perfectly still on the other side of the street looking in his direction while the pedestrian traffic parted around her. Maybe she wasn't just looking in his direction. Maybe she was looking at him. Watching. Him.

He took a closer look. She was taller than average, with a mass of black hair that was wavy like Litha's. She was definitely looking at him, looking with an intensity that reminded him of the way people described him. It was a girl who… who…

Storm stepped off the curb without thinking about oncoming vehicles. An electric blue, electric car honked and he narrowly avoided being hit. He held out his hand and dodged cars to get across the street. When he got to the other side, he was close enough to see Litha's emerald green eyes staring at him from a slightly younger, feminine version of the face he shaved every day.

Rosie. Completely grown up.

As she came toward him, looking teary-eyed, he felt his own eyes burning and it was getting hard to breathe. She walked straight into him. Just before she made contact with her cheek to his chest, arms wound around his waist, he saw her bottom lip tremble and her eyes spill over.

"Daddy."

He hugged her to him. "I missed it," he whispered to the top of her hair and she heard him even with all the crowd and lunch hour noise. She sensed every one of his conflicting emotions: relief and happiness to be found, disappointment and sadness that he missed her growing up.

She hugged him tight, clinging like she might lose him again if she let go. He hugged back and rocked her just a little, remembering the last time he saw her.

Found.

After a while he pulled back so he could get a close look at her face. "Let me see you," he said. He reached up and pushed a lock of hair back while he studied her features. "How old are you?"

Her expression said she felt like a failure for not being able to give him a straight answer to that and didn't want to disappoint him.

"I don't know. Monq thinks maybe twenty-three. He did tests on skin elasticity and bone density. That's his best guess."

Storm smiled, his eyes sweeping over her features again, drinking her in. "Looks good on you."

"There's a gang of people who might as well be wearing black arm bands," she laughed. "Everybody has been so scared you were lost forever and nobody wanted to even think it or say it out loud. They'll be dying to see you."

"They can wait. I need to see your mother first."

"I need something to tie you to me."

"We'll find something. I need to take care of one thing before we leave anyhow."

On the way to Halcyon, he told her about his job at the bar.

When Storm didn't get Hal, he left a message saying, "It's Storm. I've got to go. I'm leaving the keys and the story I owe you. I wrote it out. And this phone. Give the clothes to charity, I guess. I, ah, don't know how I would have gotten through this if… Just wanted to say thank you for everything." He stopped and cleared his throat. "Anyway. Thanks. Oh. And, if four guys show up sometime asking for me…" He raised his eyes to meet Rosie's, "…just tell them I made it home and put their drinks on my tab."

Storm knew exactly which cupboard held the duct tape. He hesitated before he put it on Rosie's skin. "I don't want to hurt you, but I don't want to get lost again either."

She laughed. "I don't care."

When their wrists were locked together to his satisfaction, he picked up the bag that held the necklace and its case and wound a length of tape around that, too.

"What's that?" she asked.

He grinned. "Present for my wife."

"Shhhh.," she said smiling. "Not so loud. I'm sure that'll break some Council rule of another to transport goods across dimensional lines."

"I'm in a mood for rule-breaking."

"Yes, sir."

When Hal opened up that evening, he wasn't surprised to find a phone, a set of keys, and a letter. He was surprised to find a little over three hundred dollars that hadn't been mentioned on the phone message. The bar and apartment were both locked up tight with the keys left inside. He wasn't entirely surprised, but couldn't wait to sit down and read the letter.

Three nights later four guys came in right before closing. They stopped just inside the door, looked around, and their eyes came to rest on Hal behind the bar. They were all late twenties or early thirties with a physical presence that reminded Hal of Storm. He wasn't at all surprised when they walked up and asked for his former employee.

Hall said nothing. He went about silently setting out five shot glasses, one at a time. Then he reached up high for the top shelf Scotch. He filled each one of the glasses, set the bottle on the bar, and said, "He told me to offer you a drink and say he made it home."

The four glanced at each other and at Hal. Each took a glass, then Brandeskin said, "There's no place like home."

The other four grinned and clinked glasses, repeating, "No place like home." Then they drank to the salute. And to their extra-dimensional Black Swan brother.

After neutralizing all elevator operations in the building, Fennimore and Angel had sealed the entrance to S3 at the east end stairwell. Their plan was to make their way to the other end of the floor and repeat destruction of the opposite passage at the west end stairs, once they were safely above at S2. Then they were planning to double back and blow the central stair unit from above.

When Z Team heard the explosion on Sublevel 3, they raced toward it assuming that it was related to the cause of alarm. Either they hadn't heard Elora's warning that charges were going to be set or they forgot. They encountered no resistance between the Hub central stairwell and S1 so they proceeded to Sublevel 2.

At the west end of S3 Angel and Fennimore were preparing to be out of the way when the popper hit the stairs, which they would do from the other side of the landing above after climbing to the next level. So occupied, they were never seen by Z team who had just arrived on S2 and vice versa.

In a comedy of coincidence that had the Fates laughing their asses off, another group of alien visitors dropped in without calling first and appeared in the central hallway of S1 at the same time. It seemed that, on the other side of the Atlantic, the French vampire contingent was running low on vaccine. Thinking the kids could handle what should have been a simple ten minute errand on their own, they sent the four teen immortals to pick up a fresh supply for their night's work.

The vamps had just popped into the Central hallway of S2 as Z Team reached that level. On first look, naturally they assumed the boys were trainees who were in the wrong place. The fact that the four teens showed no sign of either hostility or fear, in the face of Z Team on alert with weapons drawn and aimed, certainly supported that conclusion.

Torn lowered his weapon. "You lads were told to get to cover and stay out of the way. You could have been killed. Are you gettin' that?"

Javier just shrugged and grinned. That was when Z Team was clued in that they were definitely not looking at trainees who'd lost their way.

One look at those exquisite long sharp fangs, so beautifully white they could have been veneered, and Glyphs pulled the stake out of his boot. He hadn't thought he'd encounter vampire when he got dressed for the day, but old habits die hard.

He lunged for Javier, who was not expecting an attack and made no move to get out of the way, which meant he ended up with a stake sticking out of his chest. Again.

Javier looked down at the stake and then scowled at Glyphs, saying, "Pas ça encore! Qu'est ce qui ne va pas avec ces gens la!"

The veteran hunters of Z Team were so shocked to get that reaction from a vampire that they froze in uncertainty, until Glyphs leaned into Gunnar and asked, "What did he say?"

Pierre, having overheard the question since he was two feet away answered. "He said, 'Not this again! What is wrong with you people?'"

The humans watched in stunned silence as Javier pulled the stake from his chest, threw it aside and proceeded to pet the hole in his shantung shirt like it might somehow repair itself. Having recovered from the initial novelty of a vamp not being fazed by a staking, the knights of Z Team switched to Plan B and started to raise the weapons. Since the immortals were no longer trusting of the new humans they hadn't encountered before, they disarmed them in an invisible flurry that left the hunters wondering what had happened.

Pierre said, "These people are too dangerous to clothing to be allowed to roam free. Look at them. They are ruffians with no understanding of fashion, much less haute couture. They should be confined."

"Agreed. What should we do with them?"

"There's a thing on the lowest place. A cage."

Each of the four vampire took charge of one member of Z Company who were, of course, no match for the strength of pure vampire immortals. Five minutes later, the Zed Knights found themselves deposited within the chain link enclosure that had been Blackie's kennel once upon an unpleasant time. Because the kennel was six feet tall, none of them could stand up straight. Since no lock was handy, one of the vampire just bent the gate latch so that it couldn't be opened, at least not by humans.

The vampire popped straight from S3 into Monq's lab where the stores were kept.

"No one is here."

"Should we leave a note?"

"Jean-Etienne told us to get vaccine, not write letters."

"Yes. You are right."

They took enough vaccine to last a month and popped out just before detonation of the west end stairs sent a rumble through the building.

      Throughout Jefferson Unit, everyone, friend or foe, went statue still when the intercom came on loud and clear.

      "Testing. Testing. Special announcement. Repeat. We have a special announcement." Elora looked at her watch. *Good on you, Spaz. Right on time.* "Elora Laiken would like to invite all our uninvited guests to join her on Sublevel 3. For those of you who are new to Jefferson Unit and unfamiliar with the layout of the building, that would be the lowest level."

      Elora turned to her self-proclaimed shadows. "Is he always this talkative?" Kris and Wakey both shook their heads and said no. "Some people just can't handle a microphone. Goes to their heads."

      Spaz continued. "I repeat, join Elora Laiken on the lowest level of the building, that's Sublevel 3. Once again, new arrivals, there'll be a mixer in a few on the lowest level."

      Spaz clicked off the mic and looked around. He'd never been in that part of media before. It was so well disguised, he hadn't even known it was there. Kind of looked like a broom closet from the outside.

      On the inside though, there was an entire wall of dormant monitors, six rows of seven each, all black screens silently waiting like sentries. On a whim, because fiddling with mechanical or technological things to see what will happen was a universal gender trait, he flipped a few control board switches marked as cameras.

Apparently surveillance equipment had been installed in the public areas of the building, probably as some sort of standard security procedure or precaution. The cameras weren't turned on and were obviously not monitored because there was no need, but they came online right away when he started flipping switches.

It was a spy's wet dream. He stood there grinning at the surveillance wall with eyes alight, knowing how he could be helpful.

He started by dragging everything he could fit into the room with him, then locked the door and started building a barricade. He was thin, not filled out yet by a long shot, but like all potential Black Swan hunters, he worked out like a demon and was strong. The completely nondescript look of the space from the other side of the door could be useful. No one would guess there was a high tech security operation within, but if they did, they'd have to work at getting inside.

When he was finished he turned to sweep his gaze over the rows of monitors and grabbed the microphone. "Kris. Wakey. E.T.'s around the next corner. Duck into Havvy's."

Havvy's was what J.U. residents called the coffee stop at the Hub because a woman named Havila had been running it for longer than anyone could remember. If Spaz had said, "coffee", he might have tipped the hostiles off, but they would have no way of knowing what or where Havvy's might be.

The two boys had gotten a little ahead of Elora, thinking they would protect her by drawing fire first. Not needing to be told twice, they ducked behind the coffee counter thinking Elora was right behind them. Clearly, they didn't know her very well.

She continued past coffee, where the boys had wisely taken cover, to the next corner and plastered herself against the wall to wait. One of the things about searching with long barrel weapons was that it meant the bearer was always preceded by the gun he was carrying. Elora quietly slipped her own pistol into its holster and waited, hoping she could pick off a couple without making a fuss that would bring more.

When the end of the gun came into view, she grabbed and jerked. Because of the element of surprise, it loosened in his hand enough for her to send it back into his nose with as much force as her equalized strength could muster. Elora had never thought of herself as a bloodthirsty person, quite the opposite. But hearing that crunch, seeing blood spurt like a fountain, and hearing the large man mewl as he grabbed for his face with both hands? It was satisfying.

She had no time to enjoy that little piece of victory because his partner rushed her. She was too close to the Ralengclan for his buddy to fire, so he used the butt of his own gun and smashed her in the face. He missed her nose, but hit her cheek bone. She hadn't felt a jar like that since she'd arrived in Loti Dimension. While she processed the pain, she thought about the advantages of denser bones and promised herself she'd count her blessings every day if she lived through the night.

While she was getting her bearings, broken nose stumbled backward a couple of steps which allowed his partner to bring his weapon around to fire at her like he was twirling a baton. She reached for her holster to pull the pistol and counter, but knew she wasn't going to be fast enough with her slowed reaction time.

She heard two pops, but was still too disoriented to know they were coming from behind her. The Ralengclan who was aiming at her jerked his trigger finger and fired uncontrollably when one shot hit him in the forehead and another in the groin, almost simultaneously.

Elora yelled out as one of the alien's stray bullets tore past the fleshy part of her left shoulder and knocked her back on her rear end. The jolt from the pain when she hit the floor caused her to gasp, which was the only reason she didn't scream. The good news was that, when she went down, it gave Kris a shot at the alien who had recovered from the initial shock of a broken nose and was then picking up the weapon that had been taken from him.

As he started to swing toward Elora, Kris put a bullet in his temple and dropped him on the spot.

Elora looked up at Kris and said, "See. I told you practice makes perfect."

And, with that, Wakey began to retch loudly. She knew that teenage boys ate a lot, but as she and Kris watched in horror, it looked like Wakey was vomiting everything he'd eaten for the last three weeks onto the high polish of the Hub floor.

Spaz's voice came through the intercom system loud and clear.

"E.T's at the middle ladder and the track gate. Watch out for a trio of civvies south of med. AND!

Major cleanup needed right away on Aisle Three."

Kris reached over like he was going to take a look at Elora's shoulder, but she stopped him. "Get away from that. We don't have time to play doctor."

He dropped his hands. "Yes ma'am."

Wakey got off his knees and half-staggered toward the coffee counter still looking three shades past puke green.

He flopped down and groaned. Kris nodded then turned to Wakey. "Gah, man. Do not breathe in this direction. You reek."

"Leave him alone," Elora said. "He's never killed anybody before."

"Neither have I," countered Kris.

"Yeah, well, we're all different. There's a place for heart in knighthood."

Wakey looked at her with gratitude.

"I'm gathering that Spaz has found cameras and is feeding us information." She winced when she moved her shoulder.

"When this is over, I'm going to give that kid a medal. Trying to decipher his makeshift code-on-the-go, I think he just said we've got aliens at the central stairwell and the exit to the rugby field and three non-combat personnel close to the clinic. If I've counted the number of explosions correctly, S3 is sealed off, but we don't know how many aliens are unaccounted for. I need that count.

"Let's get to a camera and see if you can get that across to him." They nodded. "Wakey, when we clear cover, you look left toward the Courtpark exit. Kris, look right toward center stairs. Moving toward Farnsworth's office on three." She looked at Kris.

"Count it down."

He and Wakey pulled their weapons and got ready. "One. Two. Three."

From where they were it looked clear to cut across the Hub to reach the short hall to Farnsworth's office, but they couldn't be sure until they were out in the open and then it might be too late. On Kris's count of three, they jumped out, adrenaline pumping.

There was no question in Elora's mind that her job was to insure those kids made it to the other side. It was a toss-up as to whether that was going to be accomplished best by going first or hanging back. She chose bringing up the rear.

Her right eye was almost swollen shut from the gun butting that crunched her cheek. That was especially unfortunate because she was a one-eyed shooter and, as luck would have it, her dominant eye was the right one. That luck was balanced with a little victory when they made it to Operations without engaging. Hearts were racing, lungs working like bellows, but they were safe for the moment.

Once there, they located the camera, and Wakey started miming the need to know how many assassins were still out there.

Spaz's voice was so strong and upbeat that no one would ever guess he was announcing a life and death battle with pithy commentary. Even though his attitude might be disturbing, he was proving to be smart and resourceful.

"Attention shoppers! Special sale in the bakery department. One dozen to-die-for doughnuts with cream fillings left and they're going fast. Come and get 'em.

"Storm and Fennimore, dos E.T's coming your way from the throne room."

Elora deduced that "throne room" could either mean the toilet or The Chamber. If it was The Chamber, then Fenn and Angel were on the same level she was. If it was the john, it could be anywhere.

Three seconds later, Elora and the two boys heard the sound of gunfire coming from the level below.

"Cat Man and Borzy, hold tight, keep low, ducks in a barrel when I say go."

Elora was writing out a sign to hold up to the camera, when Spaz said, "GO!"

She stopped dead still when she again heard weapons firing toward the west part of the building. She looked up at the camera anxiously for word. That trainee was her only link to news. When all was quiet, Spaz came back on the intercom.

"All quiet on the Western end, nine, ten, a big fat hen. Repeat, nine, *ten*, big fat hen, and all is well in the west thanks to our sponsor, Helmets by Mom. Now this for your listening pleasure from the Spazmodoc..."

Elora's eyes got wide when the intercom started blasting Wang Chung "Dance Hall Days". She turned to Kris and Wakey showing clenched teeth, which hurt with a broken cheek bone, but she couldn't help herself. Elora's Medusa face was frightening and she looked like she was ready to kill somebody, other than Ralengclan that is. She couldn't get her jaw to relax to ask a question.

"What. Is. That?"

Kris took a reflexive step back, but spoke up.

"Ah, Sir Caelian, ma'am. He didn't like the music we were playing in our rec room. So he gave us a mandatory attendance lecture on disco every night when he was here."

"Unbelievable!" Elora closed her eyes for a second

"A lot of the younger kids think it's cool. I think it's stupid," added Wakey.

She smirked. "You tell Kay that?"

Wakey ducked his head and smiled boyishly. "No ma'am."

There was an interruption in the music long enough for Spaz to say, "Link and Shay, patsies on the way. Analog four and find two more."

The song started again with, *Take your baby by the ears...*

Elora glared up at the camera before she went back to her sign, muttering, "After I give him a medal, I'm going to beat him to death with it." As an afterthought, she added, "Then I'm gonna chain Kay to a chair and psyops him with Screamo until tears run down his face." Much as she loved Kay, at that moment, the image of him crying and begging for mercy made her smile, even though it hurt her face to do it.

Link and Shay were in the kitchen. They'd seen aliens in the hall outside the Mess, but more importantly, the aliens saw them. The two boys ran through the Mess and into the kitchen which was formed by a chain of food preparation rooms.

The boys heard a few pings as they ran, bullets making contact with the stainless steel environment. Looking around, trying to decide whether to hide in cabinets or shoot it out, Link spied the freezer and had an idea.

He left Shay wondering what he was doing while he set his intelliphone on a back shelf and left it playing a wetube panel discussion on gaming. Communication was jammed, but that was a recording so its operation didn't depend on anything external. Since Spaz was playing intercom music to die by, Link had to turn the volume up to max so that it could be heard. That turned out to be beneficial. Without the music, the recording would have been recognized as exactly that, but mixed with the intercom feed, there was some doubt as to whether the voices on the recording were, well, recorded or live.

Link motioned to Shay to leave the door standing open and hide underneath one of the long cooking tables where they could see the freezer. The bottom shelf on the cooking tables was so close to the ground that only a skinny kid could get under. It was such a tight fit they had to squeeze in and lay flat on their backs, but no one was likely to suspect it as a hiding place.

Just seconds after they were in place, the aliens came through the swing door, which was kind of funny, but since Spaz was the only one to see it, he was the only one to get a laugh out of it. The first guy pushed through, but then couldn't decide whether to let the door swing back and hit the next guy or shift his heavy assault shooter to one hand so he could hold the door.

When both Ralengclan were through the door,

the first guy held up his hand and cocked his head like he was listening. He motioned toward the freezer. They both looked around and advanced on the freezer with stealth. From their vantage point, the kids could see boots and that was about it, but they could see where the boots were going. Shay looked at Link and smiled. Link looked like a cat with feathers on his chin.

It would be impossible to say if the boys moved soundlessly, but with Spaz playing Disco Deejay, the aliens never heard them before the freezer door closed and sealed them in.

There was another interruption in the music as Spaz whooped. "Link and Shay save the day. Two on ice! Sticks are nice! Calling Mother, lay them straight. That's right. Seven. *Eight.*"

The song picked up with, *And take your baby by the hair...*

Elora showed teeth to the camera and held up her sign. "Say I'm outside. In forest."

The intercom answered immediately. "No go, Mother. NO GO! Hazard route. Chill in place. Calling Sirs Storm and Fenniplus, Mother is pinned at dragon's lair."

Angel looked at Fennimore. "Dragon's lair?"

"I think that's what the kids call the Operations Office. Farnsworth can be fearsome."

Angel nodded like he knew who Farnsworth was. And like he knew where the Operations Office was. "And Mother?"

A little frown formed in the center of Fennimore's brow as he shrugged. "Could be code for Elora? Maybe? She teaches the kids. Might be an inside joke."

The sounds of "Dance Hall Days" ended. Angel blew out a relieved breath and said, "Thank all the gods and their offspring."

Spaz's cheerful voice came over the intercom. "It's the Spazmodoc, The Voice of the Fray, bringing you news of the shit storm from the bowels of J.U. Doing eighties on eight at eight minutes after the hour. Stay tuned right here to channel *eight*."

That announcement was immediately followed by the BeeGees "Stayin' Alive."

Angel turned to Fennimore. "Am I the only one who wants to murder that kid?"

"No, brother. I'm guessing by now you're at the end of a long line. Us *and* them."

Angel nodded. "So let's go get Mother."

Fennimore snickered. "Call her that to her face and see what happens. I dare you."

Angel grinned then started toward the library door. He reached for the handle to open it then stopped. His eyes scanned the corners till he found a camera. On the off chance that idiot kid could see them, he got in front of the camera and made motions toward the door.

Within a second, the music stopped. "Temporary clearing outside Squintsville. Partly cloudy in other parts of the state. Clouds returning, moving slowly, south to north. Heavy rain close to Mother."

Angel nodded at the camera and the music started again.

Whether you're a brother or whether you're a mother, you're stayin' alive, stayin' alive.

The knights opened the library door and stepped out into the west wing hall, Level 1. The way was open until they reached the bend where they drew fire from aliens under cover somewhere on the other side of the Hub.

The music stopped. "If you're looking for Elora Laiken she's headed to the great out of doors. She was last seen entering the central court forest through the south exit. Dudes in black who are not supposed to be here. Again, this message is for dudes in black who are not supposed to be here. Elora has left the building. I say Elora has left the building. Annnnnnnd…"

It's all right. It's ok. I'll live to see another day.

The gunshots ceased while Ralengclan looked at each other trying to decide what to do. The commander hadn't been seen for nearly two hours. Neither had anyone spotted the second in command. Without someone in authority to take responsibility, there was confusion about how to proceed. As is usually the case when people can't decide what to do, the Ralengclan did nothing, which meant that a brief period of silence ensued.

Elora looked at her bodyguards. "They're trying to sort out the best course of action, but they'll feel compelled to check it out. They have to. I'm betting at least two of them are going to head for the Hub exit to the Courtpark next to the Solarium. If I can get to the lounge first, I'll have cover and a view to that exit. I can pick them off from there." She started to rise from a squat, but she was lightheaded from blood loss. She swayed and had to grab onto a countertop to stay upright.

"You stay. We'll go." Kris was giving Elora a look that was so intense it almost reminded her of Storm.

"No. I'm good."

Kris lifted both eyebrows. "You're good? You know that arm that you need to hold your Cuefire up with? It's streaming blood everywhere. You don't have full use of that arm, you're getting weak, and you can only see out of one eye. You're not good. You're a mess."

He didn't know the half of it. All that, combined with the fact that the Equalizer gas made her feel like every step was a drag through water, meant she was both hurt and exhausted.

"Maybe, but I'm still your commanding officer, Falcon. I go. You stay."

He crossed his arms in front of his chest. "Wakey. Sit on her."

"No need," Wakey said. "She's too weak to stop us. And we both need to go." He turned to Elora. "No disrespect, ma'am, but he's right. You need to stay put."

The Hub erupted in rapid round gunfire. Elora guessed somebody was laying down cover for a couple of Ralengclan to get to the Solarium exit.

"Wakey. Don't go out there. It's too late. We already missed the chance."

He smiled. "Don't worry so much."

When the BeeGees stopped, Spaz's voice came right on. "Welcome back to the sounds of invasion with The Voice of the Fray coming at you with New Kids on the Block and "Hangin' Tough.""

Elora was braced with her weight on bent knees and her back against Farnsworth's supply cabinets. As the boys ducked out, she slowly slid down to the floor, unable to do much else, and Monq's words came back to her. "You wouldn't retain superior strength and speed, but others from your home world wouldn't have any advantage over those who come to your aid. There will always be people here to guard you. Capable people."

Elora wasn't very good at holding back tears when she experienced high emotion, which was often, and she usually didn't try. When the first drop started down her cheek, she swiped at it in disgust then winced because of the touch to her swollen face. Her cheek was sticking out further than it was supposed to be.

She was scared for those kids who had so much blinding bright potential. They might have been 'capable', but they shouldn't be forced to prove it at their age. She couldn't even face the possibility that they might die before they had a chance to live. Especially not for her.

Don't worry 'bout nothing, 'cause it won't take long... put you in a trance with a funky song.

She let her head fall back and hit the cabinet she was leaning against, which resulted in another jolt and another wince. "Fuck me." There was nothing in the universe worse than feeling helpless. She sat for a moment pondering that and then amended. *There's nothing in the universe worse than feeling helpless unless it's being forced to listen to this song.*

The President cleared the Oval Office before he picked up the phone when he heard who was calling.

"This is the President."

"Mr. President. It's about Jefferson Unit. I know there's a standing order of autonomy where that building is concerned, but it sounds like there's a battle taking place in there. Reports of explosions and live fire, ongoing for over two hours. What should we do?"

"Colonel. Under no circumstances will you allow the perimeter of that building to be contaminated. If something must be said to assuage the curiosity of your staff, tell them that Jefferson is conducting secret research tests with live arms and that no one is to interfere in any way. Are we clear?"

"We are, sir. Sorry to bother you needlessly."

When Storm came to rest in his own kitchen, he looked around and his breath hitched. His throat swelled with so much emotion that speech was impossible. He didn't try to talk, just went to work concentrating on separating himself and Rosie from the duct tape. By the time that job was finished he was breathing normally and had command of his voice.

He reached up and ran a hand over his daughter's head. "Rosie, I want us both to take some time so I can get to know you."

"And teach me how to ride a bike."

"What?"

"I don't know how to ride a bike. I've been waiting for you to come home."

He stared for a minute then had to look down and blink a few times to process that. "I'd like that a lot. Whenever you say. I'm buying you the best cruiser we can find. But right now, I wonder if you could give me a little time alone with your mom?"

She grinned and he thought joy was a very good look for her, but it rapidly dissolved to a look that was much more serious. "It's so good to have you here. I can't wait to see mom smile again. She's sleeping. She was up all night looking for you. Again.

"I'll be back tomorrow." And she vanished.

Rosie was smiling as she grabbed a pass to her first errand stop. Her mind was full of the happy ending she'd been afraid her parents were never going to get. She thought that, if ever there was cause for celebration, this would be the time. And, in her euphoria, she forgot to mention her dad's doppelganger, who'd been living at the vineyard for weeks.

After he was left alone in the house, Storm turned down the hallway toward the master bedroom. The shutters were closed, but he could see the shape of Litha's form under the covers, sleeping on her side of the bed which meant his side was vacant and waiting for him like the most delicious invitation.

Quietly, he slipped out of all his clothes and let them drop on the floor in a pile. The anticipation of pulling her warm, soft body into him and feeling her go pliant against him was almost more than he could stand. He pulled the covers back and crawled under. It smelled like her, rainstorms and magick. In other words, it was heavenly.

He snuggled against her back and whispered into her hair right next to her ear. "Litha. Baby."

Litha woke slowly, aware that something was off. She must have been dreaming about Storm because she almost thought she heard his voice and could smell his musk, not to mention feeling the beautiful hardness of his body pressed close to hers. When Storm's hand trailed down her side, her lungs involuntarily gasped in a deep breath. She came instantly and fully awake, whether she wanted to be or not.

That's when she realized that the warm body in bed with her was not a figment of her imagination or a subconscious recreation. She rolled toward the unwanted visitor with a growl and left a full handprint burn on his chest before she jerked away and scrambled out of bed.

Storm yelled. "Ow. Litha, what the…? Ow. You burned me!"

Storm jumped out of bed, gaping at his wife who stood on her side with her arms wrapped around her, seething and looking at him like she was thinking about turning him into a column of smoke.

"What did you expect? Get the hell out of my room. Put some frigging clothes on and get out of my room. How dare you touch me!"

"Some homecoming." He looked bewildered. "I need ice."

As he started for the kitchen, Litha's eyes wandered over his body and, even in the dimmed

GATHERING STORM

light, she could see there was nothing but smooth
skin. No ink. The only mark on his flawless hide was
the handprint she'd just left there like a red brand of
fury.

"Storm?"

She seemed to be asking the question like she
wasn't sure, which was beyond strange.

"Waking Woden, Litha. Who else?"

He wondered why Rosie hadn't warned him
that Litha had jumped the track while he was gone.
Her face looked as shocked as if he was a ghost.
Then, when she ran at him, he stepped out of the way,
not wanting to be burned again.

"Oh, no you don't. Once was enough." He
caught her, turned her around with her back to him
and captured both wrists in front of her. "You want to
tell me what's going on?"

She was sobbing and squirming, trying to
break free. "Let me go. I need to hold you."

"*Now* you want to hold me?"

"Please. I didn't know it was you."

"You didn't know it was me," he repeated
dryly.

"Let me go so I can do something about the
burn."

"If I let you go, are you going to set me on
fire?"

"I'm not going to set you on fire. I am going
to make you *so* glad you're home."

The second he loosened his hold, she turned in
his arms and gave him a kiss so sweet and slow and
deep that it exceeded what he'd been dreaming about.
It almost made him forget about the pain of the

scorching she gave him.

"That's more like it," he breathed.

She put enough room in between them so that she could press her hand over the imprint her burn had left. Then she simply wished it away. When she lifted her hand, it was gone. He had to look twice and rub his hand over where it had been before he could fully accept what he'd seen.

"You can heal?"

"No. Well, not generically. It's because I burned you. I can sort of take it back."

"Oh." He passed his hand over the healed skin again. "Thank you."

"Welcome home," she said softly with both love and warmth in her eyes.

"I'm lost, Litha. What just happened?"

"How did you get here?"

"Rosie. And, by the way. Wow"

"Yeah." Litha laughed softly. "Wow."

"She brought me home. I told her I needed some time alone with you before I teach her how to ride a bike."

"She didn't tell you anything about our house guest?"

Storm's sharp black eyes narrowed and slammed into focus with laser intensity as suspicions started to take form. He lowered his chin and rumbled, "What house guest?"

The hungry way her eyes moved over his face made him feel every bit of how much she'd missed him and ached to find him. She gave her bottom lip a suggestive lick and said, "If you come back to bed, I'll tell you the whole story. I need to feel you close."

His face softened, but his voice still sounded gruff. "Close, huh? I can go along with that. There's plenty of time for talking later. Now that I'm back home, I'm not going anywhere again." She watched his eyes darken as he reached for her nightshirt. "Let's get you out of this."

Rosie was eager to tell Glen and Elora the good news and maybe spend the night with Glen, but first, she decided to stop at the flower market. She wanted the house to look and smell like a celebration. So she took her time picking out flowers and scheduling them for delivery the next morning. She then went to the bakery and spent an hour looking through the book of cakes. When she realized that she was morphing into a raging perfectionist, she chose one and arranged to pick it up the next morning.

She asked if she could use the restroom so that she could disappear from there without a fuss.

Glen had never been so conflicted or agitated in his life. He was stuck guarding a locked door in research, hearing sounds of explosions and gunfire every now and then over Spaz and his funky shit playlist. Other than bizarre intercom announcements, he didn't know what was going on and couldn't leave to go find out because of what was behind him in that locked room. Namely the smartest man on the planet – probably - the younger trainees, and, most importantly, an elfling that meant the world to Ram and Elora. And Ram and Elora meant the world to Glen. He wouldn't want to try to survive witnessing their suffering if anything ever happened to that baby.

So there he was. He and Bo, standing with their backs against the entrance to Fire Testing, weapons at hand. Glen had convinced the younger boys to get inside by explaining that they would be the last line of defense for Elora's baby and the civilians. Thank the gods for one less worry.

Thinking about Glen, Rosie expected to come out of the passes in his quarters. Instead she was deposited on Sublevel 2 outside a closed door with an armed guard, weapons drawn. What was even more confusing was that one of those guards was a very anxious-looking Glen. The other was his soft spoken easygoing, intellectual assistant.

"Glen. What…?"

He rushed forward. "Rosie. Not a good time."

"Not a good time for what? I came to tell you we found my dad. He's… he's home."

"Wow, baby, that's great, probably the best thing I've ever heard." Glen's words were rushed. "Now go get him and bring him here as fast as you can."

The floor underneath their feet shook from the shock of another detonation and she thought she heard occasional gunshots over the weird music, which stopped. Thank the gods.

"Give it up for new kids on the block, Kris and Wakey, hangin' tough, at pick up sticks. That's five, *six*, pick up sticks. Mother will be proud. And, on that note, Spazmodoc, The Voice of the Fray, leaves the eighties behind to bring you a gooooooolden oldie. This is Three Dogs at Night for you, Mother."

Rosie just stood there in freeze frame staring at Glen.

"Glen. What is going on?"

"Rosie, go get Storm. Now."

Her head jerked in the direction of distant shouts and more shooting. She looked back at Glen. When her brows came together and her mouth set with determination, she looked so much like Storm.

"No. What are you...? No. He just got home. I shouldn't be bringing him here. I should be taking *you* away."

She started toward Glen and he threw a hand up to stop her. "Stop! Elora Rose! You're not thinking clearly. I can't leave here. This is my job."

"But you..."

"We need your dad, baby. I wouldn't ask if we didn't. If something happens to your auntie or Helm, or any of us, and you didn't give him a chance to help, he'll never get over it. Please. Go get him."

"He just got home," she whispered. Glen couldn't hear what she said, but he could read her beautiful bow mouth. At the moment she looked like the little girl he remembered. Only he'd never seen her look lost or uncertain.

"I know he just got home, but this is part of home for him. Rosie, please. You've got to understand. Your dad's a Black Swan knight. No. He's *THE* Black Swan knight. Lots of people here need him. That includes me. And your auntie. Please. Let him do what he does."

Glen saw Rosie's face transform. He didn't know what she was up to, but it was something. "I'll get him. But I'll be back, too."

"Rosie. Wait…" She hesitated. "Helm is in this room behind me. Will you please take him to Litha where he'll be safe?"

She rushed forward and gave Glen a breathless kiss while a wide-eyed Barrock looked on. She pulled back and looked at Barrock. "Take off your shirt."

Glen couldn't have been more astonished. "What?"

"You heard me. I need his shirt. It's a button up and I need a way to secure Helm to me."

"Oh." Glen nodded at Bo, who handed over his gun long enough to take off his shirt and give it to Rosie.

She grabbed it. And was gone.

Elora let out a breath she'd been partially holding once she knew that Kris and Wakey were okay. She looked at her watch. An hour and a half until the gas wore off and, if she was understanding Spaz's cipher, there were six Ralengclan left.

She didn't know the song the little shit was playing, but she didn't like it any more than she liked all the other stupid mother references.

Mama told me not to come. Mama told me not to come. That ain't the way to have fun, son.

Rosie arrived at the vineyard, after having promised her dad to give them some alone time. She walked out of a pass into the hallway outside her own room and heard the low tones of quiet talk in the kitchen. When she was just outside the kitchen door she got a glimpse of them. Her dad was shirtless, wearing a pair of sweat pants. Her mother was in her Japanese silk robe, sitting on his lap and snuggled into his chest looking safe and happy with strong arms around her. She was also clutching a black velvet box.

Rosie knew there was no time to delay, but the idea of interrupting that scene was breaking her heart.

"Did I ever tell you about the first time I saw you?" Litha asked.

"No." He kissed the hair swept back from her temple.

"I was standing on the mezzanine overlooking the grand foyer when you arrived with the entourage."

He chuckled. "The entourage?"

"You know what I mean. Ram, Elora, Kay, Aelsong, Everybody was out of their offices whispering that the great B Team from Jefferson Unit was in the house. You were looking all around like you were sizing up the place, or maybe marking the escape routes. I don't know. Anyway, your eyes drifted right over me like I was invisible. But you weren't invisible to me. I took one look and said, 'I can't live without that.'"

Storm's voice was gentle, filled with love and warmth. "You never told me that."

Rosie flicked at a tear that tried to escape unnoticed. She was thinking about how to let them know she was there when Helm settled the matter by blowing a nice noisy raspberry.

"Don't want to startle you." She stepped forward into the kitchen and looked right at Storm. "I know I promised to give you time, but it's an emergency. Glen made me come. Jefferson Unit is, um, under attack."

Storm set Litha on her feet and was already moving toward the bedroom to get dressed. Litha moved forward to help get Helm out of Bo's shirt. Rosie had put it on herself, held Helm next to her body, and gotten Monq to button them in.

It was a really good thought on Glen's part. The vineyard was an ideal place to bring the baby. It had diapers his size and food appropriate for his development level on hand.

"Who would be attacking Jefferson?" Storm demanded.

"Some men are after auntie."

As Litha took Helm and set him on a cocked hip, she looked at Storm, shook her head, and muttered, "Of course."

As soon as Storm was dressed he started firing other questions at Rosie.

"Why didn't Glen call me?"

"I don't know."

"Okay. Just take me to Glen. Drop me off and get out."

"I'm staying."

"No you're not! You can't be there, Rosie. I know your heart's in the right place, but if I'm worried about you, I'll get myself killed." She hesitated. "Promise me."

"Promise."

He wrapped duct tape around Rosie's waist,

looped it over his wrist. He looked at Litha as he took a death grip on the end just above where he tore the tape off. "I *will* be back."

She nodded, trying not to have him see that she was too choked with emotion to do anything else. Helm had leaned out and was studying her face with a little frown. When she saw it, she gave him a reassuring little smile, kissed his chubby cheeks and asked him how he felt about strained peas.

A couple of minutes later Storm and Rosie were standing in front of the door to Fire Testing. They had just arrived when a rumbling vibration shook the whole building and threatened their footing. The weird music that was blaring through the intercom was just ending.

Storm looked at Glen. "What the f…?"

He was cut off by an announcement from Spaz. "E.T.s controlling central ladder. Repeat E.T.s controlling central ladder. And the Spazmodoc is bumpin' the time machine from Early Proterozoic as The Voice of the Fray brings you Scary Kids Scaring Kids and "Losing My Religion".

When the intercom base restarted its own brand of rumble, Storm's brows pulled almost together. He looked at Glen like it was his fault and spoke as quietly as he could and still be heard over the screamo.

"Briefest possible version of the brief. First, why are you standing in this hall?"

"Monq and some civvies are inside. And some

of the younger kids. Looks like the same guys back to finish the job on Elora. We think she's pinned down in Operations. Possibly with two of the trainees."

He turned to Rosie. "Can you take me to Operations?" She nodded. "Stay behind me. The second I'm there, you're gone. Agreed?" She nodded.

Elora looked at her watch. Less than an hour until the gas wore off. Six of them to go. Six male versions of her with her enhanced abilities would be enough to raze all of Fort Dixon to the ground. She knew she couldn't let it go any further. She was what they came for and she was pretty sure that, if they killed or captured her, they'd be satisfied and leave.

She couldn't walk but she could probably crawl. All she had to do was get out the door into the Hub. She'd be in the open, helpless, easy pickings. She was moving to drop down when she heard a rustle behind her. She turned her head to see Storm sliding in next to where she sat.

The last thing she needed right then was a fake version of Storm to take care of. When she opened her mouth to tell him so, she looked him in the face and something in his eyes made her freeze.

Storm.

He reached up to touch the swelling around the cut on her cheek. "You know you're not supposed to get in trouble without me."

Big tears immediately started sliding through the grime on her face. "Is that a rule?"

"Hard and fast."

"Yeah? Well, you're not supposed to get lost in space either." She reached up to swipe at the rivulets. "Glad you're back."

"Me, too. Where's Ram?"

"Ireland."

Storm's eyes widened at that. "Ireland."

"Yep. The mum's big deal birthday."

"Great Paddy."

"Exactly."

"Okay, let's see where all this blood is coming from?" He started to rip her shirt from the shoulder, but she stopped him with a hand on top of his.

"Not serious. Leave it alone."

He decided to capitulate for the moment. "Who've we got?"

"Glen, Fennimore, Z Team, and my kids."

"Trainees?"

"They've been astounding. Some of them should get medals."

He nodded. "Z Team?"

"Who knows? Haven't seen or heard them for hours. You were right about them. They didn't want to work with any of us or listen to what we had to say. So they're off on their own and I can't begin to tell if they're helping or..."

Storm let out a string of curses. "Sounds *exactly* like them." He looked back at Elora. "So, where were you off to when I came in?"

She studied his face. "You know who they are?"

Victoria Danann

His face didn't move at all except that his mouth tightened. "The same fuckers from the woods."

She smiled and winced. "Well, not the *same* ones. Obviously. But yeah.

"Here's the thing. Monq developed this gas. He calls it the Equalizer. Installed alarms all over J.U. that disperse the chemical."

Storm looked puzzled. "What's it supposed to do?"

"What it *does* is makes them the same as you. For three hours and seventeen minutes."

Realization flickered over his face and his eyes ran over her body. "That means you, too." She nodded. "How long do we have left?"

"Less than an hour. We're almost out of time. I…"

The intercom cut her off. "Knights under fire, center ladder going up, between Hub and two. Kris and Wakey, E.T.s behind the spurt."

Storm looked at Elora. "Can you interpret that?"

"I think so. We've got people taking fire in the central stairwell between here and the second floor. Two of my trainees are approaching the fountain with trouble hiding behind it."

"Okay." He reached over and withdrew her pistol from her holster." Let's see what you've got for me." When he saw it was the snub nose, he said, "I was hoping you brought a real gun." He said that last as he was moving to the door. "Stay where you are or you'll answer to the acting Sovereign. Understand?"

He didn't wait for an answer. He plastered himself to the wall that curved around the Hub and began moving toward the stairs. The Ralengclan were busy on and near the Hub stairs and didn't notice him stop at the coffee counter, where two aliens that should have stayed home lay dead. He picked up one of the weapons and examined it quickly to make sure he understood its operation, then slung the strap over his neck and picked up the second to carry.

Checking around, it appeared that all who were engaged in the conflict were occupied and not expecting another player to jump in so late in the game. He was thinking that could be just the edge he needed to put this thing to bed nice and quick. He started toward the stairwell, hugging the wall as he went.

Across the Hub, Kris and Wakey were doing the same thing, converging on the center stairs from the opposite side. He saw the two trainees and recognized them, although he didn't remember their names. He caught their attention and signaled a gesture meaning, "Stay where you are."

They stopped and nodded. Disobeying Lady Laiken was one thing. Saying no to Sir Storm was a whole other game level they knew they weren't ready for.

When Storm was almost at the bottom of the stairwell, he glanced back at the kids. There were two Ralengclan coming from who knew where. He was about to break silence and give himself away to shout, when "Shoot to Thrill" was cut off and replaced with a broadcasted voice yelling, "Wakey! Falcon! Behind you!"

Storm's adrenaline had spiked when he saw the imminent danger those kids were in. He was too far away to give much support with what he had. The alien weapons were rapid fire, but they were heavy and surprisingly short range. All he'd be able to do was watch like the horror show it was.

Without a blink's hesitation Kris and Wakey raised their weapons and turned like synchronized swimmers then advanced on the aliens acting like they thought they were made of Shieldo instead of flesh and bone. It was just as beautiful as it was insane.

The aliens were so surprised by the display of bravado that they hesitated. They got off some shots. Wakey felt a hint of air and heat go by his face, but they never hit targets. The team of Wakenmann and Falcon weren't laying down scatter. They were into pure surgical, just like Mother said. Face and groin.

In under a minute the skirmish was done. Two kids gave each other a high five like they'd just scored in basketball while Spaz proudly announced, "And the Rising Hawk team scores! Three, four, open the door. Hope Mother is listening to this broadcast. New kids like four on the floor."

The boys turned toward a pale-looking Storm who gave them an appreciative nod and that simple gesture made each boy grow a couple inches taller on the spot.

The stairwell erupted in a near-continuous volley of fire. Storm looked around the corner to see what he was facing before he started up the stairs. For the first time in his career as a Black Swan knight he froze in the middle of a fight because of what he saw on the landing. Sir Fennimore was down, hit multiple times. He appeared to be unconscious, but it was impossible to tell because of the guy who was shielding Fenn's body with his own. That guy, who happened to look exactly like him, had an autofire in each hand, one pointed up the stairs, one pointed down. The two of them were pinned, but the lookalike was keeping the aliens off Fenn. Or trying to.

Thanks to Spaz's heavy metal blast, the Ralengclan had no idea someone was approaching from beneath them. So Storm picked them off effortlessly. When they went down, that left him face to face with his twin.

The doppelganger didn't waste time. He trained both weapons on the two above and was joined two seconds later by the Storm who belonged in Loti Dimension. The remaining two were taken out the same way Storm got number three and four. A math instructor who lived on the second floor decided he didn't want to wait inside his apartment any longer. So he loaded his Magnum and walked down the hall to the head of the center stairs.

There he found two guys in combat gear set on finishing off the knights below. He raised his weapon with both hands and shot each in the back of the head before they had any idea someone was behind them.

And the last four were over before Spaz had time to announce buckle his shoe. The music stopped. "This is the Voice of the Fray giving the all clear. That's right folks, it's over. All meds on deck. You're needed in the Hub stairwell between one and two and in Operations. Three men, um, persons, down. Again, lock down terminated. Emergency medical personnel to Hub stairwell and Operations."

Angel turned to Storm. "The Great Storm, I presume."

"And you are?"

Angel hesitated for the space of two heartbeats. It's one thing to be told there are other versions of you in the universe, but another to come face to face with one. He stared into black eyes identical to his own and said, "Impersonating you." He grimaced when he started to move off Fennimore.

"Where are you hit?"

Angel looked down like he had to check. "Nothing that can't wait. He's the one in trouble."

Storm took a closer look and had to agree. Fennimore was Swiss cheese, riddled with so many holes, there was little chance he could survive it. They hadn't retained the kind of surgical med staff at Jefferson prepared to address that much trauma. The equipment was still there, but the people were gone.

Kris and Wakey had come bounding up the stairs and gave each other a look when they saw two Storms on the landing.

Storm turned to Kris. "Go up top. Tell the pilots I said to warm a Whister. Got an emergency to go to town." He looked down at Fenn as the boys were making their way past up the stairs. "Hold on." He stopped them to add to the instructions. "We can't carry him up without doing more damage. Tell them to bring the bird down to the rugby field. Get a stretcher off one of the Whisters and bring it back with you."

When Kris and Wakey got to the top and found the pilots dead, they didn't need to have a conversation about what was going to happen next. One thing was certain, neither of them would ever complain about drills again.

They'd been taken through the paces on preflight checklist so many times they could do it in their sleep. More importantly, they could do it quickly and efficiently, in the wee hours of the morning with no sleep, and with the toll taken by stress and repeated adrenaline spikes.

The Whister's near-silent blades whirred into rotation, spinning so fast they appeared to be invisible when the engine purred awake. In six minutes they lifted off and Wakey set the Whister down on the rugby field as gently as if he'd done it a thousand times.

Kris jumped out, opened the side panel, and pulled out a stretcher. The two boys didn't dialog about who would do what. Wakey was a better pilot. Kris was bigger and stronger.

Voices could be heard all over the building as people started to emerge from lock down.

Rosie and Glen arrived at the bottom of the Hub stairs together.

Storm pinned Glen with a look. "I'm guessing cells have been scrambled so there's no calling out?" Glen nodded. Storm's gaze shifted to Rosie. "Can you go take care of Helm so your mother can get Ram and bring him here? Elora's hurt."

Rosie looked stricken. Storm could see by the look on her face that Rosie loved her auntie. "I can find him, Dad. I know Uncle Ram's signature."

"Uncle Ram." Storm repeated that. It sounded so strange to hear this young woman call his teammate Uncle Ram, but at the same time, it sounded right.

"He's at the Derry palace. In Ireland."

"No problem."

"Okay. Hurry." As soon as he said it he thought better of leaving it like that. "WAIT! Make sure he's securely attached."

She nodded and disappeared.

Elsbeth had decided she would head toward Operations, but the only way to get there was via the Hub stairwell where her new fiancé lay dying on the landing between one and two. When she came upon that scene, she sank to her knees next to him and temporarily forgot all about being a nurse.

It was clear by her reaction that Fenn was more to her than a patient who needed medical assistance.

"Elsbeth," Storm began gently. "I'm not med. You're going to have to tell us what to do."

Her eyes jerked to Storm like she hadn't realized he was there and from there to the other Storm. A thousand questions joined the shock and grief that were already present on her face, but she decided to triage her own emotions.

A crowd had gathered at the top of the Hub stairs and at the bottom. Kris was yelling, "Make way! Everybody out of the way!"

On his way by, he told a couple of the other

trainees who had gathered to run to the Whister outside and get the other stretcher.

Rosie popped into the Hub tied to Ram with a halter lead, which had been handy because she'd found that Ram had risen to an Irish dawn and gone to the stables for a ride so tack was handy. He quickly untied the tether knots and ran toward the stairs where a little crowd was gathered. They parted when they saw him coming and read the panic-stricken look on his face.

Storm and Kris were helping to move Fennimore onto the stretcher while the doc on the scene told them how to do it. An orderly was holding Fenn's unconscious head as they lifted. Kris looked up and saw Ram first. He simply said, "Operations."

Ram turned and sprinted across the Hub and down the short concourse to the open door. Kris yelled after him, "Bring her to the Whister on the rugby field!"

The first thing that came into his vision was blood pooled on the floor. Then he could see that she was sitting up, but looking like a rag doll. Last, he got a look at her face as he went to his knees and slid on the blood.

She cracked the one eye that could see. She tried to laugh, but it didn't work out. "Don't look so worried. I'm not dead yet."

"Great Paddy knows, if you're no', 'tis no' for lack of tryin'. We got to figure out a way to get you to the Whister on the rugby field."

"What was that about a winch and pulley?"

"Elora", Ram breathed, his face and voice full

of concern. He wasn't in a mood for kidding around, "Where's Helm?"

"I left him downstairs with Monq locked inside Fire Testing. Glen's guardian."

Ram's eyes closed with relief and he drew in a big ragged breath. His family was alive and, given the looks of Jefferson Unit, that was both blessing and miracle. His brain did a reboot and started functioning again. "Wheelchair."

"Hmmm."

Some of the trainees had gathered outside the Operations door. Ram looked up at them. "We need a wheelchair from the clinic right now. 'Tis the only way to get her to the Whister."

Two of the boys ran off toward the clinic.

"Ram. You can't take me on the Whister."

"Why no'?"

"The Equalizer is about to wear off. There'd be too many questions about my physiology. The med staff here can take care of me."

"Auntie?" Elora turned when she heard Rosie. When Rosie saw Elora's face she whimpered. "What can I do?"

Elora reached out with her good hand to pat Rosie. "It's not as bad as it looks, precious. Where's your mother?"

"Home."

"Could you get her for me, please?"

"No. She's watching Helm." As Ram and Elora looked at each other a silent communication passed between them. "That's the best news I've had all day."

When Storm and Kris reached the Whister, Elsbeth, and the doctor who self-appointed himself to accompany them, got on board and helped secure the stretcher to the gurney that was designed for just that purpose.

The outside lighting was good, but not good enough that it didn't take Storm a while to realize that Wakenmann was sitting in the pilot's seat, wearing a headset and looking awfully young, but supremely capable. The second stretcher, carrying Storm's look alike, was likewise fastened to the second gurney. It was a tight fit with two patients and three medics.

Storm tapped Wakey on the shoulder. "You know where you're going?"

Wakey nodded. Kris slid the panel door closed and ran around to get into the co-pilot seat. Storm gave Wakey a good-to-go sign. In response, the kid touched his head and lifted off.

Storm stood on the rugby field and watched the Whister's lights speed toward Manhattan. He wished Sol was there because he would know exactly how to take people to a civilian hospital, shut down rumors before they got started, and put the press in lockdown.

When Storm pushed through the Courtpark glass door to reenter the building, he told one of the trainees to go find Glen.

"I know where he is, sir. He's working on trying to get the front entrance open, sir."

"I see. Is Monq helping?"

"I don't think so, sir."

"Well, if not, then go get Monq and tell him I said to get that door open."

"Yes, sir."

The kid ran off, delighted to be given a direct command by a legendary hunter.

Deliverance got sidetracked after sending Rosie to see if they'd found the right Storm, which was not that unusual. Litha had threatened him with a watch a few times, but he'd just laughed and said, "Babe, I love you, but a clock attached to my beautiful body? Not gonna happen."

He encountered a group of suburbanites on a twenty-five year high school reunion trip to New York and was invited back to their hotel. What was an incubus to do? The lovely ladies had spent too much time reminiscing at Harry's Bar and had to look at key cards to remember the name of the hotel where they were staying.

Only after the demon was sure that everyone was thoroughly satisfied with his services, did he remember he was late to pick up Angel and take him to the vineyard for the night.

After Storm told that kid to get Monq to help with the front door he started toward Operations to check on Elora. He hadn't taken two steps when the demon popped in beside him and slapped a fur lined handcuff on his wrist. Storm didn't have enough time to top off a proper fury about being startled before the demon said, "Time to go."

"WAIT!"

"What?"

"Unlock this thing and have a look around."

Deliverance scanned the Hub slowly, taking in the result of the mayhem. "Was there a party?"

"Take. This. Off."

Recognizing that tone, the demon looked Storm full in the face. "It's you, isn't it?"

Storm just raised the cuff in front of his father-in-law's face and stared with a seething impatience that was barely under control. Deliverance grinned and inserted the key as he said, "What a relief. Litha's been in a really bad mood while you've been gone."

Storm said nothing, just walked away thinking he would be reincarnated a hundred times before he forgave the incubus for robbing him of seeing his child grow up.

During the time it took to convince the demon to remove a purple fur lined handcuff, which registered with Storm as familiar, Monq had the front door open for business, only a minute or two before Kay returned from his trip to Houston to commune with his wife.

Between the reduction in residents and the late hour, he'd been expecting that he wouldn't see anyone other than the minimum security on duty until the next morning.

It would be hard to say what was more surprising initially, the fact that the Hub was full of people, or the fact that the building looked like what it had been a half hour earlier – a war zone.

Kay shoved some rubble out of the way with his boot, dropped his duffle at his feet and whistled as he looked around. When Storm came striding toward him, he said, "What'd I miss?"

"Everything but the clean up. Good timing."

"Looks like you'll be off the hook for at least a day. No workout tomorrow."

"I'm retired. I work out when I want."

It took a few seconds for Kay to process that. When he did, he didn't look at his partner. He looked at his boots and said, "Storm?"

"Yeah. None other."

Kay looked away for a couple of seconds and wouldn't meet Storm's eyes. "Where's the other guy?"

"Wounded. Fixable. Fennimore's bad though. Couple of trainees flew them out of here on a Whister. Don't ask. I have no idea."

"It's a story." Glen had walked up just in time to hear that. "I made them learn how to fly as a punishment. Couldn't have worked out better if I'd had Aelsong read our future. Not that she would have." He stuck out his hand to Storm. "Welcome back."

Storm shook Glen's hand. "Yeah. I don't know about you, but I don't want to be here when Sol sees this place. I can just hear it. 'I go on vacation once in thirty years and you destroy my unit!' Where's Elora? Did Ram get here?"

"Clinic. And yes."

"Okay. We're going to go check on them." He motioned to Kay to indicate that "we're" meant the two of them.

"That was my next stop, too," Glen said.

On the way to the infirmary Storm stopped, frowned and looked around like he'd lost something.

"What's wrong?" Glen asked.

"Where's Z Team?"

Glen's expression went blank. "Haven't seen them."

"New priority. Let's go find that kid with the microphone and see if he knows."

The door to the intercom room was open and a few trainees, some still wearing helmets and Shieldo vests, were chatting and joking with Spaz. Everything got very quiet when they realized that the two famous knights and the acting Sovereign had arrived on the scene..

Storm looked them over. "Which one of you is The Voice of the Fray?" He couldn't have kept the sneering sarcasm out of his question if he'd wanted to. And he didn't.

Storm guessed right, that it was the kid whose eyes had gotten the biggest. "You, right?"

Spaz nodded. "Look. As much as everybody in the building might wish that you were a mute, we *all* know you're not. So speak up."

"Yes. It's, ah, me, sir," he squeaked.

"Do you know what's happened to Z Team?"

"Not exactly."

Storm was reconsidering whether or not he was as patient as he had always believed himself to be. "What *do* you know, Spazmodoc?"

The other trainees giggled when Storm called him that and Spaz turned pink.

"Animal House came to get something from

the lab. Z Team saw them and I guess they thought they were *real* vampire. One of them tried to use a stake, but it didn't have much effect. Animal House talked it over and took them away. I don't know where. Wherever it is, there aren't cameras."

Storm took in a big breath and let it out. "You kids need to go to bed."

"Yes sir."

"Leave the gear and weapons in the armory."

"Yes sir."

"Glen, take a phone and get outside the cellscram. When you have a signal, call Baka and ask him if his vampire paid a visit to Jefferson Unit."

"Okay."

"We'll be at the infirmary. Come find us when you know something."

Storm and Kay swung through the clinic doors just in time to see Rosie arrive with a guy sporting a shock of white bedhead, wearing paisley pajamas. She pointed toward Elora's room, indicating the passenger should go in.

It was crowded in there with two J.U. nurses, the clinic doc, Ram , Storm, Kay, Rosie and now Dr. Funky P.J.s, who acted like he was expected to take charge.

"So what have we got here?"

"We're equipped to take care of the shoulder, but we're concerned about treatment of the cheek bone."

P.J.s looked around the room. "Everybody who doesn't have a good reason to be in here, get out." Nobody moved. At all. "For cripes' sake."

Ram looked around the room at the people present, then pinned the doc with a look. "Just do your job."

Apparently the man had grown accustomed to heady treatment, but he finally decided he could work with an audience and got down to business. While he was looking at Elora's injury, Ram pulled Rosie out into the hall. Storm and Kay followed.

"Where'd you get that bugger?" Ram asked Rosie.

She nodded toward Elora's door. "He's a plastic surgeon. We don't have many working for The Order, but Edinburgh says he's the best."

"Who in Edinburgh? That quack who 'delivered' you?" Ram did air quotes on the word "delivered".

"No. The Director."

Ram seemed satisfied with that. "Okay. You did good." He turned and walked back in to oversee the exam and hear what there was to hear.

Glen only had to walk a few yards away from the building to get a cell signal. He dialed Baka, who picked up on the second ring. Glen wasn't worried about getting him because he was aware that Baka's job involved working nights and expected that he wouldn't be in bed yet.

"It's Glendennon Catch."

"How are you, Glen?"

"Well, it's been an up and down day. Storm's back. That's the up part."

"All that's holy."

Glen had always thought that Baka used some incongruous expressions for a vampire. Or ex vampire. "Yeah. Holy. What I need to know right now, and this is sort of urgent, is if Animal House came to Jefferson Unit tonight for some reason?"

"Animal House?"

"Um, that's what people call your, um, vampire."

"I see. Yes. I sent them for more vaccine. Is there a problem?"

"Well, maybe. It seems they took four of our knights somewhere and left them, but we don't know where."

Glen could hear that Baka had distanced his phone from his mouth and was cursing. When Baka came back on he said, "I'll call you right back."

Glen paced up and down a base street in front of J.U. while he waited. Ten minutes later, the intelliphone face lit up like a night light.

"Yes?"

"It sounds like they took them and put them in a sort of cage on the level where the pool is?"

"Okay. That could be a big problem. That level was sealed off with explosives. The heat and air were shut down and it may be days before we have access."

"C9? You set off explosives inside the building? What in heaven's name is going on there?"

"We were attacked. It's a good guess that it was aliens from Elora's home dimension looking for her. Anyway…"

"Is everything under control now?"

"Well, the place is a mess. We have some people hurt…"

"Who?"

"Sir Fennimore, the Lady Laiken…"

"We're coming. I'll be with them this time and we'll get it sorted out."

"Okay. Thank you."

Baka ended the call.

Angel couldn't have been more surprised than to look up and see Rosie coming into his hospital room carrying a big vase of red and pink tulips. His first thought was that she was taking those flowers to Fennimore.

She was wearing a bright smile. "Had a talk with your doctor." She leaned closer and whispered, "I told them I'm family." She giggled a little at that.

Wish you were.

"He says you're going to be good as new and you can leave in three days. Maybe. If you're a good boy. Where would you like these?"

Angel looked at the flowers in her arms and his heart swelled when he realized they were for him. "Um. Here." He nodded toward the bedside table.

"So what can I do to make this more pleasant for you?"

"Don't know what you mean. What could be more pleasant than getting out of workouts with Kay and smack downs by Elora?"

She laughed. "I don't know. Feeling good? So

would you like magazines? I could load some movies onto a portaputer. You could catch up on your chick flicks."

"How did you know I watch chick flicks?"

She looked at him with such fondness it did funny things to his feelings.

"When I leave in three days, where will I be going?"

"Home, of course."

"My home? Or your home?"

Her face fell when she took his meaning. "I don't know, but I do know you'll be staying in your own room until you're completely well." She pulled on his blanket to straighten it a little, which seemed more a nervous gesture than anything else.

"It's been such a privilege getting to watch you grow up."

"Stop. You're going to make me cry." And, from the look on her face, he could tell she meant that.

"Yeah. Well, I don't want that." His face and voice were soft. "Go get me some sappy maudlin movies to watch. Something with no guns. And bring me some of those macadamia nut cookies your mother hides in the coffee can."

Her smile was back. "Cookies and cinema coming up. Back later."

"Rosie?" She stopped. "That guy? Is he, ah…?"

She looked puzzled for a minute and then realized what he was trying to ask. "Sir Fennimore? He's alive. I don't know much more than that, but I can check when I come back."

Angel nodded. When she poofed away, he looked over at the flowers. It was just the sort of thing he would expect Rosie to take someone in the hospital. Full of riotous color and life. His heart seized at the thought of how much he'd miss her when he had to go.

Three hours later Angel was watching *You've Got Mail* on a large tablet propped up on his lap. He heard the swish of the door and glanced up expecting to see a nurse come to pester him in some unpleasant way or another. He had thought he couldn't have been any more surprised when Rosie had come to visit. He was wrong. He was considerably more surprised to see his double prowl through the door.

"The Great Storm."

Storm's lips twitched just before he glanced down at the tablet screen. His eyebrows went up. "*You've Got Mail*?"

"Nice try. It won't do you any good to act superior. If you hadn't seen it, you wouldn't know what it was." Storm smiled at that. "For some reason I'm just not in the mood for shoot-'em-ups."

"Yeah. I get that." They stared at each other for a few beats. "I came to see Fenn. Thought I might as well stop off here."

"How is he?"

"Apparently too stubborn to die. He's in love. It's a powerful reason to want to stick around and see what'll happen next."

After a few seconds Angel said, "It's weird, isn't it?"

"Looking at a twin? Weird doesn't begin to cover it." Angel grinned. Storm started to look serious. "You know what you did for Fennimore during the attack? It wasn't your job. You didn't have to."

Angel looked out the window for a minute. When he brought his attention back to Storm, he said, "When you were gone, I spent my days trying to learn to be you." Storm nodded. "I don't know. It wasn't something I really thought about. I guess I know it wasn't my job, but it kind of felt like it was. Hard to explain."

Storm nodded again. "I think I understand. So, need anything? Got enough chick flicks to keep you entertained? "

Angel smirked. "It's an education."

"It is that."

"Intel on how the opposite sex thinks that might prove useful at some point."

Storm laughed. "And now you know why I've seen that movie, too. Want me to send somebody in to give you a manicure?"

"Now, see, there's a big difference between you and me right there. I'm actually *funny* when I want to be."

Glen was talking to Storm and Kay in the hallway outside Elora's room when Baka arrived with Animal House and their sitter. With a little interrogation and investigation, they were able to sort out what had happened.

The vampire had not only caged the knights,

putting them in danger of suffocation. They had also left them caged, unarmed, and at the mercy of the aliens. Fortunately for Z Team, the Ralengclan were not bloodthirsty. Their mission was simple. Kill the last Laiwynn, Elora Laiken. If someone got in the way of that, they were a target. The prisoners were not going to get in the way of anything so they were passed by and left alone, a fact that puzzled and troubled Torn Finngarick and Rafael Nightsong, who hadn't stayed around long enough to find out that the purpose of the invasion was assassination. If they had, the behavior of the intruders would have made more sense. And they might have understood that their mission was not to protect Jefferson Unit, but to protect their fellow knight, the Lady Laiken.

The teen vamps were instructed to disarm any surviving Ralengclan, transport them to the cells on S2, that had previously been used by Monq's team to study vampire, and make sure they were secured.

They then retrieved Z Team and, as directed by Storm, left them in the middle of the Hub. Storm had decided that the first phase of their correction would begin with a public humiliation. When they were liberated from the kennel, they were almost unconscious from lack of air and freezing because the heat had been shut off to Sublevel 3, a deep subterranean facility, which would have been cold in August without artificial heat, but in the middle of winter it was arctic. They were also cramped from not being able to stand up straight for so long.

The four collapsed on the floor of the Hub gasping for breath, shivering and looking at Storm like he was the one responsible for their plight. Well, to be fair, he was responsible for the spectacle. Storm called medical to attend them where they were, then walked away, but not before saying, "You'll be notified of the time and place of your preliminary disciplinary hearing."

Monq knocked on Elora's door and poked his head in. She turned her head in his direction. "You gave my baby to Rosie and she took him through the passes."

"Take it easy. He's with Litha and he's fine. I'm the one who's not fine. I'm exhausted. That child weighs five hundred pounds."

Rammel walked over and, without a word, shocked Monq by putting his arms around him and giving him a big hug. Hugging wasn't really Monq's thing, but he allowed it and gave Ram a perfunctory embarrassed sort of male pat on the back. Ram pulled back and said, "Thank you," with such depth of sincerity that Monq blushed.

"Well, certainly. Anyone would do it." He backed away from Ram just in case another such display of affection might be impending, then added, "Once." He moved closer to the bed to get a look at Elora's face. "What's the prognosis?"

Ram answered for her. "Pain meds until the swellin' recedes, then he'll get to work to restore her unrivaled beauty."

Monq nodded. "Well, he's a good man, a little bit of a dick, but most surgeons are. He's good at what he does." And with that he left the room and closed the door quietly.

Elora said, "The pain meds are causing me to hallucinate. I thought I heard Monq call somebody a dick."

"Definitely no' on the magic carpet, my girl, and I heard the same fuckin' thin'."

After a brief pause, she said, "Well, I hope he wasn't using that sort of language in front of our son."

Elora heard Rammel laugh, really laugh, for the first time since Storm had been lost. She sighed deeply, feeling content to be alive and to be able to say the same about her baby and her friends.

Storm entered quietly and looked over at Ram as he approached Elora's bed. "How is she?"

"I'm in the room you know," she answered, opening her eyes. "What's up?"

"The little shit with the microphone says he overheard you tell Fenn and, ah, the other guy, that you had some plan for sealing off Sublevel 1."

Elora nodded. "I gave them some of Monq's new stuff, the C9. They blew the elevators, then the east and west stairs. We were going to try to lure some of the Ralengclan down there by way of the central stairs, seal it off, and shut down air and heat going to that level from the main controls behind Operations."

Storm pursed his lips and considered. "Not bad for somebody who never studied tactics."

She smiled. "Thank you. Did it work?"

"Oh, yeah. Maybe too well."

"What do you mean?"

"Z Team tried a stake on one of the Frenchie vamps who stopped in to resupply their stash of vaccine. So the crazy kids put them in lock up in Blackie's old kennel and left them down there."

After a pause Elora said, "Well, that explains why we never saw them again."

Rammel walked over and shocked Storm by putting his arms around him and giving him a big hug. Hugging wasn't really Storm's thing, but he allowed it and gave Ram a perfunctory embarrassed sort of male pat on the back. Ram pulled back and said, "Welcome home," with such depth of sincerity that Storm blushed. But he managed to say, "There's no place like home."

It was midmorning before medical cleared Z Team to leave the infirmary. Raif pushed through the clinic's swinging doors ahead of the others.

"Hey. Where you goin'?" Gunnar asked.

Raif stopped and turned. Everything about his body language said he was unhappy and exasperated, but determined. He glared at Torn. "Speed dating."

"Speed dating?"

Raif continued to glare at Torn. "Made a bet with unknown consequence with that douche disguised as an elf. If I'm late, he'll come up with something equally fucked up. So I'm going."

He turned and walked off.

Torn laughed. "You're a mess, man. Do you no' think you might shower first? Change clothes? You're goin' off half-cocked lookin' like the dregs."

"I may look like dregs, but I'm going with a

full cock." To be sure that Torn got the full measure of that point, Raif walked off giving him an air finger without looking back.

Jefferson Unit was wrecked, at least the commons. With the exception of a couple of stretches of hallways, living quarters had survived untouched. Baka, having a wide range of intellectual interests including architecture, engineering and explosives, was duly impressed that the entire building hadn't imploded given the locations and numbers of C9 detonations. On his tour of the damage, he could frequently be heard muttering something around the word "amateurs".

The Order routed every maintenance and construction employee who could be spared to the New Jersey facility. They began arriving by early afternoon. Within hours materials were being delivered and the symphony made by clean up and construction created a combination of sounds that were strangely comforting to the residents experiencing emotional aftermath from having their previously thought to be secure home invaded.

After her reconstructive surgery, Elora was released to her family quarters. She'd always said she'd logged enough days in that infirmary to last several lifetimes.

On the inside of their apartment, the elves could almost pretend that everything was normal.

They had Storm and Litha to dinner the first night Elora was home. Ram cooked Guinness beef stew from the Irish Pub cookbook and beamed when the other three asked for seconds and then practically licked their plates.

Storm looked around when he heard strains of "Somewhere Over The Rainbow". He finally identified the sound as coming from his own pocket. He retrieved his phone and looked at Litha. "Did you change my ring tone?"

"No, but I can guess who did. There's only one demon we know who makes sport of changing other people's ring tones."

"I don't think it's funny."

"Neither do I."

Storm glanced at the call info and saw that it was Glen. He rose as he answered to politely put some distance between himself and the dinner table. "Hello." He listened for a minute, then turned to the others. "Is it okay if Glen and Rosie come up for a minute?"

Elora chuffed. "Like they have to ask."

"Come on."

A few minutes later, Ram opened the door to find Glen looking a little wan and a lot shell shocked.

"What's wrong, Glen?"

"Sol."

Ram stepped aside and motioned them in. Rosie followed Glen, not looking much happier.

Once they were inside, Ram closed the door and said, "Tell it."

Everyone was standing except for Elora.

Instinctively, Litha took a step closer to Storm's side.

"He died."

Litha had reached over to put her hand on Storm's arm and felt that every muscle in his body had gone rigid. He stared straight ahead at Glen, but said nothing. His jaw was probably locked down too tight to speak.

Ram looked at Storm and then quietly asked Glen, "How?"

"It was their last day before they were coming back. They rented a dune buggy at the cape. I guess it turned over and pinned him. She wasn't hurt, but it severed one of his legs. He bled out before help could get there."

Elora reached for Rammel's hand to hold onto.

A thousand things ran through Storm's mind as he stood there trying to make sense of those words, everyone processing their own unique grief, no one knowing what – if anything – to say.

He thought about the first time he'd ever seen Sol and the car ride from his parents' house to a new life that had been an adventure few could imagine. He thought about the last time he'd seen Sol and wondered if he would have acted differently if he'd known it was going to be the last time. He wondered if Sol knew how Storm felt about him. For that matter, Storm wondered if he had recognized how he'd felt about Sol before that very moment.

Mostly he thought about the conclusions of the study Aelsong had worked on. It appeared that everything about his life was identical to Angel's right up until the day, when they were both fourteen, that they had been called to the principal's office of their respective realities. When Storm reached the principal's office in his dimension, Sol had been waiting there to recruit him. What had been waiting for Angel was expulsion from school.

The inescapable conclusion Storm drew from that was that the course of his entire life came down to that pivotal moment and that he owed every good thing that had happened to him since to one factor - Solomon Nemamiah, who was in the right place at the right time.

It seemed strange to think that so much could ride on such a small turn of fate, but that one thing had propelled Storm into a knighthood and sent Angel careening off into a series of wrong turns that dead ended into a wasted life.

Glen said, "I'm going to go call Simon. He'll need to contact the Council to appoint an interim Sovereign until a replacement can be found."

Storm blinked rapidly and tried to unclench his teeth enough to get out one sentence. He looked at Glen. "You and I both know there's no such thing as a replacement for him. Don't we?"

Glen nodded and left quietly.

A representative from The Order offered a choice of resting places for Sol, but Farnsworth wanted his body to be buried nearby because he'd spent so much of his life at Jefferson and because, regardless of appearances, she insisted he loved that job. Naturally every knight he had recruited or supervised wanted to attend the service so they delayed it for two weeks to make that possible.

Since so many knights were going to be on hand for the funeral, Elora volunteered to organize an honors ceremony the following day. She had time because she wasn't going to be able to return to teaching until her shoulder and face were completely healed. And she wanted to do it.

She consulted with Simon on several ideas that required permissions from The Council. He was an excellent contact, but moreover, he and Sol had served a tour of duty together as knights when they were in their twenties and that was a surprise. While she was occupied with those plans, Rammel was busy doing his own bit of organization unbeknownst to her.

Five days after being admitted to the hospital, Angel was released. Rosie took him to the vineyard through the passes, but went as slowly as she could. He spent the next five days recovering there.

Sitting on the side of his bed in the guest room he looked around one last time. He had a satchel of mementos, mostly things to remind him of watching Rosie grow up.

She came to the door and knocked softly. "You ready?"

He didn't think he would ever be ready, but decided there was nothing to do but man-up and say, "Yes."

Angel followed Rosie to the kitchen where Litha and Storm were waiting. He hadn't seen much of Storm since he'd been Whistered away because Storm had been busy helping Glen administrate the Unit and oversee cleanup and rebuilding.

"The Great Storm."

"It is," Storm replied. "Although people don't acknowledge that nearly often enough."

Angel smirked. "You'd be surprised." He glanced at Litha. "Is this the big speech?"

"Which speech did you have in mind?" Storm asked.

"The one where you say this dimension isn't big enough for the two of us."

Storm smiled. "Something like that. I have two things with you."

"What?"

"You owe some ugly thing named Shade money?"

"Yes." Angel's eyes cut away from Litha and Rosie. There wasn't any part of him that was proud of who he'd been and he'd rather they didn't know much about it. But sometime during his sessions with Aelsong that were so wretchedly uncomfortable, he'd learned there was beauty in telling the truth even when it revealed him for the loser he was and he even began to take a sort of perverse pride in it.

"How much?"

"Fifty thousand."

Storm set a leather bag down on the table and it clunked. "There's enough gold in there to cover that and start over. Can I count on you, knight to knight, to pay your debt with it?"

Angel hesitated and looked puzzled, but nodded.

"Good. Here's the other thing."

Storm handed Angel a letter written on heavy paper.

"What is this?"

"Take your pick. It's either righting a wrong or better late than never or my tribute to Sol. If you decide you're meant for a different life, Deliverance will take you to the Headquarters of Black Swan in Edinburgh, Scotia. Walk in and ask to speak with the director. If you give him that letter, I'm betting they'll have something for you – something besides a tracker named Litha." He smiled at his wife and she returned that smile with a warmth that made Angel's stomach ache.

He opened the letter and began to read a concise and factual account of the fact that he'd been mistakenly kidnapped from his dimension of origin and coerced into impersonating Sir Storm. The second page was so shocking it made his jaw go slack. It was a letter of recommendation.

To Simon Tvelgar or Whomever Currently Serves as Headquarters Director:

We, the undersigned, petition for invocation of the ancient and honorable Rule of Gathering so that the chivalric title of knight, with its responsibilities and privileges, may be bestowed upon the presenter of this document, Angel Wolfram Storm, by merit of deed. We, the undersigned, vouch that he has been trained in the exigency of the knighthood and that he has proven its qualities admirably, as witnessed in his performance of duty when engaged by an enemy of Black Swan, and that he has been found deserving.

The following names and titles were typed. Underneath each was a respective signature.

Glendennon Catch, Acting Sovereign in the stead of Solomon Nemamiah, Jefferson Unit

Sir Engel Beowulf Storm, Knight of the Black Swan, Emeritus

Sir Chaos Caelian, Knight of the Black Swan, Emeritus

Sir Rammel Aelshelm Hawking, Knight of the Black Swan, Emeritus

Lady Elora Laiken, Knight of the Black Swan, Emeritus, Combat Instructor Jefferson Unit, Active

Sir Dirk Ales Fennimore, Knight of the Black Swan, Active

Litha Liberty Brandywine, Senior Tracker, Arcane Division First Class

His mind was swimming with the possibilities. Yes. He wanted a new life. He was going back, but he wasn't going back the same person.

"What do you want to do?" Litha asked quietly.

Angel looked up. "I just promised your husband I would use this gift to pay a debt. Then I'd like to be dropped off at Black Swan in Edinburgh." He looked at Storm. "With my letter." His gaze returned to Litha. "Maybe there's someone like you. There."

Litha smiled at Angel, then beamed at Storm. "Maybe. And perhaps you won't need to do more than walk through the front door."

Angel turned to Rosie. "You think you might visit now and then. Maybe let me know how everyone is doing?" He glanced at Litha when he said the word "everyone" and no one in the room missed it.

"I'm keeping tabs on you from now on. Making sure you behave." Rosie smiled and gave him a hug around the middle and assured him that she would not lose touch while Litha called Deliverance.

When the demon arrived she said, "Be sure you put him back where he goes, Dad. No excuses."

Deliverance rolled his eyes like a thirteen-year-old. "Alright. Alright. I got it. Sheesh."

"He needs to run a quick errand and pay a bill before he goes to Charlotte Square."

"I'm going along. Don't worry. We'll see to it he gets to the right place," Rosie added.

The demon gaped. "I get no respect."

Litha double checked the catch on the purple fur lined handcuffs, then gave Angel a goodbye kiss on the cheek.

"Wish me luck." The way he looked at Litha made her hope there was another version of her in his dimension. One who was languishing and just didn't know she was waiting for a tall, dark, and gorgeous knight to come walking through the Headquarters foyer so that she could wake from her half-sleep and feel a rush of aliveness.

Z Team waited in the hallway until they were formally admitted to the Chamber by Glen's assistant, Barrock. A table was situated in the middle of the room. Engel Storm and Glendennon Catch were seated behind it. Off to the side, on the first tier of curved bench seating, were Thelonius M. Monq, Elora Laiken, Kristoph Falcon, and Rolfe Wakenmann. On the other side, a bespectacled young man sat with a device that looked like a miniature sound board. Barrock closed the door behind them and directed the four men to, "Stand there." He pointed to an invisible line on the floor about five paces from the table.

When they were in place, Barrock said, "These proceedings will be recorded. Do you understand?" They looked at the sound engineer and nodded. "Good. Will each of you state your name so that we may begin?"

"Torrent Finnagarick."

"Rafael Nightsong."

"Gunnar Gustafsven."

"Robert Forzepellin."

After stating their names, the four stood waiting, quietly but obviously seething about being held accountable. That collective state of mind was further antagonized by the fact that Storm made them stand waiting.

Storm didn't try to hide his contempt as he stared at them.

"Why so serious? You must enjoy proceedings like this or they wouldn't have occupied so much of your careers."

A muscle ticked visibly in Torn's jaw.

"A report has to be filed concerning the particulars of the attack on Jefferson Unit and there are a few details that are fuzzy. Part of the purpose of this hearing is to clear up those details. So let me ask. Were you aware that Glendennon Catch was in charge as acting Sovereign at the time of attack?" There was mumbling and a couple of slight nods. "Gentlemen. You're not teenagers called to the principal's office. Will someone speak up so that you can be clearly understood for the official record?"

Raif said, "Yes. We were aware that Glen was in charge."

"Thank you, Sir Nightsong. That's Acting Sovereign Catch to you. And did you make a reasonable effort to seek him out and submit to his authority?"

"No."

"Why not?" All four looked at Glen and then back to Storm. "Someone?" Pause. "Anyone." Pause. "Gustafsven?"

"All respect, sir, we didn't think that Gle… um, Acting Sovereign Catch's experience prepared him to make battle command decisions."

"I see. It so happens, he didn't think so either. That is why he placed Jefferson Unit and its defense, that includes you, under the temporary martial command of Lady Laiken. Did you make yourselves available to follow her orders?" No one answered. "Finngarick?"

"No."

"No? Why not?"

Torn glanced at Elora. "For one thing we didn't know she'd been put in charge."

"For one thing? Is there *another* thing you want to add to that statement, Finngarick?"

Torn glowered at Storm. "No."

"As a review for the record, you did not make any effort whatsoever to seek out the unit command for orders. In fact, what did you say to Elora Laiken?"

Glyphs spoke up at that point. "I told her to stay out of our way."

Having that admitted so blatantly and shamelessly made Storm look like he was going to breathe fire the next time he exhaled. As that fury radiated from every pore, he glared at Glyphs for a moment more.

Storm turned toward Elora. "Is that an accurate retelling of what occurred, Lady Laiken?"

Elora looked at Z Team as she said, "It is, Sir Storm."

"Thank you. The witnesses are dismissed."

Monq, Elora, Kris and Wakey got up to leave. Everyone except Elora went straight to the door Barrock was holding open for them, but she detoured so that she could cross in front of Z Team on the way out and took her time doing so. She stopped in front of each and held his eyes for a moment before leaving the room. She wanted to make the point that she wasn't intimidated by them or their reputation and that she didn't need daddy to discipline the kids on her behalf.

When the door had once again closed, Storm said, "It can't have escaped your notice that The Order is running out of things to do with you. Who among you understands that something went terribly amiss and can describe what that was?"

When it was clear that no one else was going to speak, Gustafsven finally said, "We should have followed chain of command. We should have made every effort to locate Acting Sovereign Catch and get our orders."

Storm nodded. "What else?"

"We shouldn't have been disrespectful to another knight even if the knight is a woman."

"What else?"

Silence.

"Very well," Storm began, "I'll tell you what else. The four of you have lived inside each other's asses for so long you've lost the ability to smell stink. Your team has taken on the worst qualities of each other and magnified them. The result is a mess.

"Your actions violated at least three of your vows to Black Swan. Further, by walking off as a team, leaving the non-combat residents of Jefferson Unit completely vulnerable, you chose to stay together and protect each other instead of them. That flies in the face of everything the knighthood stands for and is so disgraceful I can barely stand to be in the same room with you.

"I have my doubts that you have any honor or good judgment to rehabilitate, but as a last step before stripping you of hunter status and sending you to various minimum security jobs, I'm going to recommend that Z Team be dismantled and that each of you be reassigned to serve with other teams."

Finngarick and Nightsong both paled at that suggestion. It was clear they'd rather be sent to Antarctica together than be split up.

"Now hold it right there, "Glyphs said.

Storm managed to grind out, "I beg your pardon?"

"I'm retiring."

The other three members of Z team jerked their heads toward him. It was obvious they hadn't seen that coming. He saw the question on their faces.

"I stepped out with that coffee girl, Brendel. She asked me what I'd be doing if I did something else. I got to thinking that I've been taking orders from Black Swan since I was thirteen years old. I was so busy doing what I was told that I never thought about asking myself that question. When I did ask myself that question, I realized that I'm way past done. I want to work on cars. Maybe cars and bikes. Or just bikes. Doesn't matter. What does matter is I'm over this quasi-military bullshit. I don't care if I'm discharged honorably or not. I don't care if I get a pension or not. Give my place to somebody else."

"Done. No reason to ask twice."

"Just like that," Glyphs said.

Storm turned slowly and pinned him with a glacial stare. "What were you thinking? Commendation? Gold watch? You get a big adios and Catch's assistant will get the door for you on your way out."

Glyphs took a look at his longtime compadres and walked out. According to Storm's suggestion, Barrock did hold the door open for his uncelebrated exit.

"Now then..."

"Sir Storm."

Storm turned to Glen.

"Excuse the interruption. Could I have an aside?"

"Of course."

Storm and Glen walked off to the side of the

Chamber where it would be more difficult to be heard.

"I'd like to present an option."

"Sure. Go ahead."

"Well, the past weeks have made it painfully clear to me that I'm not cut out for desk work. I'm up for bidding, as of now, and I want hunter division if you think I'll be approved."

"Of course you'll be approved. No question. Surely you know it."

"Well," he looked over at the three remaining members of Z Team, "instead of disbanding them... just yet, we could try one other thing first. Let me take Glyphs's place."

"Glyphs?"

"Um, Robert Forzepellin. I dubbed him Glyphs."

"You dubbed him?"

"Yeah."

Storm studied Glen for a minute. "That indicates they might have some regard for you." Storm looked over at Z Team. "I don't have to tell you how I feel about them."

Glen barely suppressed a full on grin. "No sir."

"Putting someone like you in the middle of a rats' nest... Seems like oil and water to me. You know you already have a reputation for good judgment. Commendable at any age. Incredible at your age. But I *cannot* stress the gravity of this question enough. Are. You. Sure?"

"Like you said, they've been on a loop for too long. And, they've been living on the edge of civilization. Maybe they need some reminders about what knights are supposed to be, inject another voice."

Storm stared at the floor for a minute with his lips pursed. "I'll agree to it on a temporary basis. Three months."

"Six months."

"Done. I have a few more conditions, but I can spell out terms for the record."

Storm returned, but did not retake his seat. He leaned against the table instead.

"Well, gentlemen, and, believe me, I'm using the term loosely, Acting Sovereign Catch has suggested an alternative, but I won't sign off on it unless I have your agreement to all accompanying conditions.

"It seems that Catch here thinks his butt is getting numb in an administrator's chair." Z Team looked at Glen appreciatively. "He's throwing in with hunters. Says he'd like to see you get one more shot at this before we bust up Zed Company. So, he's volunteering to take Forzepellin's place on the team. Personally I don't see it, but I have enough respect for him to let him try"

Z Team's expressions moved from surprise, to interest, to relief, to amusement.

"Now for my conditions. There will be a review in six months to determine whether the assignment should be permanent or whether the experiment should be disbanded. Meanwhile, I would like your word, as knights, that for the next six months, you not make *any* choice or decision without first hearing and considering Glen's opinion.

"He has great instincts, keen perception, and astute logic. One of his best qualities is that he can wield a delicate touch when it's called for. I've seen him manage a testy werewolf king with the diplomacy of an angel dancing on the head of a pin. He could be your savior if you let him.

"To help with that, I'm appointing Gustafsven team leader for the probationary period of a half year."

Nightsong and Finngarick looked at Storm like he'd lost his mind.

"Yes. I know that teams traditionally don't appoint leaders, but that's one of my conditions. What do you say?"

After a couple of beats Gustafsven said, "We'd like to discuss between the three of us for a minute."

"Be my guest."

"They went into a huddle and whispered together for less than a minute.

"We accept your conditions and would be honored to have Acting Sovereign Catch serve with us."

"An excellent choice. We'll take care of the formalities and roll out the new team configuration in seven days, after the funeral and the honors ceremony. I'll add just one more thing before I close these proceedings.

"I want to be sure you understand the cause and effect that led you here. If not for your arrogance and rashness, you wouldn't have left the non-combat staff and trainees without your badly needed skills. Not to mention the other knights. You started to believe the myth of your invincible badness, which is too foolish to even dignify with discussion.

"Most importantly, if you hadn't grown complacent with your antisocial policy of us-four-and-no-more, you would have learned, through interaction with other knights during your stay here at Jefferson Unit, that the Lady Laiken was the prize of B Team and not someone to be dismissed in the event of trouble. You would also have learned about the pure, immortal vampire known as Animal House around here. Had you known about them when you encountered them, you would have asked for their help in fending off the attack rather than trying to murder our allies. Had you done that, the conflict would have been put down effortlessly without injury to any of ours.

"You would also not have ended up sitting out the battle in a freezing kennel with no air *while the women and children* WERE BUSY DOING YOUR JOB, WHICH WAS TO DEFEND THIS BLACK SWAN UNIT!"

The badass members of Z Team visibly winced at that and had enough sensibility left to look appropriately embarrassed.

"Are you able to follow all that?"

Gunnar, Torn, and Raif were wearing expressions that looked more thoughtful than belligerent. Storm took the fact that the smirks were gone from their faces as a sign that there might be something worth saving in there.

Finngarick, who was the actual de facto leader of Z Team, looked at his teammates, cleared his throat. Quietly and respectfully, he said, "Aye, Sir

Storm. We are followin'."

"Good. I'll plan to see you at the funeral and the honors ceremony, dressed like knights and not riffraff. You're dismissed."

The three looked shaken as they left the Chamber which Storm took as somewhat encouraging.

With The Order's maintenance and construction crews working round the clock, the facility was miraculously put back to rights in time for the funeral.

Farnsworth walked into Operations looking like hell, but insisting that no one else could possibly handle all the details of making the arrangements and gearing up for a horde of guests to descend on Jefferson Unit, all expecting to be fed and quartered. No one could argue with that because she was right. She alerted Simon to the fact that J.U. would need some of its support staff temporarily returned to accommodate

There was a Veterans Memorial Cemetery at Fort Dixon and Farnsworth wanted him to be buried there. She said it was fitting because of the way he felt about Jefferson Unit and the way he loved his job. Since he didn't have family that he was close to, there was no one to disagree. Simon made arrangements with a few well-placed phone calls.

While it can't be denied that sadness and loss are part of funereal rites, it is also a celebration of a person and the life they led, a statement of how they mattered and to whom. Baka and Simon flew in along with dozens of knights, who had been under Sol's command at some time or another, representing nearly every Black Swan unit in the world. The rising bustle in Jefferson Unit encouraged an optimistic sense of continuity.

Knights who had trained together as teenagers or served together as knights were reunited with whoops and hugs, chest bumps, or punishing slaps on the back. The cause for coming together was somber. Nonetheless, laughter often rang out and echoed throughout the renovated Hub that still smelled like paint and new lumber . The Mess was lively and crowded and reminded Elora of the first time she'd seen it, when there were so many people stationed at Jefferson Unit that they had to eat in shifts.

The day of the funeral was cloudy and cool. Elora thought that was somehow fitting. Rain would make emotions hard to control. Sun would feel like mourners were being mocked with the fact that life does go on without the one being laid to rest.

Except for Hawking and Finngarick, the knights all wore dark suits. The two elves wore tribal dress kilts, Ram in Blackwatch Tartan, Torn in McElvoy hunting plaid. The entire ceremony took place at graveside. Simon and Storm stood on either side of Farnsworth looking every bit as grim as the lover who was left behind.

Ram held Helm, who never made a sound as if he understood the solemnity of the occasion. Careful to make sure that Ram and Helm were on the side of the uninjured shoulder, Elora reached out, took Helm's hand, and kissed his little fingers. She'd missed holding him so much, but injured shoulders don't heal fast in close proximity to hooligan baby boys.

When Elora looked back at the service in progress, she noted that the dates on the head stone indicated Sol had been fifty-three. He kept himself in such good shape she would have guessed younger. She was sure there were a treasure trove of stories that had died with him and she felt a rush of sorrow about that. She wished those stories had been recorded somewhere so they hadn't been lost.

No one knew who was going to take over the Sovereign office at Jefferson, or even whether Jefferson needed a Sovereign since it was no longer an active hunter unit. Glen had declined. Storm said something along the lines of "not for all the tea in China". But that was a worry for another day.

The honors ceremony Elora had planned was scheduled for the following night after dinner. Knights were expected to wear their dress uniforms, which consisted of black sileather pants, black combat boots, black tees either sleeveless or long sleeved and sashes that identified them as belonging to a particular team. Those that had medals or ribbons wore them pinned to the sashes. They were an incredibly handsome gathering that the mundane world would never know about, much less see, and the air buzzed with the combined energy of powerful second sons.

Normally only knights and, occasionally, knights-to-be were invited to such ceremonies, but two guests were included. One was Baka, whose service to The Order, as vampire and man, was unquestioned. As Storm had often said, "He may not be a knight, but he should have been." He sat on the first tier with B Team. The other was Blackie, who had once been intended to be the Black Swan mascot. He wore a kerchief in Blackwatch tartan, looked magnificent, and made Elora proud enough to bust buttons with his beauty and impeccable behavior. Like Baka, he sat on the first tier with B Team, but on the other side because the ex-vamp's presence rubbed his ruff the wrong way.

The mood at Jefferson was particularly chaotic, partly because the trainees had been invited to attend and couldn't completely contain either their giddiness or their immaturity.

At the appointed hour the knights filed in. The gas torches were lit to complement the ambient lighting and remind those present that the modern organization had roots in past times. The first thing everyone noticed was the huge Black Swan banner hung high on the wall opposite the main entrance. Eyes drifted up, took it in and knew that The Chamber was a special place.

The trainees, wide eyed, but trying to hide it with a show of nonchalance, were shown to a section that had been roped off for them. The only ones not sitting with the group were Glen, because he was Acting Sovereign, Barrock, who was assisting Elora, and Link, who had been assigned to push Sir

Fennimore's wheelchair.

Fenn was far from recovered, but given the extent of his injuries, it was astonishing that he'd been released from the hospital so soon. It was either a testament to great conditioning and nutrition or to youth and stubbornness. Still, the prognosis indicated a lot of painful physical therapy in his future. Fortunately, he knew a nurse who was willing to make the effort, both constant and personal. Whether or not he would be able to return to active duty was yet to be seen.

When everyone was inside, Elora came forward. She was wearing the dress uniform with a long sleeved tee. Her sash had been refashioned as a sling to keep her shoulder immobile. The side of her face was still bandaged, but no one there thought she was less beautiful because of it.

She stood still waiting for everyone to settle and quiet before she spoke. The acoustics of the Chamber had been designed so beautifully that voice amplification wasn't needed.

"Undoubtedly there are those here who knew Sol better than I. There are knights here who served under him. There is at least one knight who served with him." At that, some of those who were close to Sol turned to look at Simon for his reaction. "Still, he had a powerful impact on my introduction to this world. In fact, the first time I encountered him was in this very room." Storm, Ram, and Kay glanced at each other in a shared a moment of camaraderie as the memory flitted by.

"I'm sure you've all noticed the veiled frame. This is part of Sol's memorial."

She nodded to Barrock. He pulled the edge of the cream silk that covered the rectangle hanging on the east wall. The tarp floated downward to the sound of collective gasps and murmurs. Those who had never been to the Hall of Heroes couldn't know that the portrait matched those in the hallowed vault in Edinburgh, which meant that it was a full length portrait, about eight feet tall. Larger than life as was befitting one of the Black Swan heroes. Elora had prevailed on Simon to have the current artist in service to The Order do a portrait of Sol quickly enough to present at the event.

The subject was set against a dark background, black with swaths of brown, reminiscent of Dutch masters. The artist had been given a photo of a young Sol in a brown leather bomber jacket and faded jeans looking supremely capable and ready for anything. It was arresting partly because of Sol's youthful beauty and stark masculinity, but also because some of the force of his personality had been captured on the canvas. The painting was nothing less than a masterpiece and Elora could hardly wait until the ceremony was over so that she could bring Farnsworth in to see it.

The silence brought on by the stunning recreation was replaced with polite applause.

When the room quieted, Elora said, "The second part of tonight's ceremony is about honors."

Apparently that was a cue because Link unlocked Sir Fennimore's wheelchair and pushed it around Elora to the rear before he brought it to a stop with Fenn facing the congregation.

"You've probably heard that Jefferson Unit

was attacked with only two active knights, Sir
Fennimore and myself, defending against twenty
assailants." She looked at Z Team as she said that.
They lowered their eyes or looked away.

Elora looked pointedly at the section where
the trainees sat.

"I need Rolfe Wakenmann and Kristoph
Falcon to come down here and stand with me."

A grin quickly replaced surprise on Wakey's
face. Kris paled, looking like a severe case of stage
fright, but with urging, he managed to stand and
follow Wakey. When they reached Elora, she beamed
at them before continuing to address the gathering.

"First let me say that, during the attack on
Jefferson Unit, all of the trainees responded to the
crisis like the knights they will be someday. But I've
been given permission to honor two of my students,
Rolfe Wakenmann and Kristoph Falcon, who
demonstrated exceptional courage under fire. Since
they saved my life, repeatedly, and survived, I've
decided to waive disciplinary action for disobeying
my orders."

There was a brief eruption of muted laughter.

"The story doesn't end there. In an effort to
emulate Sol's style of creating punishments for
trainees that befit the crimes, Acting Sovereign Catch
assigned these two the task of learning to fly Whisters
in their off time as penalty for stowing away.

"On the night of the attack, our only casualties
were the two Whister pilots on duty. When the
conflict was over, all believed that Sir Fennimore was
mortally wounded. These two, however, flew the
Whister that took him to emergency surgery and

saved his life as well. That is why he has the honor of bestowing these commendations.

"At the direction of The Council, for the first time in Black Swan history, two trainees are being cited for bravery and the medal they are receiving is the Solomon Nemamiah Medal of Honor."

Barrock came forward with two medallions attached to large loops of wide green and black striped satin ribbon. He handed them to Sir Fennimore.

"Rolfe Wakenmann." He looked at Elora. She motioned him toward Fenn. Wakey bent down so that Fennimore could loop the medal over his head. Wakey said thank you, immediately grasping the medal to look at it as he stood. "Do you have anything to say to the assembly of knights?"

Still holding his medal, Wakey looked the crowd over. He grinned, looking a little goofy, and said, "Cool," which prompted a round of good-natured laughter.

"Kristoph Falcon." For a moment it looked like Kris was glued to the flagstone floor. Elora leaned over and whispered, "Kris. Go get your medal from Sir Fennimore."

The hazy look in Kris's eyes cleared a little. He walked toward Fenn woodenly and bent down to accept his medal. Like Wakey, he was compelled to grip the precious round seal and hold it so that he could look at it up close.

"Kris, would you like to say something to the assembly of knights?"

Kris did want to say something memorable. He would have loved it. At that moment he would have sold his soul for spontaneous eloquence.

In the blink of an eye his experience unfolded and played on his heart like it was an instrument ill-used or seldom used.

Kris was second son in a family of three boys. His older brother was the golden child who could do no wrong. Beautiful, talented, smart, athletic, and popular. Kris's parents were so busy taking pride in the accomplishments of his older brother that there wasn't much left to give anyone else. What *was* left went to Kris's younger brother.

As his childhood unfolded, Kristoph was like a plant without water. He longed for attention and recognition. As his developmental years went by and neither were directed his way, that need was replaced by anger-fueled attitude. Black Swan had given him a way to channel that anger into something that might be productive, even precious, someday.

In short, public recognition was utterly alien to Kris Falcon. It was utterly alien and utterly overwhelming. Truthfully, standing in the middle of the Chamber, with the eyes of so many Black Swan knights and all his peers trained on him, waiting for him to speak, could have been his worst nightmare. And he could *not* have been more unprepared to deal with attention on that scale.

The Chamber was quiet as a tomb while everyone waited to see how the boy would answer Elora's question. He wasn't spontaneous and easy-going like Wakey, but he wanted to express what the honor meant to him in some way.

"I…"

All present looked on as Kris Falcon tried to

wade through the depth of his emotion and find voice and words. It was a battle he ultimately lost. His chin trembled slightly and his eyes grew red rimmed. In a moment suspended in time, a moment of shared empathy, everyone involuntarily held breath, waiting for the inevitable. When tears that couldn't be held back spilled out of his eyes, the entire class of trainees poured out of the risers, jumping the rope or going under. They ran forward and smothered him in a pile on of a group hug accompanied by quiet words of support and congratulations.

In the rows above, the seasoned knights who bore witness – some of them legends - looked at each other with smiles, nods, winks, and also pride, as if to say, "Yep. That's what it's all about."

Almost in unison, onlookers in the assembly rose to their feet with loud applause and shouts of appreciation. Everyone was a little emotionally wrung when they began filing out of the Chamber on their way to the lounge for drinks and billiards or drinks and cards or just drinks.

Elora was one of the last to leave. Ram walked up to her looking dazzling in his sleeveless tee that showed off sculpted arms, a sash crowded with medals and ribbons, and his beautiful signature smile. "Amazin' is what you are."

He gave her a kiss that qualified as a public display of making out, while still taking care with the injury to her cheek.

"Rammel. Not a good example to set for the trainees."

He looked around. "They're long gone, my girl. 'Tis just us and the fuck ups. So do no' be embarrassed."

Fuck ups?

She realized Z Team was still there.

"You go on with Storm and Kay. I'll stop by in a while. I'm going to go get Farnsworth and bring her to see the portrait."

He glanced back at Z Team before saying, "Do no' be long."

When Ram was gone, Z Team came forward. Torn Finngarick spoke for them, "We talked it over and decided we owe you an apology. 'Tis been a long time since anyone was expectin' us to work or play with others. And 'twas badly done."

Elora looked them over and took a minute to respond.

"Storm has a very low opinion of you. When you first arrived, I questioned him about it. Thought he was just being prissy. So I decided to keep an open mind and see for myself. And I kept an open mind right up until you..." She looked at Glyphs. "... told me to stay out of your way and you..." She motioned to the others. "...gave your implied approval of that by letting that stand.

"Fenn," she paused, "Sir Fennimore is in love with my best friend and they were planning a future together. Right now that future is very uncertain because they don't know if he's spending it in a wheelchair.

"I can't say for certain that the outcome would have been different if you'd done what you were supposed to do, which was to defend Jefferson Unit according to authority of command, which was me.

"I get rash behavior. I married somebody given to Irish hotheadness. Lots of people can live their lives controlled by their aberrations. But not Black Swan knights. More is expected from us.

"If Fennimore recovers completely, then I'll accept your apology and we'll be good. If not, there won't be enough words or deeds in your collective lifetimes to *ever* make it right."

She turned her back on them and walked out.

When she returned a half hour later with Farnsworth, there was no one else in the Chamber. Elora had thought to bring some tissues. Even though Farnsworth had not shed a tear publicly, not during the funeral proceedings or while directing the traffic of so many guests converging on Jefferson Unit at one time, Elora anticipated that, sooner or later, she would let go.

Farnsworth wasn't given to emotional displays. She wasn't dramatic and wasn't hysterical. She did have a little bit of a temper, but it took some doing to draw out of her. She stared at the portrait transfixed then looked at Elora with bright eyes. When one tear spilled, Elora handed her a tissue. Farnsworth accepted gratefully, but that was it. One tear. Elora thought that meant that Farnsworth had probably been ideally suited to the man whose visage was hung proudly on the wall like a guardian in spirit.

Looking back up at the painting with admiration clearly written on her face, Farnsworth's eyes moved downward to the gold plaque.

In honor of
Solomon Neuhm Nemamiah
Jefferson Unit Sovereign
Knight of The Order of the Black Swan

Farnsworth turned to Elora. "Thank you. It's perfect."

Elora just nodded. "He was one of a kind."

Farnsworth laughed quietly. "Oh yes. Indeed."

The following morning, Elora was cooing, exchanging gurgles and baby talk with Helm as he sat in a ray of sunshine that seemed to seek him out. Nanny had come early to bathe, dress, and feed him. Helm had just learned to sit up and was enjoying showing off his new trick. He got excited about his mother's rapt attention, waved his arms fast like he was trying to fly, lost his balance, and tumbled over on the side. It didn't hurt him in any way, but his face crumpled at Elora's laughter and he cried.

Ram came striding out of the bedroom at that moment. "Ram. Thank the gods. You're just in time. I hurt Helm's feelings and can't pick him up to comfort him and say I'm sorry."

Ram went straight for the baby. "Sensitive are ye? Just like the ole man."

Elora snorted at that.

Ram picked Helm up, groaning. "Ack. Monq is right little one. You *do* weigh a ton." He cuddled the baby into his chest and rocked him a little. "Now tell your da about the trouble. Is mum bein' mean to you again?"

Helm rubbed his nose into Ram's chest, grabbed one perfectly pointed ear with his little fingers, and looked over at Elora as if to confirm that, yes, indeed she was being mean to him.

"I'm sorry, Helm," she began, "I truly didn't realize that you can't take teasing."

Ram smiled at Elora over their son's head.

Meeting his eyes, she said, "So what are the plans for today? Nanny tells me she's on duty the rest of the day."

The smile left Ram's face just as Elora heard commotion outside in the Courtpark four floors down. "What's going on out there?"

She opened the French doors and stepped out onto the balcony. The portable bleachers had been hauled out of storage and were stacked along the rugby field sideline where they were being set up by trainees. She wheeled around on Ram and narrowed her eyes.

"'Tis a memorial. You know Sol always loved the annual game."

She gaped. "You're really going to play *that* card, Ram? You have no shame at all." Helm's head jerked at his mother's tone. Ram shrugged, bouncing Helm, and did his best to look innocent. "How did you manage to hide this from me?"

"You've been busy."

"Ugh!"

"About the plans for the day…"

"What time?"

"One."

Elora gave Ram a dirty look before storming

into their bedroom and slamming the door. Ram felt Helm jump a little in his arms when the door slammed.

The baby looked at his dad to gauge whether or not he should be alarmed. "Well, 'tis no' exactly a surprise, is it?"

Elora called Litha from the bedroom. "Did you know about this?"

"Just found out."

"So what are we gonna do about it?"

"Show up and cheer?"

Elora barked out a laugh. "Yeah. We're too easy."

"We are."

"Come early for lunch. Just us. If they're going to play, they shouldn't eat first."

"Okay. I'll drop Storm off at your place and we can grab something in the solarium."

"We should make them watch us eat something they love and make yummy noises the whole time."

Litha laughed and disconnected.

Ram was right about one thing. Sol did love the annual celebration of masculine strength and stupidity. Testosterone at its finest.

With all knights playing, except for Fenn and Elora, they were three short of the forty four players needed, twenty two on a team, fifteen on the field at a time with seven replacements. In order to come up with the right number, they had to press Baka into service along with the recently retired Glyphs and the newly active Glen.

Everyone in Jefferson showed up. The bleachers filled with cooks, meds, clericals, researchers, trainees, maintenance, instructors. Everyone.

Simon was tapped to coach one team and Fenn got the other. They were playing old school, which meant no referees. Captains decided on rules and the knights would honor them, on their honor. The first order of business was a coin toss for which team would be shirts and which would be skins.

The knights who weren't American would have been fine with short shorts and knee socks, but the Americans refused to wear the traditional "sissy garb". So most played in jeans. It wasn't a practical approach to ease of movement. But it looked good.

Just before the game started, a couple of the trainees raced out carrying a card table and folding chair. They had just finished setting it up when another showed up with a portable P.A. Spaz walked in front of the bleachers waving his microphone in an exaggerated farce of a victory lap. Elora's groan was voiced, but not heard above the crowd's cheer.

When she'd told Kay exactly what she thought of the results of his series of trainee lectures on disco, he had just laughed and walked off.

Spaz plugged in. "Testing. Testing. And it's a fine day for a game at Jefferson. Let's strike a match and get this game started, gentlemen!"

No one on B Team was surprised that Storm was chosen to captain his side. He faced off the other captain, a Frenchman named Sinoret, and called heads. It was tails, which meant that Sinoret was privileged to choose shirts.

Elora's lips pressed together. To her chagrin, that meant Rammel would be shirtless, which in turn meant that it would be another year of overhearing women use her mate's name in the same sentence with phrases like "wet panties".

A rain the day before had left the grass vulnerable to punishment. Within half an hour they had torn up the field so that it was beyond repair and would have to be re-sodded. They'd also torn each other up so that, with players covered in mud, sweat, and blood, it looked more like war than sport. The boys seemed to take perverse pleasure in bashing the opposition until the end, when they were so exhausted they could barely reward each other for a game well-fought with stomach bumps and beer spray.

Most of the women were appalled and fascinated at the same time.

Spaz was clearly biased toward B Team's side and announced the game accordingly, but nobody seemed to mind.

Glen got pulverized twice because of glancing at the sidelines to see if Rosie was watching. Rosie jumped up and down and cheered like a, well, like a cheerleader. She didn't question why Glen was included in the game when no other trainees were playing, probably assuming it had something to do with acting as temporary Sovereign.

He was delaying telling her that he was being inducted into active hunter duty, that he was a new member of Z Team, and that he would probably be assigned elsewhere. He just had a feeling none of that was going to go over well. There was no question in his mind that his chemistry with Rosie was the once-in-a-lifetime kind. He just wasn't ready to settle in one place and take a job that didn't include hazard pay. Someday, sure. Just not yet. He had some more living to do first.

Storm could have been a professional athlete. Litha knew he was a beautiful male at the peak of physical perfection, but she didn't know he could move with the grace of a dancer and the fluidity of water. Though he'd never been that interested in sports, it looked like there was some pleasure for him in "letting the horses out".

On the last play, he went down with a muscle strain, and had to be helped off the field by Ram and Kay. Still, his face was a vacillating conflict, grimacing because of the pain and grinning because of the victory. Somebody took a snapshot of the three of them coming off the field together that would be treasured by the respective families for generations thereafter.

Litha gave Elora a hug being careful to avoid both shoulder and face. It didn't need to be said out loud. The rugby game turned out to be just what was needed to restore a sense of optimism and life. The boys were banged up, but feeling great and there was a sense of buoyancy in the air.

"It doesn't mean our original objections weren't legitimate," Elora said.

"No," Litha agreed. "It just means things change."

Elora looked into Litha's eyes with warmth and affection. "Some things don't."

Litha smiled and shook her head. "No. Some things don't change. They're forever."

"By the way, gorgeous necklace. Looks incredible with your eyes."

Litha automatically reached up to touch the jade stones and beamed. "Thank you. It's a gift from Storm. Souvenir."

Rosie came bouncing over, breathless. "What's going on here? Group hug?"

The women brought her in to form a circle. They were still basking in the essence of familial sorority when Glen came up.

"Hey," he said, looking at Rosie like the sun didn't rise before she got up.

"Ew." She scrunched up her nose and jumped away from him. "Talk to me after you've had a shower."

Glen looked down at his mud-streaked body, smelled his armpit, and then looked up at Rosie, grinning wickedly. "Come on. Give us a kiss."

She squealed and darted away while he gave a mock chase. While her mother and auntie watched, Litha said, "She could do worse."

"No doubt. I take it Storm agrees with you?"

"Um, well, we haven't really had time to…" Litha's eyes scanned the crowd and came to rest on Storm who was watching the chase with dark interest. And intensity. And something else less definable. "Uh oh. I guess we should have *made* time to tell him."

Victoria Danann

EPILOGUE_I

The twenty Ralengclan sent to assassinate the former Briton princess never returned. The entire team had been wiped out. Gone. Vanished. No survivors.

It was a bright sunny morning when Rothesay barged into Archer's lab to say that the project was pronounced a failure. Officially. That wasn't the only news he brought. The rest of it was that Archer was to go back to square one and start again.

He turned toward Rothesay with a blank look, then told his assistants to take a break before he stepped a few paces away to open a cabinet door. He withdrew a very old bottle of whiskey and began to pour into two glasses. As he watched the amber liquid transfer from one container to another, a hundred thoughts coalesced in his brain, which was, of course, faster and more complex than any artificial intelligence in the foreseeable future. The whirl of words and images was distilled down to a single word.

Rothesay.

Archer knew he had been complicit in a campaign of insanity that could only have been fueled by passion so misguided that it had either originated as psychosis or wandered there from pressure. It was a given that Rothesay hated Laiwynn. Every single

Ralengclan had stories to tell and reasons to hate the former oppressors. But the result of Rothesay's obsession had brought the total of dead Ralengclan to forty. So far. With nothing to show for it. And, apparently, the Council was going to continue to go along with missions conceived by a madman, no challenge being strong enough to dissuade them from pursuing a path of lunacy.

Nodding at Rothesay, he said, "Let's drink to success."

Rothesay smiled, but it did nothing to warm his expression. "Sure."

They clinked glasses and drank.

Four minutes later, Rothesay was crumpled on the composition floor with lifeless, vacant eyes staring at nothing. And everything. Archer had slipped a couple of drops of his priceless potion into the drink. It was a masterpiece if he did say so himself. Untraceable. No residue. Flawless mimicry of a heart attack.

Archer threw the rest of his untainted shot back and savored the slow burn all the way down his esophagus. As he looked at his victim, he thought about his crimes and knew that Rothesay's execution went on the shorter list of good things he had done in his lifetime.

In another minute his assistants would return and he would have his speech ready. *Poor fellow. It was quick and severe. Shame. Not a thing Archer could have done.*

POSTSCRIPT

"Do no' be thinkin' the irony is lost on me." Elora looked at Ram with a blank expression full of innocence. "I know you're dyin' to say it."

"Okay. If it'll make you feel less guilty, I'll say it. We came here so that we'd be safe from Stagsnare assassins. Guess what? We're not."

"Yeah. So look outside in the hallway."

Elora opened the apartment door and stepped into the hall. There was an entire set of vintage Louis Vuitton trunks stacked one on top of the other. She turned back to Ram and grinned.

"We're going home."

"Does that smile mean I'll be gettin' lucky tonight?"

"You're lucky every night, elf."

He laughed. "And that would be the truth of it."

AFTERWORD

As to Kellan Chorzak, some things, especially things with vast potential to embarrass, take on a life of their own and sometimes that life seems to be eternal. One day Chorzak's grandson would be recruited by Black Swan and be initiated into the knighthood where stories of legendary exploits are told and retold. And sometimes in his old age, when Sir Chorzak was alone with that grandson, the young knight would playfully refer to him as Spazmodoc, The Voice of the Fray.

EPILOGUE_II Excerpt from *Solomon's Sieve,* Order of the Black Swan

COMING SPRING OF 2014

CHAPTER 1

Regrets? Well, sure. Nobody dies without regrets.

The only way to avoid that would be to sleep even less than I did and be rearranging your priorities every minute. Of course, if you rearranged your priorities every minute, then there'd be no time for anything else and, at the end of your life, you'd regret that you'd wasted your time working so hard at trying to reach the finish line without regrets that you never got anything done.

What's my biggest regret? The first thing that comes to mind isn't exactly a regret, but more a disappointment. I wish I'd had more time to spend with Farnsworth.

I never expected to find love so late in life. Neither did she. I asked her once why she'd never married. She said she was waiting for the right crusty old bastard to come along. I liked that answer. Honestly, I liked just about everything about Farnsworth. I wish I had told her that. Just like that.

Victoria Danann

All those years I would stop off at the Hub
and grab one of those rank strong coffees with a
cheese and ham and egg thing they nuked while I
waited, which was never long because the way I
stared at them made them so fidgety they could
hardly wait to give me my order and get me the hell
out of their space.

Makes me smile just thinking about it.

Every morning I was just steps away from
where Farnsworth was working in Operations, really
running the whole show at Jefferson Unit while I was
taking credit for it. Fuck me. She's one of a kind.

It's funny to think that all those years she was
right there. I must have seen her from time to time,
but we just never made *that* connection. I guess it's
not exactly funny.

Now that I have one foot on the other side, the
pieces all fit together better and it's easier to see
things clearly. Got to stop and laugh at my own jokes,
because who else is going to?

Oh. Well, I guess to get the joke you'd have to
be aware that, at the moment, I only have one foot.
Looks like the godsdamn dune buggy cut off one of
my legs. And my life. I'm bleeding out. The worst
part is that, while I'm doing it, I'm listening to the
weeping of the only woman I ever loved.
Criminently. That's the hardest part.

The only reason I can joke about this is
because it's temporary. If I thought it was permanent
there'd be nothing funny about it at all. But I can't
stay gone. There's too much going on right now.

I was planning to wait until I got back from
the first vacation I ever took in my life to inform the

interested parties, that would be almost everyone I know, that the great bright promise of curing vampirism with a vaccine… well, it's not working. And, unfortunately, the conclusion is that it's not going to work. Ever.

Victoria Danann

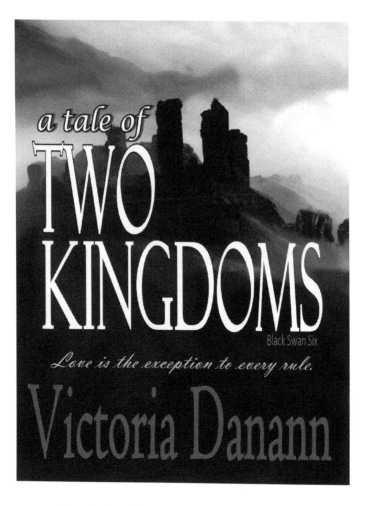

a tale of
TWO KINGDOMS

Black Swan Six

Love is the exception to every rule.

Victoria Danann

Book Six, Coming December 2013.

The fae and elves of Loti Dimension have been at war for two thousand years even though the current environment is more "cold" war. The Lady Laiken, as an outsider, has undertaken a search for answers as to what started it all. The saga returns to pure romance as we follow the quest of star crossed lovers, progeny of the two royal houses, for a happy ever after.

Books 1-5,
The Order of the Black Swan

For more on Victoria's books visit my website, www.VictoriaDanann.com or my blog at http://victoriadanann.me.

To all of you who have helped make this serial saga a success, I am so humbled and so grateful to be able to spend my days spinning tales.

The Witch in the Woods,
Victoria Danann

You're always welcome to write.
vdanann@gmail.com

35145530R00202

Made in the USA
Columbia, SC
20 November 2018